I0658092

TILL DEATH ZOO US PART

ELLEN RIGGS

BOUGHT-THE-FARM
MYSTERIES

FREE PREQUEL

Rescuing this pup could bring Ivy a whole new life... if it doesn't kill her first.

Discover how big city executive Ivy meets Keats, her crime-solving sheepdog, in A Dog with Two Tales. Ivy Galloway doesn't know how desperate she is to escape the big city and her soul-sucking corporate career until she meets a sheepdog in need of rescue, too. This short prequel to the laugh-out-loud Bought-the-Farm Mystery series is a page-turner for lovers of animals, humor and spunky amateur sleuths. Join Ellen Riggs' author newsletter at **ellenriggs.com/opt-in** to get this FREE prequel.

Till Death Zoo Us Part

Copyright © 2025 Ellen Riggs

ISBN 978-1-998742-16-5 Paperback - D2D
ISBN 978-1-998509-35-5 eBook
ISBN 978-1-998509-36-2 Book
ISBN 978-1-998509-37-9 AudioBook
ASIN B0D2NNLJTJ Kindle
ASIN 1998509362 Paperback

Publisher: Ellen Riggs
www.ellenriggs.com
Cover designer: Lou Harper
Editor: Serena Clarke
2512231316D2D

CHAPTER ONE

I was on top of the manure pile skillfully wielding a spade when my best friend Jilly Blackwood shouted my name from the porch.

"Already?" I complained to Keats, my border collie, who stood looking up at me from a safe distance. One of the few things my dog and I disagreed on was manure management. He didn't see the point of creating fertilizer when we could be doing something more interesting. Moving livestock around needlessly, for example. Or searching the meadows for clues to mysteries we had yet to uncover. Lately, he'd been trying to herd me out to the old dump where we'd excavated evidence to solve our first murder at Runaway Farm. After losing my breakfast and fainting there, I wasn't in a hurry to indulge my dog's curiosity.

His odd mumble below sounded like a reminder that his curiosity often led to grand adventures a regular hobby farmer would never experience. Most wouldn't want to get into the predicaments we did. Yet our little gang, including Jilly and Percy, the marmalade cat sitting on the barn roof, continued to accept the gauntlet fate threw down.

Jilly's next shout was louder but I still couldn't make out the words. Like my pets, I had selective hearing. She'd said we were leaving at five o'clock and I was holding her to it. There was a good hour before I needed to shower and make myself presentable for dinner at Dundonald Mills. The local wedding venue was the only site that had passed Jilly's initial screening but I doubted their cuisine would make the cut for my exacting maid of honor. Once a headhunter with a taste for fine dining, Jilly had become the chef at the inn we ran here together. Three potential venues had already been scratched from the list, and not because of me, or my betrothed, Kellan Harper. All had fallen short for Jilly, which made me wonder if she regretted taking a back seat with her own wedding plans. My event was fast becoming a Jilly Blackwood-Galloway production. I was happy with that and Kellan was too snowed under with police work to notice. The wedding didn't interest me nearly as much as the marriage. Maybe that's how Jilly felt when she tied the knot with my brother.

"Ivy Galloway, stop ignoring me." The shout was louder as she walked to the barn to collect me. "Hurry! It's a 911."

I groaned before starting down the stairs carved into the manure pile. "A family meeting? Now? How?" Despite being pleasantly preoccupied I couldn't have missed the dozen or more texts that followed what we called a Butter Tart 911 alarm.

Keats shot me a look with his eerie blue eye and then turned his warm brown eye on Jilly. Circling my feet, he gave me one chance to get moving of my own accord. If I didn't, I'd get a nip of encouragement.

"What's so urgent?" I directed the next question at Keats. The dog had been with me all afternoon, almost as if he sensed a change coming. Normally when I was busy with manure, he made his own fun. He never went far, however. Keats had many self-assigned jobs but managing me was chief among them.

Pulling off my gloves, I dropped them on a shelf before walking ahead of the dog through the barn and out the other side. Jilly stopped beside the truck and bent to collect Percy, who had beaten her there.

The site visit had clearly dropped off our list for today. Jilly would never scout a place wearing yoga pants and a T-shirt liberally dusted with flour and daubed with egg yolk. Her curly blonde hair was in a frizzy topknot.

I unlocked the doors before asking, "What's going on?"

"It's not your family. There's a Rescue 911." She hopped inside and called back, "A penguin problem."

My boots moved a lot quicker as I circled the truck. "A penguin? For real?"

"Two, according to our favorite rescuer." Jilly's voice rose until I opened the driver's door and let Keats jump in. "She texted and apparently you didn't answer."

Cori Hogan wasn't necessarily my favorite among the Dorset Hills pet Rescue Mafia, but she was the hardest to ignore. Under her watch, I'd gotten into plenty of scrapes and acquired more animals than I could technically accommodate. "I was in the zone and missed her. Obviously, penguins trump manure."

"And baking." She started to brush flour off her shirt and gave up when the animals settled in her lap. "Cori said there wasn't time to change. Mission critical."

I got the truck rolling before asking, "Where to?"

"Honky Haven." Jilly cracked the window open for Keats. "She said you'd know."

Dust drifted up around us and I slowed down to be sure I could see vehicles coming up the lane. We'd had so little rain this spring the farm was at risk of blowing away.

"It's the wedding venue you cut first from my list." We passed under the old iron arch. It read "Runaway Far," and with the dust cloud surrounding us, I could imagine the rusted out "m" had returned to its rightful place. "The zoo, remember?"

"That place? You told me it was tacky."

"It *is* tacky but I still thought we should give it a chance."

She tried smoothing the tendrils of hair that blew free. "The chief of police can't tie the knot at a petting zoo, Ivy. He's a public figure in Clover Grove."

"If Kellan worried that much about his dignity he wouldn't have proposed. I've given him more to be embarrassed about."

"Well, I worry *for* him. Besides, the site you choose reflects on the inn. If we're not holding the wedding here, the alternate venue needs to be fabulous. And if this is a plot to get me to Honky Haven to reconsider my ruling, it won't work."

"It's Happy Haven, and there's no plot. Is Cori already there?"

The breeze picked up when we turned onto the highway and Jilly gave up on her hair. "She's in the middle of raiding a puppy mill with the rest of the Mafia, so we're running lead. We need to collect Edna. Gertie is meeting us there, and the rest will come as soon as they can."

Edna Evans, our octogenarian neighbor, was standing at the bottom of her front stairs wearing a camouflage jumpsuit and army boots. There was a backpack slung over one arm and a helmet over the other.

"Why a helmet?" I asked, as she tossed it into the back seat with the pack and swung in after them.

"You know my motto, Ivy." Edna buckled her seatbelt. "Preparation saves lives. We're going to a zoo. Anything could happen."

Jilly tried smoothing her hair again without much success. "It's not a real zoo. Cori said penguins are as exotic as it gets."

"The hippo is long gone but there's a zebra," I said, as we drove back to the highway. "That's pretty exotic."

Edna patted her own tight curls. Her perm stood up to helmets and gale force winds. "Zebra's gone. Escaped nearly two years ago. Animal services captured it in a farmer's field and refused to return it."

"What?" I stared at her in the rearview mirror. "Why didn't I hear about this?"

"The zoo managed to keep it quiet because it made them look bad. Naturally that useless reporter missed it. She never covers real news. But she did report that you dined at the Berry Good Café last week. How was the vegetarian shepherd's pie?"

"Bland." Justine Schalow was the only reporter at the Clover Grove Tattler and she had an annoying obsession with me. Date night was her best chance of surveillance because Keats and Percy stayed home. "Where is the zebra now?"

"Safe. The Mafia liberated it from its temporary home and sent it to a sanctuary out of state."

"Thank goodness," Jilly said. "The last thing we need is a zebra at the farm."

"Please. We need a zebra. Who doesn't?"

Keats' mouth dropped open in a happy pant. He was game for big game. Exotic animals delivered new challenges for an ambitious sheepdog.

Edna chuckled. "Perhaps it's with your kangaroo family, representing two large foreign continents stateside."

The thought made me smile, although I was still mad at Cori for kidnapping the kangaroos from the farm while I slept. The tiny trainer was clever, devious and stealthy. She'd neglected to mention the zebra on purpose. Why couldn't she leave the cool animals with me instead of regular livestock? "I guess we're only hearing about the penguins because Cori's otherwise occupied."

"Quit sulking," Edna said. "We're second tier rescuers and that suits me just fine. I need to allocate my remaining time on earth among many worthy causes. Honky Haven isn't one of them."

"Happy," I corrected, catching her eye again in the rearview mirror. "Did you know it's on the top ten list for wedding venues in the state?"

Edna's nearly permanent frown deepened. "That says so much

about the state of humanity. What kind of fool wants to marry in a zoo?"

My best friend's hand came up in a pistol aimed in my direction. "This kind of fool. Haven't you been reading my posts in the wedding planning group?"

"Jillian, I'm busy planning for the end times. When Ivy's big day arrives, I'll put on my dress, march up the aisle and even give her away to the chief. But I do hope that aisle isn't at Honky Haven."

"Only if the penguins are back," I said. "And Jilly approves the food."

The topknot swayed a negative. "I've set the bar high for both food and ambience."

"Why on earth would you choose such a cheesy venue, Ivy?" Edna sounded truly befuddled. "I may not always say so, but you're marrying a class act."

Edna never said so. In fact, she rarely missed an opportunity to slag Kellan. I knew she liked and respected him, but he'd confiscated her driver's license for infractions yet to be disclosed. Further, he'd cancelled her prepper classes and banished a couple of bunkers. They were friendly adversaries who liked to keep each other on their toes.

Now I aimed a finger pistol back at Jilly. "Because my maid of honor shot down nearly every site available this year or next. She's the Goldilocks of wedding planning. Nothing is 'just right.'"

My best friend shrugged. "Guilty as charged. This will be the event of the year for the entire region. It needs to be perfect."

"You don't want Justine reporting we're *basic*," I said, happy to take my nephews' slang for a test drive.

"Need I remind you that at least two mayors will be there." Jilly's voice had its schoolmarm edge. "We have a reputation to uphold."

"You certainly do." Edna's snicker suggested she meant something far different. "Murders, poisoning, animals behaving badly... The list goes on. *That's* why you don't want to hold the wedding at the farm. Surely, it's the obvious venue in every other respect."

"It's because of the pond," I said. "Dad hit a few snags while excavating and it's a big dusty crater. Hardly the image I want preserved in my wedding photos."

"I offered to douse for a natural water source but Calvin thinks it's quackery," Edna said. "He'd rather tear up your whole meadow for a spring."

"Did I miss the vote for a pond?" Jilly was still cranky. "People will track mud and slime all over the hardwood floors." She ran a hand over each pet. "Keats vetoes it, too."

Jilly was right about that. My dog detested water and wanted no part of the pond project. I'd envisioned a small, sweet pool with ducks paddling, but Dad's backhoe was so thirsty it would be a small lake by the time he struck gold.

"I'm sure you'll find a better site for the 'I do's' than Honky Haven," Edna said. "You'll see that for yourselves soon enough. Why not do the sensible thing and elope? You'll save a bundle and have more fun."

Jilly turned quickly to glare at Edna. "Don't give Ivy ideas. Eloping is cruel. Loved ones want to share a couple's important milestone."

"Looks like someone's overinvested," Edna said. "But at least this has stopped the baby talk. It was getting old for this old lady."

Keats' next mumble seemed to suggest I change the topic. We weren't far from the zoo now and I still hadn't been briefed. "What happened to the penguins, Edna?"

"Two went missing from the colony sometime today. They're rare African penguins. Guess what they used to be called?"

Jilly tapped her phone to check. "Seriously? The old name came from the sound of their call. Apparently, it's like a braying donkey."

"Donkey penguins?" I guessed. "Burro penguins? Give me a hint."

Edna threw her head back and gave a passable imitation of Bocelli, the donkey I'd adopted out to my grandparents. "Here's your hint. Jack—"

"Let's just call them by their proper name," Jilly interrupted. "African penguins."

I laughed. "They deserve more respect. Did these two toddle off on foot? Follow a zookeeper out of the enclosure?"

"That's for them to know and us to find out," Edna said. "All eighteen were present at breakfast roll call and by afternoon fish snack, two were MIA." She read Cori's words aloud. "Check security feed. Deploy Keats."

The dog sat up straight in Jilly's lap. He loved little more than being assigned a mission by Cori, a respected trainer and born leader. Normally he had to compete with her own border collie for attention, but today it was the Keats and Percy show. I had no doubt they'd uncover these penguins in short order. No security feed required. How far could flightless birds get, even with some lead time? Surely, no one would want to steal a seabird in hill country. It was a long way to the nearest aquarium, let alone the ocean.

The visitor parking lot at Happy Haven was almost empty, except for a limousine near the door. I parked a little further away. No need to make my truck feel bad sitting next to fancy wheels.

We walked up the ramp to the front entrance. Happy Haven would normally be open till five but the closed sign was already turned. A man with graying hair and a pleasant face stood waiting for us. The logo on his tan shirt featured a prominent zebra in the design. Rebranding everything from the signage to swag in the gift store after the striped equine star departed was probably too expensive. Maybe they were hoping to land another one and make things right again.

The man introduced himself as Fergus Shay, assistant manager, and gestured for us to follow him down a set of stairs to the basement. The foyer had the vibe of an elementary school, with lots of posters of animals and a banner asking for donations. Jilly was probably right about holding out for a more romantic ambience. The large aquarium filled with tropical fish was fun, though. A trio of large angel fish with gaping mouths gawked at us curiously.

My best friend raised her hand to slow Fergus down and then pointed to closed double doors. "Is that the party room?"

He nodded. "There's a wedding rehearsal in progress. The manager asked us to keep the penguin problem quiet so the bride and groom don't worry about tomorrow's ceremony."

Jilly started walking toward the doors and then stopped. Her topknot flopped to one side, as if she were straining to listen.

"What's wrong?" I asked, joining her.

She slashed her hand for me to be quiet before whispering, "That voice. No. It can't be."

Keats cut in front of Jilly and eased her back gently with a low mumble. That was unusual. My bossy sheepdog didn't wear kid gloves when he was on assignment.

Percy meowed eerily from the cat carrier in my arms. I'd confined him until we got our bearings. Normally, he only hunted depraved humans but a large, waddling bird might be tempting.

"Jillian, this can wait," Edna said. "There's a time for weddings and a time for—"

"Quiet." Jilly's tone was sharper than I'd heard since our corporate days. "I just need to check something."

I adjusted the carrier and caught her sleeve. "Keats wants you to wait, too, Jilly. Has he ever steered you wrong?"

The double doors to the party room swung open and another staffer walked out. The doorway framed a small wedding party gathered in front of an officiant. A woman in a blue suit with highlighted blonde hair turned. She was probably in her late fifties and looked vaguely familiar. If we'd met, I couldn't recall. Maybe she'd been in my mother's dating class and found her match. Mom would be thrilled.

The bouquet in the bride's arms was exquisite. Red roses and freesia were my first choice, too. If she kept squeezing them so hard they wouldn't last long enough to be tossed to her friends, though.

I wondered if the bride also recognized us. Her mouth dropped open in surprise. It closed and then opened again, like the angel fish in the lobby. Finally she said, "Jilly?"

My best friend's hand went to her throat. Then she croaked, "Mom?"

CHAPTER TWO

An awkward silence dropped over everyone and it took a loud mumble from a canine to break it. Keats nudged my leg, his muzzle turning into a poker. At least, that's how it felt, because I didn't want to be the one to speak first. This wasn't my party. But it wasn't my best friend's party, either, and it should be.

With assistance from my canine manager, I walked into the room and offered my hand. "Mrs. Blackwood? I'm Ivy Galloway, Jilly's best friend. We've spoken before when you two were on the phone."

She transferred the bouquet to her left hand and shook mine. "Ivy. Of course. I go by Brighton, my maiden name."

"Not for much longer." A tall silver fox in a sports jacket slung an arm over her shoulder and pulled her close. "Tomorrow Brina will become Mrs. Lenard Pembroke."

Keats poked me again and I offered my hand to Lenard, too. "Congratulations, Mr. Pembroke. If Brina is anything like her daughter, or her mother, Bridie Brighton, you've found a wonderful partner."

"I'm not," Brina said. "Like my mother, that is."

"She's not," Jilly muttered from the doorway. "Like me, that is."

Edna clomped over in heavy army boots. "That's what we all think, isn't it? I would have hurled myself off Garnet Point before conceding even the slightest resemblance to my mother." Patting her curls lightly, she laughed. "Here I am with hair like hers. And I knit like the wind, just as she taught me."

My prepper friend didn't often grease the wheels of social interaction—quite the opposite—but her loyalty to Jilly ran deep. Possibly deeper than Brina's, given she'd flown in from San Francisco without letting Jilly know.

I added my laugh to Edna's and picked up the conversational baton. "I look just like my mother only supersized, and that's not all we have in common."

"Is that where you got your giddiness?" Edna's laugh turned into a cackle. "Dahlia Galloway isn't known for her subtlety."

Giddiness wasn't one of my failings but I pretended to think about it. "That's a clever cover. Mom is stealth personified when she wants to be. Some say I inherited that trait."

Lenard looked confused by the discussion but it served the intended purpose. Jilly's wilted composure revived and she came toward us.

"Mom," she said. "Are you actually getting married here tomorrow?"

Lenard answered for her. "She is. My beautiful bride indulged my whim to marry here. I grew up in hill country and felt a little homesick." He squeezed Brina's shoulder. "Right, darling?"

"Yes, Len." The words came so quickly that I guessed Brina agreed with her groom often and automatically.

Jilly's pretty face scrunched as she tried to make sense of this situation. "You hate hill country, Mom. You said you'd never come within a thousand-mile radius of Wyldwood Springs and the Brighton manor. That's why you skipped my wedding."

"I didn't skip it, Jilly." Brina plucked absently at the baby's breath in her bouquet. "I was sick."

"Sick of Wyldwood, you mean," Jilly said. "So sick you've never even met my husband and weren't going to introduce me to yours."

Lenard raised an imperious hand. "Ladies, it's not the time to bring up old grudges."

"It's the perfect time," Edna said. "That's what weddings are all about, Len. Funerals, too. Any old grievance is up for grabs."

The balding officiant and another middle-aged couple in smart suits retreated to the large windows to give us space but the remaining woman came over. She had a rainbow of highlights in her unruly mop of hair and nearly as many colors in the frames of her oversized glasses. "You're not wrong about that, Miss Evans."

Edna turned to her. "Do I know you? I never forget someone I've vaccinated."

The petite woman's smile had a trace of smugness. "I'm Lacey Byle. We were in your catchment area but my mother always pulled me out of school on vaccination day."

"Ah, vaccine dodgers." A scowl formed on Edna's face. "If you suffer the scourge of preventable disease, now, in your declining years, you'll get no sympathy from me."

Lacey didn't look much over forty and her lips pursed. "None required." She turned to Jilly and me. "I'm the event planner at Happy Haven as well as a couples therapist. You might know me as Lovebirdy, my handle on socials. I share relationship advice and videos of my lovebirds."

"Speaking of birds, we're here on business." Edna grabbed Jilly and me by our upper arms. "Let's deploy."

Jilly didn't move and Keats didn't move her. In fact, he swished around, tying us together in a sheepdog love knot.

"Ivy, I need..." Jilly's voice drifted off but her fingers twitched in my direction.

"Percy, of course." I set the carrier down and released the cat. He wasted no time scaling my best friend and collapsing into the arm that curled to receive orange fluff. "Edna, would you mind taking a preliminary look into our business matter? The rest of us can chat a little longer."

Edna began to do as I asked but stopped to lob a last shot at the couple. "The place feels like a classroom, Lenard. Sterile. Dreary. A Brighton deserves better."

"We love it," Len said, unfazed. "Lacey's arranged everything nicely. You're all welcome to join us tomorrow evening, if Brina agrees." His brown eyes jumped from Edna's camouflage to my stained overalls, and finally Jilly's floury shirt and leggings. "It is black tie, though."

Jilly's face flushed at the implication she didn't know how to dress for a wedding. My sophisticated friend could outshine most guests at a coronation. "Mother, may we have a word alone?"

Len's fingers tightened on Brina's shoulders. His whitening knuckles made me worry the bride could bruise. "We're a team, Jillian. There's nothing you can say to Brina that you can't say to me."

The color on Jilly's cheeks advanced to her hairline. "Oh, really? You have no idea, Mr. Pembroke."

Edna was still near the doorway and a family with young kids walked through the foyer behind her. There were obviously stragglers left in the building. They slowed to stare into the room and I worried someone would recognize us. Jilly wouldn't be happy if this story reached the big ears of Justine Schalow.

It was my duty to intervene and I had the means to do it. I flicked my fingers. "Keats, doors."

He raced over and nudged each door closed, shutting Edna inside with us. I flicked again and the dog ran back and introduced his teeth to Lenard's pantleg.

The silver fox yipped. "Back off, dog. That's a cashmere blend."

It was enough to make Len release Brina. He bent to swat at Keats, who circled just out of reach. The dog's flattened ears and lowered tail told us the groom scored a big fat fail in the character department.

Edna clomped back to collect the bride. "Come sit down, Ms. Brighton. Did you know your mother is a student of mine? She's preparing for the end times. You'd be very proud."

"The end times?" Brina sounded dazed. "I'm not sure what you mean."

"Let me tell you more." Edna steered Brina to the single row of folding chairs. Lacey started to follow and Edna shook her head. "This information isn't for you, Ms. Byle. Disease will claim you long before the zombie uprising."

The elderly officiant backed away discreetly and then slipped out of the room through another door. When the other couple came over to Brina, the rest of us followed.

"Brina, what's going on?" the woman asked, scanning Jilly, Edna and me. "Do you know the custodial staff? Or are they zookeepers?"

Lenard Pembroke's laugh reinforced my dog's verdict. Percy's tail twitched a warning, too. If he weren't on emotional support duty, the cat would be adding orange fur and punctures to the cashmere blend. My pets weren't waiting for the ceremony to state their objections to the union.

No matter how the rest of us felt about the groom, however, Brina must love him. It wasn't our place to pass judgement. We would leave that to the angel fish in the lobby.

"I'm Ivy Galloway," I told the newcomers in their smart suits. "Becoming a zookeeper is my secret dream, but for the moment I'm just a hobby farmer and innkeeper. Please meet my best friend, Jilly Brighton-Blackwood-Galloway."

"Of the Wyldwood Springs Brightons," Edna said. She introduced herself and offered her hand to the woman, who ignored the camouflage glove. "Your girl Brina tried to slide the wedding past her own daughter. Good thing we happened to be in the neighborhood."

Another silver fox who was even taller than Len spoke first. "I'm Theo Radcliffe, the best man, and this is Vanessa Greer, the maid of honor."

"Brina has a daughter?" Vanessa scanned us again at closer range, stenciled eyebrows rising over cat-eye glasses. Her dyed auburn hair was twisted into a tight bun. Instead of returning my smile, she looked down and plucked several feathers off her dark suit. They probably came from the large flocks of geese that gave the zoo its nickname. "I didn't know."

"Are you actually friends?" Edna asked. "Or one of those rental bridesmaids for secret weddings?"

Vanessa's eyes came up and she blew a feather in Edna's direction. "I'm Lenard's friend and haven't known Brina long. In our circles, we don't fling open all the closets and let the skeletons dance. If Brina held this back, there must be a reason."

My temper burbled a warning in my belly. Left unattended, I'd unleash fiery words that would upset Jilly even more. Keats sensed the risk and locked his eyes on Vanessa, ready to deliver a death blow to her hosiery. I snapped my fingers to stop him. "Jilly isn't a skeleton in anyone's closet, Ms. Greer. She's a chef of renown and runs an inn with me."

"Never heard of her," Vanessa said. "But then, I avoid the social media your generation worships. It's a blight on polite society."

"On that we agree, Vanessa," Edna said. "Too many people spew garbage online." She glanced over her shoulder to make sure Lacey was listening. "Some use their platform to manipulate the gullible for personal gain."

Lacey pushed her glasses up her nose with a sharp tap. "I take offense at that, Miss Evans. My followers benefit so much from

Lovebirdy advice that I'm writing a book. The working title is *Radical Romance: Blow it All Up for Love*."

Edna snorted. "Keep working."

Len shoved Lacey out of the way rather rudely and pushed in beside Edna to set a big hand on Brina's shoulder again. "We're getting off track, here. Way off track. Brina and I decided to have a private ceremony with our best friends as witnesses. It's nothing personal, Jillian."

I'd never seen Jilly more flushed and Percy's squirming told me this was beyond his capacity to soothe. He hung on, but not without a hiss in the happy couple's direction.

Lacey Byle bravely shouldered in beside Edna. "Domesticated cats aren't permitted at Happy Haven. Nor dogs, for that matter. They could carry parasites or other toxins that are lethal to the zoo's collection."

"We came at the request of your assistant manager." Swiveling, I realized Fergus had vanished. Perhaps he was with the officiant waiting until the dust settled. "My pets have unique gifts Fergus wants to exploit, so he was willing to take the risk."

Vanessa pulled a tissue from what looked like a designer purse. "At least put the cat in the carrier. I'm allergic."

"The cat stays where he is," Jilly said, hugging Percy closer. "I need him."

Ignoring her, Vanessa fished out her phone. "I'll speak to the manager myself."

"Ms. Greer, as a licensed therapist, I recommend standing down," Lacey said. "Jilly just suffered a huge betrayal. An abandonment. It's the type of thing one never gets over. Let her have her cat."

Brina blinked a few times. "It's not a—"

"Jillian, *relax*." Len spoke over his bride again. "There's nothing at all to be distressed about. We just wanted a private romantic moment. Then we were going to drop by your agricultural outfit on our way back to the airstrip. I promised Brina we'd surprise you."

Edna chuckled. "Agricultural outfit? You'd have been surprised, too, Len."

"You'd be most welcome at Runaway Farm," I jumped in. "In fact, why don't you hold the wedding there? Brina, my brother is anxious to meet you and I know you'd love to see what Jilly's been doing since your last get-together."

Len patted Brina's shoulder firmly. "She knows. The local news coverage comes straight to our inbox. Exactly how many people have been murdered on that farm, Ivy?"

I pretended to ponder as the burble in my gut tried to turn into a geyser. "Just two. Technically."

"And a third on my property next door," Edna supplied cheerily. "Plus that lumberjack on the other side. Are we missing anyone?"

"Miss Evans, I'm all about radical honesty," Lacey said. "It's the cornerstone of my program. But that's probably honest enough for the occasion."

It was enough honesty to puff Len's chest under his cashmere blend. He was an imposing man and probably used to getting his own way. "Don't downplay this threat. An old friend sends regular updates on the body count in the region and your involvement. He strongly advised severing ties with Jilly for our own safety."

"Lenard." Brina shook off his hand. "I'm not severing ties with my only child. Long ago, Jilly was my purpose in life. My only reason to get up in the morning."

"Not anymore, darling." His big mitt landed on her shoulder once more. "You have a groom who adores you. Love is all we need."

Lacey raised her hand. "In all honesty, that's just the beginning, sir."

"Lovebirdy's not wrong," Edna said. "Decades of watching

marriages crumble have told me that most break down over miscommunication and money."

"A gross oversimplification, Miss Evans," Lacey said. "If it were that easy, I wouldn't have close to a million followers."

Percy squirmed harder and Jilly finally loosened her grip. The cat pushed off against her stained shirt and landed on Len's shoulder. The groom stepped away from Brina to fight off the unwanted visitor.

Jilly loosened her tongue, too. "There's not much of a tie left between us to break, Mom. Not if you cut me from your wedding guest list."

"It's not like that." Brina's voice was strained. "This was spur of the moment. I didn't even—"

Theo intervened since Len was occupied with Percy. "We're businessmen, Jilly. Investment advisers to folks in high places. Given the scandals, Len thought it would be best to keep a distance. To safeguard our clients."

"It's a high-stakes game," Vanessa added. "Any doubt from investors can spell disaster."

"Exactly right." Len's words were muffled by orange fur as Percy moved from shoulder to shoulder across his face. "It's about me, Jillian, not you."

"I see." Jilly stared at her mother. "All the good work we've done here is an embarrassment to you."

Brina shook her head quickly. "Not at all. I'm proud of you."

"So proud that your bridesmaid doesn't even know I exist?"

Vanessa pulled out a compact and checked her makeup. "It was better that way, dear. Knowing you apparently comes with great risk."

"With risk comes reward," Edna said. "Isn't that how the saying goes?"

Lenard wrapped his arm around Brina. "I can't risk my sweet dormouse. That's what I call her, you know."

"Dormouse?" Edna said. "Brina's mother would take you down with one swing for calling her that. What does Bridie think of you, Lenny?"

His teeth were surprisingly white for a man of his age but there were a couple of crooked ones to prove they were original. "To know me is to love me. And she will when she meets me. We'll visit the Briar Estates when the weather cools down."

"Bridie will be thrilled," I said. "I hear Shelley is still there. Janelle's mom."

Brina winced at the memory of her sister and their decades-old rift. "It'll be a short visit."

"A drive-by," Edna said. She gestured around the room with one glove. "Lenny, what's your deal? A wedding to a Brighton is something to celebrate, not hide."

"No one's hiding anything," he said. "Our best friends in the world are here. Theo can attest to my good character."

The best man offered a set of teeth equally bright. Their investments were going well enough to cover professional whitening. "Brina's the best thing that's ever happened to Len, and he was wise to move quickly. If he hadn't swept her off her feet, I certainly would have. She's beautiful and biddable. The whole package."

It wasn't clear if Theo and Vanessa were a couple, but she lowered her compact to glare at him. "Biddable?"

"Biddable?" Edna echoed. "Did you gents time travel here from the Victorian age?"

"It's a compliment," Len mumbled, as Percy made another pass. "She really is the best thing that ever happened to me."

That may be, but I doubted Lenard Pembroke was the best thing that had happened to Brina. What was his hold over her? Was there time to help her see she could do better? "Brina," I said, "please come stay with us tonight. It's unlucky for the groom to see the bride before the wedding, so we'll get ready together and come back. It'll be fun."

Len managed to shift Percy. "We have reservations. Why don't you join us for breakfast tomorrow?"

He was a master of deflection but I'd find my way through it eventually. "Lenard—"

"We really must be going," he said. "It's getting dark and my dormouse needs her rest."

His dormouse stared down at Keats and then touched the dog's ears. I couldn't help wondering if she'd been drugged and was determined to find out. "Brina, please. It would mean so much to—"

"Ivy, it wouldn't mean anything," Jilly interrupted. "If she wants to go, let her. We have work to do."

Lacey adjusted her glasses again. "Why don't we all sit down and get to know each other a little better?"

"That ship's sailed, Lovebirdy," Edna said. "And we're shoving off, too."

"Don't. Please." The two words came from Brina. "There's champagne. Join us for a toast, at least."

Jilly backed away. "I don't think so."

I summoned an HR smile from my corporate days. "We'll go do our work and come back. Save Jilly a glass."

Lenard let out a huffy sigh, also muffled by fur as Percy resumed warfare. "I'll ask the restaurant to hold our dinner reservations. It's one of the finest restaurants in the area, Brina."

"Not saying much," Edna said. "Your future daughter-in-law can out-cook any chef you're likely to meet, Lenny. Shame you won't get to learn that from experience."

"I'll live," he said. Then he used his massive mitt to shove Percy off his shoulder with unnecessary force. The cat went flying, landed with his usual grace and directed a hiss at the man.

By then, Jilly was advancing on Len. "How dare you throw my cat?"

Len held his ground. "He's a menace."

My friend formed the same hand pistol she'd aimed at me earlier. "If you *ever* do that again I will—"

Jilly's threat jammed in the barrel when Edna grabbed her and turned her by force. My best friend struggled as we practically carried her away. Fergus Shay was already opening the door to the foyer.

"She won't deliver on that threat but I will, Lenny," Edna called over her shoulder.

There was a highly satisfying man scream as Keats had the last word.

CHAPTER THREE

J illy was virtually unherdable as we went down the staircase
and into the hallway below. Keats ran ahead and circled back
but she repeatedly sidestepped him with ease. In this dance,
Jilly was leading and Keats didn't like it. Normally, she was his most
cooperative sheep. She hated nips and holes in her pants and
worked hard to anticipate his moves. Today, she was willing to risk
her leggings. The only reason they remained unpunctured is that
my dog chose to spare her.

Percy, on the other hand, had tried to leap onto her back twice
during our descent and because I was worried she'd stumble, I
stopped to put him back in his carrier. Perhaps it was for the best as
we moved among the indoor exhibits.

When we entered the main hall, two river otters swam up to the
glass of their enclosure to greet us before somersaulting and pushing
away again. Their aquatic gymnastics would have made me smile
on another day. I loved otters and didn't see enough of them. One
thing the farm lacked was a creek. That's why Dad was working so
hard to fill the pond with fresh water. Rain alone would turn it into
an outpost of Huckleberry Marsh.

Keats came back to me grumbling. Even thinking about swamps seemed enough to earn me a reprimand. His temper was already short because of interruptions and tension. Now his best human sheep had gone rogue, charging down the hall ahead of us.

"Is she okay?" Fergus asked.

"She'll be fine," I said. Our corporate career had thrown bigger problems at Jilly and she'd stepped over them easily in heels and a pencil skirt. She'd kick this one to the curb in sneakers. Perhaps not today, but soon.

I waved to the otters with a silent promise to come back. Seeing wild animals in captivity was hard for me but I would focus on the educational value for visitors, particularly kids. While otters and the beavers in the next enclosure were not threatened, many creatures exhibited here were likely close to extinction in the wild. There wasn't much wilderness left for them in the world.

Fergus slowed to match my pace. "Most of our animals were born in captivity. A few are rescues from rehab facilities. We care for them well and our mission is to educate and inform. Wait till you see the aviary. Our collection is a who's who of Psittacidae."

My heart sounded a sad trombone. I knew too much about the plight of parrots to enjoy hearing about Happy Haven's gallery of stars. "Tell us about the penguins, Fergus."

"Most come from a zoo in the Pacific Northwest. Their colony of African penguins is prolific, probably because they've nailed the environment. Even with more temperate varieties, it's hard to get the details just right. Climate change has decimated their population in the wild. Most hatchlings never—"

Edna's camo glove rose to cut him off. "Spare us the details, Fergus. We're rescue soldiers today. Emotion will hamper the mission."

"Understood." He picked up the pace, hustling past enclosures containing a variety of amphibians and reptiles. On her best day, Jilly wouldn't have given them a second glance and I doubted she noticed them at all today. Some were hard to miss, at least for me. This was the first time I'd seen a Burmese python since I broke into the dogcatcher's basement lair soon after moving to the farm. While the visit gave us a valuable clue to solving a murder, if I never saw another constrictor, I'd be happy.

A poke in the calf brought me back to the present. Keats wanted me to pay attention. "Fergus, this place seems very secure. How would a pair of penguins escape? They don't have prehensile thumbs to work the locks. Did they follow a keeper out?"

Edna answered for him. "What's rare is valuable so theft is more likely. Probably an inside job."

"Our staff have been thoroughly vetted and cleared by police," he said. "I trust all of them."

I glanced up at the cameras in the corners. "Was the security feed disabled?"

He shook his head. "Only the right staff went in and out. It's baffling."

We were at the penguin enclosure now, where a group of birds huddled on a fake rock looking forlorn. Were they trying to console each other or protect each other? Either way, it was hard to see them as the adorable creatures they were. Not the largest or most striking breed of penguin but cute nonetheless.

"Going with the theft theory, why would someone only grab two?" I asked. "They're small enough to be easily transported in a carrier like this." I patted Percy's shoulder bag and he responded with an eerie meow. "There are bird backpacks, too. I used one for a while with a feathered friend."

"Even two penguins would be a handful outside the zoo. To be healthy, they need to swim and get a steady stream of fish. And quite frankly, they stink. On top of all that, they're loud. There's a reason they earned the name jack—" He stopped. "Never mind. It's not a word to use in front of ladies."

"We know what donkeys used to be called, young man," Edna said. "And please don't call us ladies."

I gave Fergus a smile. "You see, the term 'ladies' might make people underestimate us."

He smiled back. "I know better than to underestimate you. Cori Hogan is a longtime friend of Happy Haven. I hoped her, uh, organization could spare us from calling the authorities. We won't be able to avoid it for long, however. If this isn't resolved by morning, we'll keep the zoo closed and interview all staff. Still, the news will get out eventually. We barely kept a lid on the... Well, never mind."

"The zebra," Edna said. "Don't pussyfoot around, Fergus. We can't help if you're being evasive."

"Have you lost other penguins?" I asked.

He shook his head. "Mostly reptiles and parrots. We've recovered some of them on the black market."

"So, it's about money?" I asked. "Would a black market penguin attract a good price?"

He rubbed his forehead. "With only twenty thousand left in the world? Definitely. This pair has bred successfully, both here and in their previous home. Two of their eggs are in an incubator now. We control what we can."

"Are the eggs safe?" I asked.

He pulled out his phone and scanned his messages. "I assume so. No one said otherwise."

"Never assume, Fergus," Edna said. "Give us the key and go check with your own eyes."

The florescent lights overhead showed the man's hesitation. "I can't let you inside with the penguins. You might be carrying viruses or parasites that would decimate a fragile colony. Not to mention the damage your pets could do."

Jilly had gone down the long hall to the very end, presumably to be alone with her thoughts. There was no solitude to be had with an officious pet duo around, however. She beckoned us. "Keats has a lead."

When we joined them, my dog was facing an exit with one white paw raised. "Where does this door go?" I asked Fergus.

"To the trash bins. We store them behind the zoo so they don't impact the visitor experience."

"Part of keeping the mystery alive," Edna said. "And that's how your thief escaped."

Fergus pointed up at the security camera. "There's no escaping the feed."

She patted his back. "Sweet, naïve Fergus. Your feed has likely been tampered with. I trust this dog over technology."

"Keats is onto something," I confirmed. "We'll head outside while you go and check the eggs. See if anyone had access to the cameras."

"Okay, I'll let you out first, so the alarm doesn't— Oh."

Jilly had already cracked the door open without so much as a warning beep. "There's your next clue," she said, striding outside. "Ivy, I'll take my cat baby now."

As soon as my feet hit pavement, I released Percy. Instead of running to Jilly, however, he joined Keats to bound away from us down the path. They moved onto the grass and picked up speed.

"Where are they going?" Fergus called from the doorway. "A thief would have parked in the lane behind the building."

"Eggs, Fergus," Edna shouted as she clomped after the pets with Jilly. "Save the babies."

I moved more slowly, studying the grass, which was crushed in spots. The earth was moist here. A large puddle had formed in a hollow. Either they'd had a very localized thunderstorm or the sprinklers were generous. Bending, I saw boot prints, some larger than mine and some smaller. Unfamiliar swooshes in the mud made me stoop even more. That's when I saw the other prints. Webbed with long claws. No need for Edna's tracker apps to interpret those findings.

"What's down there?" I called out, hoping my suspicions were wrong.

"Babble Creek," Edna replied. "It babbles nicely here but gets a bit vicious further on. Runs all the way down to Capshaw Lake, and based on Keats' cue, I'm afraid that's where our penguin friends will end up."

"I'm afraid of that, too. There are webbed footprints in a puddle that don't resemble geese or ducks."

Jilly turned back from the water. "What do we do now? Wade after them?"

"I don't stand down often, girls," Edna said, "but I suggest waiting for Cori to come with gear and reinforcements. Even if you could grab a swimming penguin with your bare hands, their beaks are meant for stabbing."

Normally the voice of reason, Jilly crossed her arms and sulked. "We have to do something. These birds are precious. And parents. Ivy, you must agree."

Normally the voice of impulse, I shook my head. "I vote with Edna. Cori will be here soon. And if I were a zoo penguin, I'd have vamoosed out of the vicinity fast." Keats herded Jilly over gently and I added, "Let's go back inside and join the toast."

"Not a chance." Jilly's green eyes were full of rage but tears leaked from the corners. "My own mother ditched me from her wedding."

"It's a honking shame," Edna said, pointing to the flock of Canada geese grazing in the distance. The zoo had several acres of luscious grass to keep them multiplying. "Eventually they'll be the only thing left on exhibit. Few natural predators."

One such predator crouched beside me now, aching for permission to send them flying. This dog adored seeing a wave of geese rise and flee.

"Leave it," I said. Keats looked up at me with his blue eye, when I expected pleading brown. Were we missing something bigger than penguins on the lam? "Jilly, there's something going on with your mom. She didn't look happy to be here. Maybe she doesn't want to marry Len."

Edna scowled. "Who would? That man had her transfixed, like a cult leader. I've seen that glazed look in people's eyes before."

"Can we break his hold before the vows?" I said.

Keats gave up on the geese and decided to try. Either that, or he just wanted to be away from the water. Even here, Babble Creek could carry a midsized dog away without much trouble.

"Not my business," Jilly said. "We'll wait here until Cori comes."

Edna gave her a pat most would consider a shove. "Don't let them best you, Jillian. Soldiers don't whine."

"My mother didn't invite me to her wedding, Edna. I'm allowed to take a moment."

Apparently, she was not. My dog disliked wallowing intensely. Wallowing meant inaction and we had things to do.

He cut between Jilly and the shore in an exaggerated arc.

"My friend, you're being warned," I said. "That was a herding shot across the bow. Your ankles are in imminent peril."

She backed toward the creek in a blatant ploy to use his fear of water against him. The dog's ears went back and he took a mock dive at her shins. One more pass and her yoga pants would be toast.

"Keats, stop," Jilly said, now on the water's edge. "I'll go into the creek. Don't think I won't. I'd rather drown than face my mom right now."

I didn't think she'd wreck a new pair of sneakers but she didn't get the chance. Instead of nipping, Keats reached up for the edge of her oversized shirt and yanked with such force that Jilly lost her balance and staggered a few steps toward us. Then the dog circled and drove all of us toward the building. Edna and I looped our arms through hers and started walking.

She didn't go without a fight, but Edna squeezed and lifted till one sneaker dragged on the ground. I couldn't bring myself to do the same. Supporting Jilly to face her family was one thing. Brute force was another.

"You'd do the same to us, Jillian," Edna grunted. "Wouldn't you?"

"I would not." Jilly tried to go limp and got a nip for her efforts. "This is different. You can't even imagine."

Edna grunted as she hauled my friend along. "Seeing your mother fall for the wrong man is no worse than the family drama I've faced. Nor what Ivy's faced. Buck up, little camper."

"Besides, there's still time to bring your mom to her senses," I said. "There's more going on here than romance, I'm sure of it. It's not like you to give up so easily, Jilly."

We got to the door where we'd come out and found it locked. Jilly's resistance subsided and she shook off our arms. "Where's my cat baby? I'm not going in without armor."

I looked back and saw Percy emerge from the decorative shrubs. There was fresh, moist soil on his paws. He'd been digging, or perhaps swishing to announce an unsavory find. I hoped it wasn't a dead penguin. After the others arrived, we'd expand the search.

Jilly went to collect Percy, while I exchanged texts with Fergus and did some research on penguins. Edna called Cori to fill her in on our discoveries.

When we put our phones away, Jilly was gone. "Meet me round front," she texted.

Fergus opened the door in the same moment, so I just thumbed up her message.

"Show me everything," he demanded, after we briefed him.

Keats was only too happy to do so, and while I wanted to check out what Percy had found in the bushes, the cat had been carried off to add dirt to Jilly's already-stained shirt.

Finally, we left Fergus at the side door and walked around to the front, where Jilly was still waiting for her escort inside. Keats led the way up the ramp, his gait more prowl than prance. Percy's tail lashed under Jilly's arm as we walked to the door side by side. Fergus was already waiting to let us in.

My best friend stepped ahead, digging deep for a show of strength. Her chin was high, and her shoulders back as she strode through the foyer and into the party room. I knew, in her own mind, she was wearing her second best dress and heels, saving number one for the big day. She was ready to take on the new man in her mother's life.

Lenard Pembroke would be an easier target now. In the time we were gone, he'd become quite drunk. He staggered around the room, muttering incoherently.

"I hope he's not driving," Jilly murmured.

Edna harrumphed. "He won't be. I'll make him walk a line and then seize his keys. That'll take his ego down a notch."

My feet slowed long before we reached the wedding party. Brina's brow was furrowed as she watched her intended hit a wall and bounce off. Then he tried walking into it again. Theo and Vanessa had their heads together, laughing over a private joke. Maybe they were dating, despite Theo's open admiration of Brina. Lacey had the officiant cornered, perhaps interviewing him for her book. If today was any example, he would have plenty of stories to tell.

"Lenard doesn't look well," I said. "His face is—"

"Ugly?" Jilly said, falling back to join us. "His character is showing."

Edna studied the groom. "Ivy's right. Len isn't just tipsy. Look at his pallor. His eyes are puffy and he looks like he's going to—"

Len bent and parted ways with what was left of his lunch. He was unlikely to enjoy fine dining tonight, either.

I puffed out a sigh of relief. With Len ill, the wedding would be postponed. We'd have a bit more time to find out if Brina actually wanted to go through with it.

Keats moved in front to hold us back, though no one was in a hurry to rush to Len's aid. Even Edna, proud field medic, was inclined to let him get it all out.

Brina seemed frozen but eventually she said, "Len? Are you all right?"

"No, Brina, he's not all right." The snappish words came from Vanessa as she hurried toward the groom. "He's obviously very ill. Someone call an ambulance."

"Done," Fergus called from the doorway. "It'll be about fifteen minutes."

"Too long." Edna's tone was brisk and businesslike as her boots thudded toward Lenard, now on his knees. When push came to shove, the retired nurse wouldn't neglect a patient, even someone obnoxious. "This is serious. Very serious."

"A heart attack?" Brina's voice was high and tight.

Edna eased Len down to the floor and rolled him onto his side. "Everyone move back."

No one did, so Keats deployed medic dog herding moves. The only one permitted to pass was Percy.

With Edna hurriedly loosening his tie, the prostrate man gurgled, thrashed a few times, and then stilled.

"He passed out," Theo said, watching Edna take Len's wrist in her hand. "Must have had a bad oyster at lunch."

Vanessa touched her midriff. "Oh, dear. I ate the oysters, too."

Lifting her eyes from Edna, Brina turned to her daughter. There was horror in the green eyes they shared. "Is he okay, Jillian? Is Lenard okay?"

Jilly was staring down, not at Lenard but the cat. Percy's paws still held a little soil from his earlier excavation. Now, he sprinkled it over Len's splayed hand and moved around to the fallen man's face.

"What is that cat doing?" Theo asked.

Brina glanced at the cat and then back at Jilly. "Can't you stop him?"

"No, Mom. When Percy gets like that there's nothing I can do."

"Of course you can," Vanessa said, trying to get past Keats and earning a run in her hose. "Get that thing away right now. Len doesn't like cats. Or dogs."

Edna released Len's wrist. "Len doesn't like anything. Not anymore."

CHAPTER FOUR

It took a long moment for the truth behind Edna's words to sink in.

Then the screaming began.

Vanessa got the ball rolling, then Lacey joined in. Finally, Brina offered a stifled squawk. It sounded uncertain. Had Lenard been so controlling that without his direction she didn't know how to react to his loss?

"I'm so sorry," Jilly said, crossing the short distance to her mother. She started to reach out and Brina stepped back. It looked like she was moving away from the body but Jilly took it as a rejection and turned to me, eyes filling with tears once again. "You'd better call the police."

Normally that was *her* role when someone died unexpectedly in our presence. It was a common enough occurrence to have a routine. While she observed protocol, I usually dealt with the pets and took a look around. In this case, it wasn't a crime scene, of course. It was just an unfortunate and untimely demise from natural causes.

Except that Keats remained at the dead man's side with one white paw in the air. Fluffy orange paws continued to scrape at the carpet with feverish zeal. Was it possible the cause of death wasn't natural after all?

I pulled out my phone and pressed Kellan's direct number. It was easier than dealing with central dispatch. No matter what time I called, the woman I'd nicknamed Bunhead Betty answered. She found me lacking as consort to the chief of police, an opinion she'd formed even before I showed up at reception carrying someone's femur in my handbag.

My fiancé answered cheerfully. "How goes wedding scouting? Anything survive Jilly's scrutiny?"

I turned away from my best friend and lowered my voice. "Well, we've ruled one place out. Honky Haven."

"The zoo? I thought you'd already ruled it out. Are you desperate enough to risk dragging your wedding dress in goose poop?"

I wanted to laugh but it would have been inappropriate. "Not *this* desperate, no. We were deployed by Cori Hogan to look into a penguin disappearance. But when we got here, we ran into Jilly's mom at her wedding rehearsal."

There was a silence. "Back up, please. Jilly's mom is there? And she's getting married?"

"Yes and no. She's at Honky Haven—Happy Haven—but she's not getting married. At least not to Lenard Pembroke. That was her groom, but unfortunately he..."

When my voice faded, Kellan tried to help. "Flew the coop? I wish the geese would do the same."

This was why Jilly made the calls. She was better at getting to business. But it was partly to spare her that I was soft-pedaling the news. I moved further away from her, only to find myself standing over Lenard's body, where Percy tirelessly swept invisible litter.

"Percy, stop that," I said. "We all get the point."

"What point?" Kellan's next words were louder and Edna overheard.

"The usual point, Chief," she said, straightening and grabbing the phone. "Ivy's trying to break it to you gently that the groom expired from poison."

"Poison!"

The communal exclamation brought a small smile to Edna's face but she wiped it clean before she turned.

"Most certainly," she told both the group and Kellan. "Look at Lenard's face. He's unrecognizable." I tried to grab the phone back but she jumped nimbly over the prone form. Percy let out an indignant meow as boots landed too close for his liking, and then resumed the mock burial. "You'd better get a move on it, Chief," Edna continued. "We've got everyone contained in the party room and—" Another joint scream from Vanessa and Lacey drowned her out but she concluded, "Oh, good, Gertie's here."

Gertie Rhodes strode into the room pulling her rifle over her shoulder with one smooth movement. It was all the more impressive because she managed to toss her knee-length braid from front to back in the same moment. A ratty brown poncho concealed the upper half of camouflage that matched Edna's.

Edna's brief distraction allowed me to grab my phone back and say, "You're coming?"

"On my way," Kellan said. "Do. Not. Move." There was thudding as he ran to his car. "Do you hear me, Ivy?"

"Of course I hear you. Even without the phone I could hear you. You're yelling."

The car door slammed. "Our definitions of yelling differ greatly. But I am asking you not to leave the room and go chasing pigeons—"

"*Penguins*, Kellan. Rare African penguins on the verge of extinction. We wouldn't be staging a massive rescue effort for pigeons." I thought about it. "Maybe we would."

"I'm sure it's only a matter of time till you do. For the moment, just try to keep everyone calm."

"That ship sailed when Lenard keeled over. And then again

when Gertie walked in." Glancing at my dog, I murmured, "Keats says it's foul play."

He sighed. Given that the engine was roaring, he must have put some lung power behind the gust to make sure I heard it. "Keats is not always right."

The dog's eerie blue eye turned, perhaps sensing treachery in his fiancé. "He's right when it matters. And detecting poison is well within his skill set. We did scent work back in Boston, you know."

"How would the groom get—" Kellan stopped. "Never mind. Don't answer that. A proper investigation will reveal all we need to know."

I pretended he hadn't shut down the discussion. "They were drinking champagne when we came back from looking into the penguin problem. Maybe someone sprinkled tragic dust into Len's glass. He didn't seem like a nice guy."

"Speculation. You didn't know the man." There was a screech of tires on his end and I let him execute his act of derring-do on the highway. "Or did you? You've never mentioned Jilly's mom's better half."

"Worse half, trust me." I turned with my back to the door, watching the others. "Although you're correct, I didn't know the guy till today. We all agreed he wasn't good enough for Brina Brighton."

"You've barely mentioned Brina before."

"We haven't formally met. In all these years, I've only spoken to her the odd time during Jilly's calls. They weren't close but I never thought Brina would exclude her own daughter from the wedding." A mental python squeezed my throat and I had to force the words out. "Jilly was heartbroken, Kellan. She had no idea. About a month ago, Brina mentioned visiting the farm but didn't follow through. If we hadn't come about the penguins, we may have missed her entirely."

A roar of air whooshed over the phone line as he cracked open his window. "That seems like a strange coincidence."

"If there's a connection between a pair of penguins and a heart-broken bride, I can't see it." Keats joined me with a mumble. Perhaps he sensed something I couldn't. Luckily, the noise on Kellan's end was too loud for him to hear more speculation, this time of the canine variety. If my fiancé got suspicious enough, he'd revoke our penguin pursuit privileges. "Just good timing, I guess. Although it doesn't feel good."

I hoped he'd drop the subject but my fiancé's brilliance was as attractive as his tall, dark and handsome packaging. Maybe more so.

"What did you find out about your feathered friends?" he asked. "Do penguins have feathers? Or fur, like seals?"

"Feathers. Super dense for warmth, although these birds are from a temperate climate. That makes them easier to maintain in zoos. Did you know that the African penguin—"

He coughed conspicuously. "I don't know anything about any type of penguin and I'm content with my ignorance. There's only so much room in my mental filing cabinets and they're stuffed to the brim. My job is taking more than its share right now."

I knew that was true. Keats and Percy had recently found a makeshift crematorium that saw the fiery finale of some hill country criminals. Sorting out teeth and bone fragments and pairing them up with unsolved cases was a huge job. That's why Kellan had surrendered wedding decision-making to Jilly and me.

Mostly Jilly.

"I'll keep the fun facts to a minimum," I said, although we both knew that was a lie. When *my* mental filing cabinets overflowed with animal lore it was impossible to contain. "As for the missing penguin duo, staff found nothing suspicious on the security feed but a door near the enclosure was unlocked. Keats and Percy traced the penguin trail to a creek behind the zoo. Maybe someone set them free, thinking it was best for the birds. They won't survive in the wild, though."

"We'll check security feeds thoroughly and I'll share whatever I find about the missing birds." I started to thank him but he wasn't done. "In the meantime, I'd ask you and your rescue colleagues to avoid my crime scene." Rolling up the window, he sighed more audibly. "Presuming it is a crime scene."

"It's possible Lenard ate a bad oyster at lunch, like his best man suggested. That would be a form of poison, too, right?"

"Either way, we need to investigate." I heard the sound of sirens in the distance. "I'm still a few minutes away. Can you stay out of trouble till I get there?"

"Chief, I'm just an innocent animal lover. Would it be okay if we—?"

"No. The only acceptable action at the moment is for you, Edna and Jilly to huddle and hush."

"Huddle and hush?" I repeated. "You do know the word 'hush' doesn't belong in a marriage?"

"In a marriage like ours, it's the kindest way to say button up. And trust me, Ivy, I've had to hush myself more often during this courtship than most men do in a long marriage."

I knew that was true so I hushed myself and ended the call with a mere whisper. "Love you."

CHAPTER FIVE

"Huddle and hush?" Edna asked. "Does he know you?"

"Or us?" Gertie added, now thoroughly briefed by Edna.

Keats backed them with a ha-ha-ha. It was his first pant-laugh since we arrived at the zoo. There'd been nothing fun and joyful about our visit to this family attraction.

"Exactly. I'd like to ask a few questions before he gets here." I gestured to Jilly, who was standing alone, looking wilted again. "But I also need to support Jilly. She's miserable."

Edna nodded. "It's hard when parents let us down, no matter our age. You're one of the few who saw them turn around and surprise you. Calvin and Dahlia aren't the average parents."

"No argument there." We walked over to Jilly, who stood with arms crossed for comfort because Percy was still working. "The police will be here in a few minutes, my friend. How are you doing?"

Her normally sharp green eyes were dull and glazed. "Hanging in there." She jumped a little as a black-and-white muzzle nudged her thigh. "Keats keeps checking in on me."

I looked around at the others. Fergus Shay was chatting quietly with the officiant. Theo and Vanessa were also whispering to each other. Meanwhile, Lacey, licensed therapist and social media sensation, was trying to make inroads with Brina and utterly failing. The bereaved bride was determined to remain an island. No one could blame her for that.

"Jilly, the police are going to need to interview everyone to find out how he died," I said. "Including your mother."

"Of course." Her voice was as dull as her gaze, but then her stress hormones kicked in and her eyes sharpened. "You're not suggesting Mom had anything to do with Len's passing?"

"She wouldn't be the first bride to get cold feet," Edna said. "Lenard was detestable and she may only have realized at the last minute."

"Or a little earlier," Gertie said. "Poisoning takes planning. I doubt Brina keeps it in her purse like peppermint candy."

The look my prepper pals exchanged made me wonder if they carried toxic bonbons in their go-kits. I wouldn't put it past them.

Jilly scowled at all of us. "My mother did not kill anyone. How could you suggest that?"

Keats' ears arrived under my fingertips to ground me. "I know she didn't, and we don't even know it's foul play."

She studied the fallen man for a long moment and then sighed. "If it weren't, Percy would be in my arms. And I saw what Keats signaled."

"That's why I brought it up. Based on experience, it's worrying when someone you love is lumped in with the real suspects. You'll want to be prepared."

Jilly glanced over at Brina, who was trying to shuffle away from Lacey. "We're not close, but Mom isn't capable of something like that." Her fingers twitched, probably craving fluffy consolation. "Mind you, I didn't think she was capable of eloping, either."

"If you were marrying someone like Len, wouldn't you keep it quiet?" Edna said. "I can't understand what Brina saw in him."

"He took care of her. Isn't that what every woman wants?" Lacey had given up on Brina and ambushed us. "It's a universal fantasy."

"Not mine," Edna said. "Quite the opposite. My fantasy is to look after myself and only myself."

That wasn't the whole story. Edna looked after us all the time and had saved my life half a dozen times. But it was a choice, not an obligation. As far as men were concerned, despite her notable quirks, Edna had admirers yet she continued to evade ties. Her fantasy truly was independence—something that had been harder for women of her era to find.

"Not my fantasy, either," Gertie said. "I was fortunate to find a good man and we looked after each other very well until his passing."

I nodded. "That's all I want, too, Gertie. My fantasies involve winning a lottery so I can rescue even more animals."

"What about you, Jilly?" Lacey asked. "If you didn't know about Len, it must have come as a terrible shock to be displaced. I understand your mother is quite wealthy."

Jilly turned from Lacey to me. "Is she suggesting what I think she's suggesting?"

Edna answered for me. "Well, you *have* poisoned people before, Jillian."

She meant it as a joke, but Jilly would need time and distance before she could laugh about any of this. "I only *served* the poison and you know it."

"Quiet, both of you." It was probably the first time I'd ever silenced Jilly and she was startled. "Lacey is trying to stir things up and you're walking right into her trap."

"I'm a certified therapist, remember," Lacey said. "It's my honor and privilege to help people process difficult emotions." She directed her gaze at Theo and Vanessa. "Those two are distraught but they have each other. It's Brina I worry about." Lacey tried to touch Jilly's arm but my friend jerked it away. "I was just going to suggest you talk to your mother."

I signaled to Keats and he inserted himself as a shield between Jilly and Lacey. He took it a step further and gently relocated my best friend to the open window to catch some air.

"The chief of police asked us to remain calm and quiet until they arrive, Lacey," I said. "There will be plenty of time for Jilly to reconnect with Brina later."

"That's your fiancé, correct?" Lacey asked. "Brina mentioned you still haven't married, after a very long engagement."

I snatched the bait she tossed at me. "It hasn't been *that* long. Chief Harper and I are busy people."

"No doubt. And yet your best friend married a police officer in short order. I'm just curious about what's holding you back, Ivy. Or is Kellan the one stalling?"

The burble in my belly was back but this time the rage mingled with anxiety. What if Lacey were right? Most couples could get this job done in a reasonable time frame. She was playing on one of my deepest fears—that Kellan would change his mind. Luckily, I had my human resources arsenal within easy reach and hoisted a bland smile into place. "Lacey, if you're looking for business for your therapy practice at a time like this, it's a little—"

"Tacky," Edna concluded. "Never recruit clients over a dead body. That comes straight out of an etiquette book."

"Which book is that?" Gertie asked. "Because I'd like to get my hands on a copy. Never too late to learn manners, old friend."

Lacey's flush resembled the mottled rash I got if I stayed in the sun too long. "No etiquette lessons required, thank you very much. I simply wanted to help Ivy ease the chief's trepidation and achieve wedded bliss. Work like this is so fulfilling I do it for free. In fact, I'll enter your names in the zoo's upcoming draw for a free package of six couples therapy sessions. That's usually enough to get the most reluctant groom to the altar. If it isn't, you'll have your answer and can both move on with grace."

The burble in my gut was on the verge of becoming a volcano that would rain lava down on Lovebirdy had Keats not intervened with a nip to her calf. The dog tore a hole in her flesh-toned hose without drawing blood. Still, it had the desired result of making her back away quickly. "How dare you? Try that again and—"

"Hush, now," Edna interrupted, chuckling. "That's what the chief ordered, Lacey. Not idle threats to animals. The job that pays your bills is a zoo, after all."

"I'll pop your name into the draw for counselling, too, Miss Evans. And add Mrs. Rhodes. It's never too late to dig deep into your feelings. Radical honesty frees everyone."

Edna and Gertie took a synchronized step in Lacey's direction and the therapist scurried back to Brina.

"No digging for me," Gertie said. "Feelings are best left to sort themselves out."

"Agreed, old friend. Navel gazing is a complete waste of our precious time on this planet." Edna shook her fist at Lacey. "It'll drive our species to extinction."

Keats nudged my hand and my memory. "That reminds me about the missing penguins, whose species is under threat of extinction. Our best chance of helping them is to cooperate with the police."

Edna turned to me. "Since when did we cooperate with the police when animals are in peril?"

"Always? Or at least often," I said. "Mainly it means not trampling the crime scene."

"Which we've already done," Edna replied.

"Inadvertently," I said. "Which doesn't count."

Gertie laughed. "Is that right?"

"I just want to be a little more careful this time. That's all."

My two senior friends stared at me in silence for a moment before Edna asked, "Why?"

"Because this is about Jilly's mother and her friends. Kellan and Asher are going to want to get this sorted out as quickly as possible."

Gertie smoothed her long braid and then tossed it back over her shoulder. It flopped heavily down her back and twitched around her knees, a fleeting reminder of the Burmese python downstairs. "And how will your newfound common sense affect the penguin search?"

"It won't, really. We just need to be respectful of police activity. Stay out of their way as they work."

Edna's thin eyebrows rose. She had them professionally tinted at the salon but they were still faint. "You're giving mixed messages here. One thing we can always count on is that you'll put animals first."

"Nothing's changed. I just want to be a little more discreet about it."

My senior friend pursed her lips as she pondered. Finally, she exclaimed, "Dagnabit, Ivy, you let Lovebirdy get in your head, didn't you? Now you're worried about chasing Kellan away from the altar."

Keats' mouth opened in a blatant pant-laugh and I glared at all of them. "It's not that. I'm only worried about making things harder for Jilly."

The police started coming into the room and Gertie flipped her rifle over her back, sending Minnie off duty. Then she patted my shoulder. "I don't often give unsolicited advice—or even solicited advice—but I'll make an exception here, Ivy. As someone who was very happily married for more years than you've been on the planet, there's no use trying to hide or change who you truly are in a partnership. Just continue doing what you're doing." Her pat turned into a shove in the direction of the tall handsome man framed in the party room's doorway. "Be a thorn in that man's side. He loves you for exactly that."

Did he though? The doubts had started long before Lacey churned them up like silt in a stagnant pond. When Kellan fell for me in high school, I was more rose than thorn. Quiet and polite. A studious nerd. It took a severe conk on the head and the love of an amazing dog to turn me into the thorn I was now. Mostly I was okay with that but I did worry it was why our wedding hadn't happened. No matter what Kellan said, I wondered if he wanted the old me back. The one who didn't make waves, as I might very well do in pursuit of rogue penguins.

"Maybe you should hang out your shingle and charge, Gertie," Edna said. "The prepper coffers could use it. Saving up for a tank."

Kellan gave me a nod and a mere hint of a smile. It was enough to send most of the silty doubts back to the bottom of my mental pond. "Gertie, did you wear a poncho while Saul was alive?"

"This very one." She ran her fingers over the nubby fabric. "Haven't been able to part with it for that reason. The braid came later, in case you're wondering. He liked my hair to blow free, as long as it didn't obscure his vision on road or trail. Saul was a wise man in hippy packaging. You'd have liked him."

This time I patted her shoulder. "I know I would, and I'm glad to be your first client at Poncho Psychotherapy."

Asher pushed past Kellan and raced to Jilly's side. He hugged her but her arms hung limply at her side. It probably felt like embracing a crash test dummy. "I'm so sorry about all this, honey," he said. "Don't worry. It'll be okay." Turning, he flashed his brilliant smile in Brina's direction, turning down the wattage when he realized it wasn't the time for beaming. "Hello, Ms. Brighton. I'm sorry our first in-person meeting happened this way."

"Me, too, Asher," she said. "I'm not at my best."

Once Kellan reached the body, Percy called it done and resumed his place in Jilly's arms.

My brother steered Jilly over to her mother, stepping around the dead man's feet. "What a terrible shock for you and your friends," he said. "I hope you'll all stay with us at Runaway Inn while you recover."

"Asher." The name came from two people. His wife and his boss.

My fiancé joined them and took over. "You'll have accommodation in town, at least for tonight. We'll need to speak to everyone and it will take some time. You'll be able to visit the farm soon, Ms. Brighton."

"Good. Thank you." Her voice was a mere whisper. "I've wanted to come but Len—"

Kellan coughed to cut her off. "Officer Galloway will find you a spot to sit down and have a chat. Perhaps Percy could be of assistance."

The cat refused, sticking to Jilly like a big fluffy burr. I could see his claws digging into her shirt but she didn't complain.

"Jilly, I could use some fresh air." I tilted my head to the door. "How about we see if the Mafia's here?"

"Been and gone," Kellan said. "I met them outside and told Cori I'd let her know when the site's cleared."

Keats mumbled objections. Crime scenes were Kellan's turf and animal rescue ours. I considered speaking up but Lacey Byle caught my eye and pressed a finger to her lips. It irked me but I did subside, and that irked me even more. Edna was right. Lacey had gotten in my head.

"Let's just go home," Jilly said, slipping out of Asher's grip. He offered his arm to Brina and she let out a shaky sigh as she took it. "I left cookies cooling and we could all use some tea."

"Actually, I'd prefer you stay here, at least for now," Kellan said.

Jilly was always respectful of Kellan when he was in chief mode, but today she shook her head. "I feel faint and I'd rather leave in the care of our medic. You know where to find us when you need a statement."

I gave him an apologetic smile before Keats herded the four of us away.

"Don't look back," I muttered. My head turned anyway and I found Lacey watching us with a sly smile. It was all I could do not to borrow a famously rude gesture from Cori.

"Focus, Ivy," Jilly said, striding through the foyer and outside. "Call Cori to come back and let's get to work."

"Now? You said you wanted to go home and drink tea."

She rolled her eyes. "My mother's a suspect in a murder investigation that may somehow be linked to the missing penguins. Is this really a time for tea?"

"Is that a trick question?" Edna said, laughing. "Deploy!"

CHAPTER SIX

C ori hadn't gone far, as it turned out. Being told by the police to disperse only sent the crew a quarter mile downstream to a home owned by a Mafia ally. For a caustic individual, the tiny trainer had plenty of supporters who threw open their doors—and their boat launches—without hesitation. Compassion for animals created strange bedfellows and boat fellows.

"Ivy, straighten out," she called from the dock. Her black gloves with orange middle fingers gesticulated and the message wasn't flattering. "You're going to run into—"

I ran into the opposite bank. The creek wasn't wide but it was deep in spots and the water moved faster than expected. I could barely coordinate the oars to steer the rowboat.

"You said you could row," Edna called, deftly spinning her kayak in circles.

"I *can* row." So far it had only happened once before in a calm pond, but still, I'd gotten us from A to B, passing a crocodile and a dead body en route. I could row, had rowed and would row again. For the moment, however, the bow of the old aluminum boat was stuck in rushes.

"Remember to feather," Cori shouted. "Turn those oars."

"Relax," Jilly said. She sat facing me, in the stern seat with Percy in her arms and Keats between her knees. "Just take a few breaths and push off. Nothing you haven't done before. I was there to see it."

It meant a lot that my best friend was cheering me on in her own time of need. "Sorry, Jilly. There's so much going on here I got flustered."

Our friends and Mafia colleagues had arrived with canoes, kayaks and inflatable dinghies and enough equipment for a naval deployment. We could survive for days on the water, a mere stone's throw from a string of small, pretty towns. With just a little more practice at docking, we could stop somewhere for coffee. I could really use a hit of caffeine.

Keats' mumble was subdued but firm. It sounded like he didn't want me getting too comfortable. He certainly wasn't comfortable in the canine life jacket Cori had insisted he wear. Percy wore one, too, fluff bursting around it like sunrays. Unlike most cats, however, he relished aquatic adventure. In fact, Percy was the one who'd discovered the body in the pond at the Briar Estates, where Jilly's grandmother lived.

"Just give the bank a shove with the oar," Jilly said. "We'll catch up with everyone else."

That was unlikely. We'd been assigned the stodgiest vessel partly because of our skillset, but mainly because of the pets. Keats didn't try to hide his convulsive shudders of terror despite his deep desire for Cori's admiration. Clem, her own border collie, had no qualms about taking the empty seat in her double kayak. I'd assumed it was a breed preference but apparently this was all Keats.

His next mumble had slightly more attitude, as if warning me about the hazards of the high seas. Come to think of it, I'd never been that comfortable around water myself. Repeatedly getting swamped by swamps only confirmed my boots were best planted on dry land.

"Ivy! Get moving, dagnabit, or I'm coming aboard. We're losing the light."

I shoved off and rowed in the direction of Edna's voice. It didn't make sense to me that rowers faced away from their target. No matter what navigational advice Jilly gave, I ended up in the wrong place.

Edna wasn't wrong about losing the light. At best, we had an hour till sunset and already, the tall trees on either side of the creek filtered the last rays. It seemed unlikely we'd find two expert marine swimmers who had more black feathers than white unless they wanted to be found. They might be missing their easy fish dinner, but I suspected they'd enjoy freedom a while longer. If I had mixed feelings about zoos, they surely did, too.

"Good, you're finally moving," Cori said, paddling up beside us in her kayak. "Tell Keats to stop shaking and get sniffing."

"He can hear you." I glanced at her and realized her busy gloves were stifled. Rude gestures would only send her careening into rocks and a kayak was more fragile than a tin rowboat. A black life jacket with two neon orange stripes basically broadcasted the same message, anyway. "How can the dogs smell birds in the water?"

She nudged our boat with her paddle. "If a trained scent dog can detect a killer whale one nautical mile away, our brilliant dogs can smell a large bird in a creek."

"Ah, it's about the poop, isn't it? I read penguins can deliver every twenty minutes or so. A big colony produces so much guano it can be seen from space."

Jilly shook her head. "How about you two share your fun facts later? This isn't how I wanted to spend my evening."

"Could have been worse, right?" Cori said. Her short, sleek dark hair was handling the dampness better than ours. It always surprised me how attractive she was, given her testy temperament. "Like a wedding rehearsal dinner."

I paddled backward to stay in place. "Too soon for jokes, Cori."

Pushing frizzy tendrils off her forehead, Jilly smiled. "Jokes permitted. And no, that's one affair I would have been happy to skip."

"An affair might be behind what happened," Edna said, paddling in circles around Cori. "Lenard seemed full of himself. Maybe Vanessa slipped him a kill-pill with a last illicit kiss in the aviary."

Cori tapped Edna's kayak with her paddle. "Priorities. Animal rescue first, murder mystery second."

"Then stop blocking me and let's get going," I said.

They fell back alongside the rowboat and Edna smirked at me. "We're doing this for your own safety. Like bumpers. Keats and Percy will thank you."

"We'll be fine, just go on ahead. As long as I can keep the boat centered, heading downstream will be easy enough. Getting back up is another story."

"Fear not, I have a plan," Cori said. "We'll scan shallows and shores till we get to Stoat Crossing. Vans are waiting there to drive us back to the launch point. Tomorrow morning we repeat as needed."

"Genius," Jilly said.

"I know." Cori smirked before spinning the kayak. "This isn't my first river rodeo, Jilly. And make no mistake, Babble Creek turns into a river. You'll need to get your sea-legs before then, Ivy, or you'll end up in Wyldwood Springs."

"At least we'd have a place to stay." The other two paddled off and I looked at Jilly. "Did you let Janelle know about your mom?"

"Not yet." Jilly's voice was tight and tense. "If Janny's the amazing psychic everyone says she is, she'd have known about this already, wouldn't she?"

"Maybe." I'd witnessed some strange things in Janelle's company and was open to believing she had a special gift. "She's had her hands full in Wyldwood, though. People are dropping like flies there."

A canine grumble made Jilly and me laugh. People were dropping like flies here, too. We often mentioned visiting both Janelle and Jilly's grandmother, but there was so much going on. The inn had welcomed more guests lately and with Daisy expecting, we needed to hire help while my clean freak sister was still available to train them to her exacting standards.

I concentrated on keeping the rowboat aligned in the center of the stream, watching for signs of wildlife on either shore. Soon the creek expanded, as Cori had warned, and the current picked up speed. That was worrying, but we were less likely to hit rocks. At least, I hoped so.

Finally, Jilly spoke again. "Why didn't my mother tell me she was here, let alone getting married? We weren't close but we weren't at loggerheads, either. I wanted her to come to my wedding." I let that slide until she added, "Mostly. At least I didn't elope under her nose. If Cori hadn't sent us to Happy Haven, who knows when I would have found out?"

"I'm sure she'd have come to the farm before flying home. Even Lenard said so." I tipped the oars this way and that to stay centered. There was little need to row now. The boat floated along nicely on its own as long as I kept it steady. "Do you think she may have been embarrassed to tell you about him? You know, in case you tried to talk her out of it?"

"I would have made a strong case for waiting a little longer, that's for sure. You know the old expression: 'marry in haste, repent at leisure.'"

"It did seem out of character for your mom, from what you and Bridie have told me. She sounded as determined to stay single as my mom was determined to date. I'd have been upset if Dahlia hooked up with someone like Len."

She hugged Percy closer and he didn't complain. "It isn't about what Lovebirdy Lacey said. I'm not a child feeling displaced by my mom's new guy and I don't need an inheritance. I invested wisely when I sold my headhunting company and Asher will have a pension. We'll do just fine for ourselves without the Brighton gold."

So Lacey had gotten under Jilly's skin, too. With therapy skills like that, it was no wonder she had to take a gig as a wedding planner at a zoo.

"Absolutely," I said. "There's more to the story than we know. I can't help feeling Len cast some sort of spell over your mom."

"A spell? You know my mom didn't believe in that stuff, either. It's the reason she fell out with my aunt and Janelle."

"Not *that* kind of spell. Just the regular romantic kind. Maybe Len love bombed her, with his fancy dinners and impulse decisions."

"Red flags all over," Jilly said. "The maid of honor was Len's friend, too. Mom didn't really believe in friends."

I tried to slow the boat down and failed. "How can you not believe in friends?" It was the exact opposite of how we lived, surrounded by—and reliant upon—a large group of friends.

"Family trauma, I guess. After she fell out with Aunt Shelley and Gran was relocated for safekeeping, Mom stopped trusting people. She was suspicious of everyone. Even Asher."

"Ash? Why?"

Jilly shrugged, but it turned into general squirming that made Keats yip in protest. "He's too nice, apparently. Too handsome. Too charming. Too good to be true. Since there were no red flags, Mom warned me about green ones. And then she did exactly what she warned me to avoid."

"Why didn't you tell her about Asher's faults?" I said. "He has some."

"None that would have counted with Mom. He's a good man who treats me like a queen. I guess she fancies a different kind of guy. Or did. Now what will she do?"

"After she's cleared as a suspect, she can come and stay at the inn for a while to recover. Then you can get to the bottom of it."

She bent carefully to pull a flashlight from our go-kit. I was so intent on the conversation I hadn't realized how dark it had gotten, or how close we'd come to the bank again. "Mom didn't kill him, Ivy. Even if she wised up in time, that's not in her nature. She is a bit of a dormouse, but she has common sense."

"I would never think otherwise."

A silent "but" hung in the air between us and she snatched it. "But *what*?"

I set the oars on the boat and grabbed a long branch overhanging the water. Using both gloved hands I could hold position. "At the risk of making you mad, I'm just wondering if the Wyldwood side of the family might have found a way to take Lenard out of the equation. You know, to save your mom from making a mistake."

"Janelle's not a killer either." Her voice rose and then dropped to a whisper. "Wouldn't put it past Aunt Shelley, I suppose. But that would presume Mom told her and as far as I know, they haven't spoken in two decades."

"What about Bridie? Would your mom have told her?"

Jilly shook her head while continuing to scan with the light. "Gran can't keep a secret. If Mom told her about Len, she'd have told me. Especially if she knew what he was like. My mom isn't exactly warm, but she didn't deserve a creep like that."

"My money's on Len's friends," I said. "Theo didn't even try to hide he admired your mom so maybe he offed Len to get to her. Not sure what Vanessa would have to gain but she's hard to like."

"I shouldn't have turned them away from the inn. We could have kept an eye on everyone more easily there. The killer will slip up and we won't be around to spot it."

I grinned at her in the dusk. "When has proximity ever stopped us before? If the police haven't cuffed someone by the time we've dealt with the penguins, we'll stick our noses in where they don't belong. How about that?"

It was a bold promise, given the fears Lacey had stirred in my heart about Kellan. But Jilly was the best friend in the world and I would never leave her hanging if there was something I could do to help. She often flouted Asher to do the same for me.

She managed to grin back. "Okay, but if you're cracking the case, I want to be around this time. Usually I miss the exciting parts."

"Because I don't know they're going to be exciting until I'm in over my head, thanks to the boys." My eyes dropped to Keats who was shivering hard despite the balmy evening. It was like this when we last rowed, in Bridie's gated community. The memory made me shiver, too. Maybe it was contagious because Jilly joined the general shudder. The only one unfazed was Percy, who gave an irritable meow before breaking free and jumping from Jilly's arms to the branch I was using as an anchor. "Percy, don't! You could be swept right down to Wyldwood Springs and you're no fan of Mr. Bixby."

To be fair, Percy was fine with Janelle's dachshund. It was the latter who said harsh things to my cat. At least, that's how I interpreted their spirited exchange. Mr. Bixby was even more vocal than Keats but I couldn't understand him at all. Janelle sometimes translated, proving she was as nuts about her dog as I was mine.

The cat sashayed along his fir catwalk in the glare of Jilly's flashlight. When he reached the bank, he dismounted and picked his way down to the water. Standing on a rock, he fished a baseball cap out of the creek with his claws. Then he dragged it back to the shore and used flashing paws to sprinkle it with sand and drive his point home.

This cap belonged to a person of interest.

Someone who'd hopefully be brought to justice long before their next baseball game.

CHAPTER SEVEN

I t felt good to be behind the wheel again. I enjoyed adventure as much as the next hobby farmer but, like my dog, preferred it on dry land. These days I was quite proficient behind the wheel of the truck, which was more than I could say about a rowboat. Getting towed by Edna to the dock in Stoat Crossing was embarrassing but the mockery stopped when we revealed the potential clue. No one recognized the logo but I took a photo before dropping it off at the police station. The discovery seemed to take the edge off Kellan's annoyance that we'd gone penguin hunting against direct orders. As far as I knew, the wedding was still on.

"He probably would have gone easy on us anyway, given Jilly's stress level," I told the boys as we turned out of the lane before the sun was fully awake the next morning. "The fact that he didn't repeat his order proves it. He knows we mean to pick up the search today. Our gang will leave no stone unturned in that creek until the penguins are found."

We had nearly two hours before heading to the meeting point. Jilly took her frustrations to the kitchen to cook up savory delights, whereas I craved the sweet breakfast of rescue and sleuthing champions. Mandy's Country Store was nearly always my first stop after a crisis. She frequently had a tidbit of information that set me on the right path.

Probably not today, however. Brina Brighton and her unpleasant groom fell outside even Mandy's vast sphere of knowledge as the most popular purveyor of baked goods around. Her skills were lauded far beyond Clover Grove, but likely not in San Francisco.

"Good morning," she said, unlocking the door and welcoming us in. "Maybe not-so-good if you haven't found the missing penguins."

I was impressed by the accuracy of the town's grapevine. It had always been fast but often more fiction than fact. Perhaps in the old days, when people had to walk next door for news, the truth had more time to fragment. Mandy was a hub for information and sifted through it like a supercomputer. Back in school, I'd seriously underestimated her capacity for data capture and analysis.

I'd seriously underestimated my own capacities, too.

"No luck," I said, following Keats to our favorite stool at the counter overlooking the parking lot. Before too long, it would be full of vehicles. The window to fill up on sugar and intel was short. "And not for lack of trying. We had a good turnout and worked for ages. But penguins can swim up to fifteen miles per hour and they may be long gone by now."

"You'll find them. You always do." She walked to the counter and collected the breakfast she'd already plated in anticipation of my visit. Sliding it in front of me, she left me to take in the splendor while she went back for the coffee.

"Usually the credit goes to the boys," I said, watching Percy scale the grocery shelves. Since Mandy set him free from his carrier recently, he was making up for lost time exploring. The country store probably held more secrets than any building in town, other than the public library. Mandy's grandmother, Myrtle McCain, had seen a lot in her decades of running the post office. "Ooh, you made my favorite!"

A double slice of coconut cream pie dominated the plate, with a few chocolate cookies on the side. It was the perfect jumpstart to what would undoubtedly be a busy day.

"Figured you could use the extra boost." She brought over a coffee mug so large the contents steamed the window glass and created a convenient shield from passersby. "On top of the bird theft, there's the family stress." Perching beside me, she added, "How's Jilly doing?"

"Trying to cook it off, but this is bigger than frittatas. It's brought up years of resentment." I thought about it while slicing into the pie. "I get it, but I don't think I'd be that upset if my mom eloped." Taking a bite, I mumbled, "Guess I'd almost expect it from Dahlia."

"What was the groom like? The grapevine wasn't kind."

I closed my eyes to let sugary bliss push away disgust over Lenard Pembroke. "Unpleasant. Domineering and chauvinistic. You haven't heard of him?"

She shook her head. "The name isn't familiar. And I'm surprised any Brighton woman would give him time. From what you've told me, they're all firecrackers."

"Those I've met certainly are. Jilly. Bridie. Janelle. Shelley. Cousin Liberty, especially. Brina must have inherited the tame genes."

"Or she's sitting on a powder keg of repressed emotion." Mandy stared out the window as she sipped her own coffee. "I know what that feels like. Used to be so afraid I'd detonate. Now, I have a whole strategy for letting off steam a bit at a time."

"Tell me more. You know I have a little buildup myself. Hence, the manure pile. Wood chopping. Manual labor of any kind."

She laughed. "My main outlet isn't that much cleaner than yours. I visit Happy Haven."

"The zoo? Why? It didn't look like much of a retreat to me."

"How much did you see? The butterfly garden is so peaceful. The aviary is the opposite, but I love the bright parrots, even though I never escape without getting hit by poop. Did you know they run a flight school? The macaws are stunning."

My eyes narrowed. "Why am I just hearing about this now? You know I love tropical birds. Broke my heart when Hannah left with Duncan, her African gray."

Mandy shifted uncomfortably. "Happy Haven is almost a hidden treasure. People only focus on the cheesy wedding aspect. There's a whole contingent of us with annual memberships who know better. We call ourselves zoobies."

"You're in a zoo club?" I set my fork down. "What other secrets are you keeping, Mandy McCain?"

I was joking but her pale cheeks reddened. One of Mandy's secrets had very nearly gotten me killed.

"You always talk smack about Happy Haven, so I didn't want to admit I'm a huge fan." She lifted her coffee and sipped. "Plus I like that it's not overcrowded. It's just like the name... my happy haven. I go for a couple of hours most Sundays, and I try to get to some of the talks. Meet the Keepers is my favorite."

"I didn't realize they had events like that. If you don't mind my crashing, I'd love to check them out." Turning back to the pie, I added, "When the penguins are home and the crime tape is gone."

"I'd be happy to take you on my private tour. If I ever get married, I'd love to hold the ceremony in the butterfly garden."

"Do they allow that?"

"Yeah, and I don't understand why most people choose the party room. Weddings aren't cheap there, though. I guess Brina will lose that money." She tipped her head. "Unless she could convert it into a credit for you and Kellan."

My fork clattered against the china. "It wouldn't be my destination of choice after what happened."

"Wait till you're surrounded by butterflies or exotic birds. You might change your mind."

"Even if I did, the event planner is an odd duck."

"Lacey Byle? Yeah. I know her from the events. Always trying to psychoanalyze people. She's writing a relationship book, you know."

"Oh, I know. She mentioned it several times. Seems like anyone can write a book these days, but will anyone read it?"

"Probably. Everyone's looking for a quick fix for romance." She drummed her fingers on the counter. "Lacey says the key is radical honesty. Can you imagine someone like me embracing that concept? I don't even know what *I* think half the time, so I'm not going to drop any truth bombs."

"Hard pass from me, too. I'm too honest already." I grinned at Mandy. "Except when I'm not."

She grinned, too. "Perfect balance." After taking a long sip of coffee, she added, "Lacey says I'm *choosing* shyness as a shield to avoid getting into a relationship when I could just *decide* to do something different. Isn't that ridiculous? Who would choose to be this way?"

The luscious coconut custard nearly stuck in my throat. Lacey's words had the ring of truth in relation to Mandy. It was possible my friend could choose a new way of being, especially with her grandmother out of the picture. There was no one to hold her to the timidity she'd worn like armor as long as I'd known her. But if Lacey was right about Mandy, was there validity to what she said about Kellan and me? I suppose even a fake guru might hit the mark once in a while.

The pie finally cleared the obstruction and I sliced off more. "It would be nice if our challenges were so easily resolved, wouldn't it? Lacey didn't hesitate to share her unsolicited advice with me, too. It's like she plants seeds of doubt so that she can pull the weeds out after they take root and grow. I've been questioning my relationship since I met her."

"Your relationship with Kellan? Why?" Mandy was indignant on my behalf. "You two are the 'it' couple in Clover Grove."

Laughing, I picked up a chocolate cookie. "Travis and Poppy are a hot ticket these days. Not sure how I feel about that."

The bearded woodsman and I were getting along better since rescuing each other recently, but we both liked to keep the embers of conflict warm. I still wasn't thrilled he wanted to marry my sister and he wasn't a guy to jump through hoops to prove himself worthy. Not even to Poppy.

"Travis is the kind of guy you'd find in a romance novel. Rough around the edges and soft on the heroine. You and Kellan are less cliché."

Now I set the cookie down beside my fork. "In a bad way? Isn't cliché good when it comes to romance?"

"Sounds like you let Lacey climb right into your head, Ivy. Your relationship with Kellan is unique in all the best ways. Don't let her undermine your confidence." She glanced out into the parking lot and then gestured to my fork. Our private moment would end soon. "Those seeds of doubt grow quickly. Why not get married before they can? I hear they've had a cancellation at the zoo today."

"As if Kellan would tie the knot in the middle of an investigation."

She leaned over and put the fork in my hand. "You're nearly always in the middle of an investigation. At some point, you've just gotta jump. There are worse places to do that than Happy Haven."

I lifted the fork and got back to work. "It wouldn't go over well with my maid of honor, given what happened. Besides, we haven't even chosen dresses."

"No one pulls an event together faster than Jilly Blackwood. All you have to do is catch the penguins, help solve the crime and smooth things over with Brina. Then get yourself hitched in the butterfly garden."

"Mandy, that's your fantasy and you should hold onto it. I'll check out the aviary, though. I'm always eager to learn more about birds and it's good luck to get hit by poop."

Keats lifted his paw and Mandy noticed. "Bird knowledge. That's where I can help, Ivy. Professor Tapley Horn gave a talk on penguins last year. Maybe he'll have some tips about finding the escapees."

I jumped off my stool but then realized there was too much on my plate to leave. Wasting pie like this would be a genuine crime. "Where can I find him?"

"He lives outside Dorset Hills. A retired ornithologist. I think I have his address."

She went behind the counter and rummaged in her purse. Eventually she came back with a business card. Beside Professor Horn's number were the words, "Call me." A little heart served as the period.

"Mandy, was this dude hitting on you?"

She shrugged. "I don't notice things like that, if I'm being radically honest."

"He used a heart as punctuation. It's hard to miss."

Her flush came back. "If I were interested in dating, it wouldn't be Professor Horn."

By this point, I was shoveling pie into my mouth. "Too old?"

"Too much. You'll see."

"There's no such thing as too much." I lifted the last bite of cookie and opened my mouth. "Lacey said—"

Mandy tapped my hand firmly, plugging my mouth with chocolate perfection. "Let Lacey date Professor Horn, then. Relationship gurus shouldn't be single. It sends the wrong message."

I swallowed the last bite. "The message she's a quack. Remember that the next time she gives you advice."

She walked me to the door. "Quack. Got it. The problem is

what she's already said. There's no getting it out of my neural circuitry."

Outside, Keats gave a pant-laugh. "That's where you're wrong, my friend. You need to embrace the mental vacuum concept. I'm writing a book about it. Turn it up to high and voom! Trash be gone."

Her smile lit up her blue eyes. "With my luck, your mental vacuum would take my recipes along with Lacey's tripe. I don't write anything down, you know."

"Get Lacey's ghostwriter to help you out. We could sell copies of your cookbook at the inn."

She started closing the door and stopped. "If I published my recipes, no one would come here."

I walked down the stairs. "Oh, Mandy. No need for a guru like Lacey to call you out now. You've become hill country's favorite confidante. People come here for *you*, not the pastries."

A gentle click told me Mandy wasn't ready for a truth bomb like that.

CHAPTER EIGHT

No one answered the door at Professor Horn's house when I knocked. Was he still asleep? It was barely eight o'clock but felt like the day should be half-over. Fretting about the penguins and Jilly's mom had kept me awake much of the night and now I was running on caffeine, sugar and adrenaline—my favorite cocktail on tough days.

"Do you think he's home?" I asked the boys. "Maybe he's out with his binoculars. The early birdwatcher catches the worm."

Keats' grumble suggested he wasn't taken by my humor. His paw came up in a brief point toward the side of the house. Percy's tail was already disappearing through the railings. Maybe we early birds would find the bird expert out back.

The man on his hands and knees beside the garden didn't acknowledge our arrival in the yard. Nor did he react when Percy added orange paws to his excavation. The professor simply brushed the cat aside gently and said, "Would you mind? Unless you know how to plant a ranunculus, you're a hindrance."

"Percy knows a lot about a lot of things, Professor Horn, but he isn't a gardener," I said. "I'm Ivy Galloway and this is my dog, Keats."

His broad-brimmed sunhat didn't tip up. "I expected you, though perhaps not quite this early."

"I couldn't sleep for worrying about the penguins. You?"

He reshaped the hole to fit requirements, tipped a plant from a little pot and then placed it in the ground. "The birds should be fine for a day or two. I expect your rescue colleagues will find them before natural predators." His fingers paused. "Not seals and sharks, obviously. I think a coyote would feel pretty lucky to nab a plump penguin." He sounded blasé but a tremor in the plant gave him away. "They won't stay plump for long in Babble Creek. A few minnows will hardly suffice."

"So, they can survive in fresh water?" I asked.

The hose was nearby and he squirted enough into the hole to make Percy scoot backward. My cat wasn't afraid of mud but it did create more fluff maintenance. He stalked away and stared at me from some flowering shrubs at the rear of the garden.

"They can and they have been," Professor Horn said. "It's not the preferred option for marine birds and I've been advocating for years to move them to a facility with a saltwater system. A zoo as small as Happy Haven can't afford that."

The bitter edge to his tone made me ask, "And the zoo's administration refused?"

"You got it. The penguins are the most popular exhibit at Happy Haven, so they're willing to risk the birds' health to keep visitor dollars rolling in. Meanwhile, the world population of this species is at an all-time low."

"It's a shame they won't listen to an expert," I said.

"My advanced studies are with Trochilidae, you see. Hummingbirds. That undermines my credibility with aquatic species. As if someone with a doctorate can't learn all that's worth knowing about another bird. Or any animal. Knowledge is my vocation."

"How frustrating, sir. I only read a little about the African penguin last night because it made me so sad to learn about their plight."

Finally, his hat tilted back and I caught a glimpse of his face. His features were attractive but his dark eyes had a haunted look. "You can't turn away from a sad read, Ms. Galloway. If more people persevered, maybe these birds wouldn't be on the brink of extinction. I've been to South Africa twice and helped rehabilitate thousands of penguins after oil spills. Still, they're on the brink of extinction because of human impact on the environment." Looking down, he scooped dirt into the hole and patted it around the roots. "We're a blight on this planet. It's people who need to go, not birds."

"I feel the same way sometimes. The way some people treat animals breaks my heart."

He pounded the dirt until the little plant tipped over. "I should have stuck with ruby-throats. Their population is increasing, thanks to backyard feeders. Meanwhile, the only place African penguins thrive is a zoo. Not *this* zoo, but other zoos."

I clicked on my phone. "I read Happy Haven had produced quite a few chicks. Enough to share with other zoos." Scrolling, I found something else of interest. "Huh. I see you've been in the news, Professor. Justine Schalow has profiled you nearly as often as me."

"There's another blight on society," he said.

I laughed. "No argument there. But the Tattler's not the only paper. What's with all the headlines?"

"A rash moment." Both his palms came down and his head drooped. "A rash of rash moments, I suppose. I'm passionate about penguins and lost my temper when zoo management refused to put the birds first. These aren't like parrots who thrive in captivity."

"You threatened Fergus Shay?" I asked.

He sat back on his heels and met my eyes squarely for the first time. "Not just Fergus. Handlers and even the board members. The police came and evicted me from the premises. I'm barred from Happy Haven for life." There was a slight quaver in his voice. "That's my reward for years of selfless service. Zoobie no more."

"I'm sorry it came to that. I've hit plenty of roadblocks while protecting animals, myself. If it weren't for—"

"Your long-suffering fiancé," he interrupted. "He bails you out when you overstep."

"I was going to say my pets and like-minded friends. Kellan certainly wouldn't spare me if I threatened to blow up a zoo."

Pulling off his sunhat he threw it halfway across the yard. "Gross exaggeration. I would never risk hurting the animals."

Keats rarely lowered himself to retrieving, but he fetched the professor's hat and set it on the grass beside the man. Without the hat, he looked much younger. I'd pegged him as late- fifties but overshot by at least a decade. His interest in Mandy McCain was less of a stretch, but their temperaments didn't seem aligned. "Since you're retired, Professor, maybe you have time to join our search party today."

"I'm not retired. I was fired by the college after the zoo incident." He gestured to the little white house. "This used to be my vacation home. Luckily, I'd saved enough to make it permanent."

"Well, we'd be lucky to have you on the team."

"I'm not a fan of teams anymore. People just use you and then stab you in the back."

He moved on to the next plant and I felt sorry for the poor thing getting tossed around by his grief and angst. Professor Horn was like others I'd met since coming home—doing his best for helpless animals and struggling to understand the humans behind their plight. Sometimes this friction went the right way and other times, far wrong.

Keats nudged my leg to put words to my thoughts. "Professor, you could turn this situation into an educational opportunity. No one can stop you from searching a creek for penguins, and since you don't represent the zoo or a college, you can shape the narrative. Do some good for penguins."

His hands stopped moving as he considered my spin. "It's too late for the penguins."

"Too late! You said they could likely survive a couple of days in the wild."

Scooping dirt around the seedling, he patted it down more gently. "Not too late for Beatrix and Bertie, I hope, but for the species at large."

Their names weren't Beatrix and Bertie, I was quite sure of that. He could call them what he liked but that didn't mean he was right. I wouldn't know for sure until I actually made their acquaintance. "While penguins are hatching in captivity, it's not too late. There are rehabilitation programs and sanctuaries. From what I've read, lots of people are committed to this species. It's harder to be heard from our part of the world, but not impossible. Good news travels, sir. Slower than bad news, but it does get around."

Giving the plant a last pat, he moved on to the next one. "You've made a good case, Ms. Galloway, and I'll think about it. I'd be a huge asset to your search party thanks to my special talent for attracting jack—"

"We don't call them that. Some of my friends have delicate sensibilities."

None of my friends had delicate sensibilities, but the old name wasn't respectful of these threatened creatures.

"Fair enough. Now, if you'll leave me in peace, this is my time for contemplation."

Percy came back from his shrub inspection and passed under the professor's arms before dusting the man's face with a fluffy orange tail. By the time he sneezed, the cat was turning back for another assault. Apparently, we weren't quite done here.

"Professor, do you have any idea who might have stolen the penguins?"

He tried unsuccessfully to push Percy away, his movements gentler than my persistent cat probably deserved. "Not me, if that's what you're thinking. I would never put vulnerable birds at more risk. This is the work of amateurs."

"But why? What would they hope to gain by releasing them into a creek?"

Since the cat could not be deterred, Tapley Horn crawled away pulling his box of plants and equipment behind him. "I've been pondering that myself and haven't come up with a plausible answer. There were disgruntled people on the zoo's board. Perhaps you could start there."

"Could you tell me more?"

"I never do the student's work for them. Show some hustle and you may find people are grinding different axes. Some may not believe events like weddings should take place at a zoo. People bring in disease." He added in a mumble, "Some *are* a disease."

Keats' paw came up and I decided to keep pressing. "Do you think the timing of this penguin theft was deliberate? Was someone trying to make a statement?"

"Are you always a lazy student, Ms. Galloway? Try doing your homework and more may be revealed."

"I've been a straight-A student all my life, Professor Horn. It wouldn't kill you to give me a few hints when time is short."

He stayed silent, hands moving, but the pets were having none of his coy act. Four paws got busy excavating and sent dirt flying. The hole was soon big enough to bury a man's reputation. He tried to push them away, with a loud "Off, off!" All that got him was dirt in his mouth.

The boys' enthusiasm made me switch gears. "Do you know something about the murder, sir?"

He wiped his mouth on his sleeve. "How would I know anything about that? I'm banned from the facility."

It wasn't a "no" and Keats' paw, speckled with damp soil, rose again.

I persisted. "How about the zoo staff? You were around a long time."

He spit a bit of dirt onto the ground. "I'm sure the police will do their jobs. Maybe your fiancé will pick up some relationship tips from Lacey Byle in the process." He grinned and there was dirt on his front teeth. "If I'm being 'radically honest,' there was no hope for that couple even before what happened."

His dark eyes widened, as if he regretted saying so much, and he went back to work on his planting.

"Did you know the bride or groom, sir?"

Dirt flew from his trowel in my general direction and I figured I'd earned it. "Never met them. But it's hill country and you hear things. An A-student like you must have good ears."

There was more. I knew there was more and he wasn't going to hand it to me on a silver platter.

Pulling out my phone, I sent him a text that pinged in his pocket. "There's my contact info and details about the penguin search party."

He turned quickly. "How did you get my number?"

"Homework, Professor. Unlike most people, I enjoy it." Letting Keats herd me away I called back, "Hope to see you at Babble Creek. Maybe you'll score a story worth publishing."

"Don't use academia against me, Ms. Galloway. I'm done with that world."

"Never too late to have the last word, sir. In a good journal. That's all I'm saying."

"All I'm saying is get out of my yard." The words had a staccato quality as he spit out dirt. "And stay out."

I slowed at the corner of the house. "The penguins need a hero. It could be you."

Keats gave me a nip that moved me out of the way before a trowel clattered against the downspout.

"Next time I won't miss," he shouted.

"You will, though. If I'm being radically honest, you wouldn't hurt my animals."

"True. But I wouldn't mind cutting *you* off at the knees."

"Too much honesty, sir," I said, exiting quickly. "All it gets you is headlines."

CHAPTER NINE

Jilly was waiting on the porch beside a hockey bag when I came back to pick her up.

"Gonna hit the rink later with Asher?" I asked, carrying the heavy bag down the stairs. "The couple that plays together stays together. Tell Lacey to footnote me for that in her book."

"It is sporting equipment but not what you think," Jilly said, as I hoisted the heavy bag into the bed of the truck. "Asher had a couple of sets of hip waders. I borrowed them for us."

"Nice. Does he know you plan to wade into Babble Creek in his oversized galoshes?"

She walked around to the passenger door and let the pets inside. "You know my sentiments about radical honesty."

We'd been best friends since freshman year and there was plenty we didn't know about each other even today. That didn't trouble either of us. We knew enough to trust each other implicitly and had proven our loyalty countless times. The current trend of oversharing, especially online, was leading younger generations astray. It had nipped plenty of applicants and employees in the butt when I worked in HR.

"I share those sentiments," I said, getting behind the wheel. "But if I can be radically honest for a moment, I could do without spending the day in hip waders. Keats won't be happy."

The dog shuddered convulsively on Jilly's lap and gave a miserable mumble.

She stroked his sleek fur. "It's okay, buddy. You can probably stay on the shore and point out good spots to fish for penguins. I won't let Cori shame you into doing more." Her phone pinged and she checked the screen. "Good news! Cori says there's been a sighting close to Thistledown. The birds swam further than we thought."

"Must have traveled all night without a clue where they were going, poor things. Luckily, we'll have lots of support there. Wendel Barrick is an expert fly fisher who probably knows all the nooks and crannies in the river system. Rickie and Madge Merriweather relied on fishing when they were off grid, too."

The formerly homeless senior couple now lived on Wendel's farm property while the older man stayed in town. All were animal lovers and had become great friends.

"We'll be searching in regular library hours, so Thelma will need to sit this one out," Jilly said.

When we arrived in the picnic area outside Thistledown, however, a woman in a bright silk kerchief waved from the water. Thelma Tilrow was wearing a fly fisher vest and hip waders. The clawed cane in her hand was something the senior librarian didn't use often anymore. I hoped it would help with slippery rocks.

Edna hopped out of Gertie's white van and called out, "How's the roller set holding up, Thelma?"

Patting her kerchief, Thelma shrugged. "Mind your own curls, Edna. We'll see who looks better at the end of this soggy ordeal."

"Ten bucks says it's me." Edna tugged a broad-brimmed khaki hat over her perm. "And younger, too. Can you really afford sun damage?"

Thelma got back to work. "We won't be here long, I'm sure. The dogs will find the birds and all we need to do is net them."

"Is it okay to net penguins?" Jilly asked. "I wouldn't want to hurt them."

Cori Hogan walked over, gloves gesticulating. Today they were waterproof black vinyl, with both middle fingers wrapped in neon orange tape. "Netting is likely our best option, but first we need to get close. They're usually docile in captivity, but they may be reactive after being bird-napped and chucked into a river." She pointed from Jilly to me and back. "What are you waiting for? Suit up!"

Jilly and I argued briefly over who should get the better set of waders. I insisted on taking the older pair, even though they were shapeless and cracking in spots. Waders had come a long way, judging by our well-appointed friends. Cori's were trim and black, likely child-sized, whereas Evie Springdale—doing more filming than searching—wore leopard print. I waved to my rescue friends, who were stationed at intervals in the water. It was similar to regular search formation, only aquatic. Maybe there was an underground manual for rescue. That's a book I would buy.

Asher was a tall man and his old waders had enough room for two of me. I added his oversized rubber gloves, knowing I was unlikely to get through the day without falling. If there was a body of water around, I generally toppled, even without a floppy costume.

"I hate this," Jilly grumbled as she shortened the straps on her shoulders. "Still beats sitting around at home wondering why my mother would elope under my very nose. Like I said before, eloping is cruel."

I stooped to wrestle Keats into his life jacket, wishing I'd done that first. Now, I was at a disadvantage in the coat game. "She'll tell you the truth in time. And if she doesn't, we'll tag team to draw it out of her. How many people have we interviewed successfully?"

"Hundreds." She snapped Percy into his adorable tiny jacket. "But my mom's a tough read."

"Tougher than a criminal?" The words came out as a grunt because Keats had gone flat and limp on the bank. His technique to avoid all garments was to play dead. It didn't stop me from trying to keep him alive, safe and warm, but it made the job harder.

"That'd be a yes." Jilly released Percy and he trotted happily down the slope to the water with orange fluff exploding around the life jacket. "Mom's as slippery as a wet penguin. At least, what I imagine a wet penguin to be."

"Guess we're going to find out. As for your mom, we love a challenge. Keats and Percy will help. She'll underestimate them."

Keats was still flat on his side and didn't seem like much of a threat. He rolled his eerie blue eye up at me in silent protest. He was on strike.

"Get up, Keats," Cori yelled. "Or I'll make you."

He was typically quick to obey Cori but his life jacket was overstuffed with attitude.

With a whistle and flick of her glove, the tiny trainer delivered the threatened motivation. Two border collies descended on mine and a glint of teeth in a pure black muzzle brought Keats quickly onto his paws. Annie, his blue-eyed dam, growled a message to stop being a baby. Frost, Keats' sister from another litter, gave a pant-laugh she'd learned from her brother and frolicked around them. She was a mother herself now, but that hadn't diminished her zest for adventure. They didn't share Keats' aversion to water and Annie had jumped into a pond to rescue me once while her son whimpered on the shore. He was the only one who actually needed a life jacket, which heaped burning coals onto his pride. The look he cast my way was scalding.

Maud Gentry, owner and breeder of Keats and family, laughed and headed down river to her local colleagues. We saw each other often enough that we didn't need to chat now. In fact, I probably felt more at home in Thistledown than Clover Grove these days.

Edna and Gertie shut themselves in the back of the van and emerged wearing scuba suits. I expected them to be prepared for most encounters, but scuba diving opportunities were few in hill country.

"What are you staring at, Ivy?" Edna asked. "Never seen an octogenarian in a wetsuit before?"

"You wear it well, Edna. I'm just surprised you'd splash out on high-end gear that won't get used much."

She shook her head. "Do you think the apocalypse comes without tsunamis? We're fully certified to dive."

"Saul and I used to take diving trips to the Caribbean," Gertie said. "Edna and I are thinking about a little getaway."

"Sweet," Cori said. "Like a honeymoon."

Gertie gave her a long, cool stare, its impact diminished by the poncho covering her wet suit. Minnie sat on a checkered picnic blanket within easy reach. "Don't think I won't shoot you, Cori." She flipped her long braid over her shoulder. "But I'll keep you alive long enough to capture the penguins. You're our best hope."

Cori laughed. "Normally I'd agree but I think the dogs will have better luck today. We have four border collies with above average noses and a beagle with a stellar schnozz. Surely they can tell us if two oversized birds are in the area."

"Incoming factoid," I said. "Penguins poop seven or eight times an hour and shoot it three feet or more."

"Stop." Cori gave me two orange flares. "You'll scare the volunteers away."

"It's only fair they know it stinks. Like *really* stinks. All that fish, you know."

"That's me out," Jilly said. "I'll hoof it back to the farm."

"It'll take you a while to get there, Jillian," Edna said. "I've got a bunker midway where you could ride out the night."

Cori's gloves got busy again. "Get in the water, Jilly. You're Percy's chief wrangler and we need all paws on deck."

As we took our assigned positions, Cori floated Leo to the opposite bank on a paddle board and worked that side with Remi Malone. When Bridget arrived a few minutes later, she splashed over with Beau, her setter mix, who was probably the only dog here who truly loved water. The rest of us combed our side with Keats, Annie and Frost. My dog kept his paws dry and Percy did reconnaissance from the trees lining the creek.

We worked in silence, our group moving up the river and away from the people who got here first. It was a beautiful day and aside from the awkward gear, I didn't mind the outing. Working in solidarity with so many good people always gave my heart a lift, which it needed after yesterday's tragedy.

An hour or so later, the cat's eerie yowl from overhead let us know there was something worth seeing. A few seconds later, Keats' white paw came up. When he was satisfied I got the message, he loped along the bank into brush while I followed in the water. The footing was slippery and Asher's sloppy waders made it hard to get traction. Still, I was faster than everyone else, and a yip told me I was nearly there. A subsequent mumble then advised me to halt.

There on a rock in the shallows sat a tuxedoed bird. It was around two feet tall, with a black head and back, a white speckled belly, and a bold pattern of contrasting markings. At first, its flipper wings stuck out, perhaps ready to dive, but then it seemed to slump on the rock.

Alone.

Two birds were gone from the zoo, two sets of prints were in the mud outside, and they were a bonded pair. Why was this one on its own?

"Where's your partner in crime, buddy?" I asked.

The long slightly hooked beak turned this way and that, before drooping to its breast.

"Oh, the poor thing," Jilly whispered behind me. "He's lost his wife."

"Other way around," I said. "Pippa's lost her husband."

"Pippa?" The question came from Cori on the opposite side of the creek. "We've discussed this, Ivy. You can't go assigning names arbitrarily. The zoo called the female Beatrix."

I shrugged. "They were wrong. This is Pippa and obviously something's happened to her mate. Polo, I think, although I won't know till I meet him."

"Let's bring her in and worry about that afterward." Cori signaled the others to stay back. "A bird in the hand is worth two in the creek."

"How are we going to catch her? If I walk up to her with a net, she'll dive and be gone in a second. It looks a lot deeper there."

"Five feet at most," she said. "You're the tallest. Just walk over and grab her."

I turned with a glare. "Grab her? Did you get a look at that beak? It can cut through metal."

"Animals always like you. Or so you say." There was a collapsible net strapped to Cori's back. She pulled it around and sent it floating across the water to me. "Splash and scoop, Stretch. Use the net only as a last resort."

"What's the first resort? I mean, how exactly do you hold them?"

Cori sighed audibly. "Do you only retain poop facts? You gotta grab the scruff gently and support its weight under the butt. Then you scoot the bird under your arm like a football."

"I don't see a scruff. She's as sleek as a seal."

"Grab that net and quit stalling." Her gloves got more assertive. "And don't forget to turn its beak away if you want to be a beautiful bride."

Keats mumbled cautions above me on the bank. He thought it was a bad idea, too. No one wants an ugly bride.

Putting vanity aside, I said, "What if she panics in the net and bangs herself up on the rocks?"

"That's where the football grip comes in. Hold her close, turn her head away with the other hand. Easy-peasy, although in deep water, it really is a job for the tall. That's the only reason I'm giving you bragging rights. No one here's nabbed a penguin."

"Nice try, Cori. You know I'm the clumsiest one in our crew, even without hip waders. But if you're willing to risk Pippa's welfare, I guess I'll give it a try."

"You can't call her Pippa unless you catch her," Cori said. "And you don't even know it's the female. They're identical, give or take a few inches and ounces."

Jilly lost patience with Cori. "If you want Ivy to do it, let her focus. You're not sending her because of her height. Bridget is tall, too. You're finally conceding Ivy has some skills you don't."

That earned my best friend a double shot of neon tape. "Ivy's no penguin whisperer. I'm just giving her a chance to prove herself as a rescuer."

Edna came to my aid, too. "Zip it, shortie. Ivy's proven herself countless times. But every new animal's a challenge. Let her do it her way so we can move on."

I waited for a gap in the bickering. "My way is to let Pippa come to me. For her safety and mine."

Cori snorted. "How do you propose to incentivize her? Are you packing herring and smelt?"

"You'd smell the smelt," I said. "I have another idea."

Pulling my phone out of the front pocket of my overalls, I extracted it from a sealed baggie and cued a clip. Then I jacked up the volume and hit play on the courting call of an African penguin.

The grating vocalization was an odd combination of braying and barking and it got Pippa's attention. Her beak came up and her head swiveled. She didn't move, however, and in the gap after the clip, my dog made a sound rather like a raspberry.

"Struck out," Cori said. "Points for ingenuity, though."

Jilly was more optimistic. "Try it again. You can't expect her to trust you right away."

"Just cut to the part where you wade over and grab her," Cori said. "That's where this is going. Bag the phone first, because you'll fall at least once. Tick-tock, Ivy."

"I'm not trying to get out of it." I *was* trying to get out of it, but for honorable reasons. "I truly think it would be less stressful for the bird if she came willingly. Let's give her one more try."

I played the clip again and when it was done, tried to imitate the sound myself. I wasn't a gifted mimic but I'd mastered a decent version of Bocelli the donkey before. This was similar enough.

Pippa wasn't swayed. On the contrary, she shuffled to another rock even further away. It was hard to see a creature who looked like a cartoon come to life in such apparent despair.

Keats mumbled something cautionary but I wasn't ready to give up.

Instead, I tried the call again, putting my heart into the woo. Behind me, another call chimed in and then rose to drown me out. It was far closer to the recorded clip but had a different tone and rhythm.

At first, I assumed it was Edna because her voice was naturally grating and she didn't hesitate to use it. As a choir leader, she had a good range and strong lungs. Edna was an alto, however, and this voice was most definitely bass.

The call grew louder and I turned in time to see a broad-brimmed sunhat appear over the bank of the creek.

Professor Horn had belly-crawled toward us from above and Keats had tried to warn me in the gaps.

"Stay still," the man whispered. "I'm imitating her mate, Bertie. African penguins recognize each other from their unique vocalizations. You're a stranger to her, Ms. Galloway."

"Or just strange," someone muttered behind me. Probably Cori.

Professor Horn resumed his siren's song and everyone else fell silent.

After a long minute, Pippa waddled forward again. She cocked her head and this time seemed more willing to take a chance. The professor released another braying serenade and she toddled to the edge of the rock, webbed feet poking over the side.

"Come along, darling," he murmured, as if she could understand the words. Who knows, maybe she could.

Either way, she decided to take the plunge, quite literally. Her sleek form darted through the water toward the professor, and as he was now nearly behind me, she passed me on the way.

It was as easy as netting fish in a barrel. One scoop and I had her.

There was no time for the scruff and tuck before Professor Horn came down the bank on his backside. He landed in the water in tall rubber boots but the water went well past his knees. That didn't slow him down at all. He reached me in two strides and seized the net from my hands. The transfer was fast, but not fast enough to avoid a healthy squirt of the foulest poop ever to meet my nostrils. Since I'd bent to hold onto her, the stream of guano went into the gap of my hip waders.

Professor Horn left as quickly as he arrived, clambering up an easier slope with his precious cargo and crooning a tune decidedly more musical than the penguin's own song.

I waved to Edna. "Follow him. Pippa needs to go home to Happy Haven and the professor's been banned."

"Stop right there, Tapley Horn," Edna called, moving faster than he ever could, possibly even in his prime. She was the cheetah of seniors and the wetsuit reduced friction.

He was still running, clutching the penguin like the football Cori mentioned. "You can't take her back there. The conditions are inhumane."

Edna caught up with him quickly. "Penguins have been living

and breeding at Happy Haven for decades. Pippa's produced plenty of offspring. Right, Ivy?"

"Right. Her eggs are incubating right now. She's not ours, Professor. And no one here is equipped to house penguins."

"Thank goodness," Jilly muttered. "If you could create a sea to float your ark, Ivy, you would."

"True, my friend." I threw a smile over my shoulder at her. "It's a shame I can't keep Pippa but I'm learning my limitations."

Cori followed Edna, complaining. "Me, too, and I don't like it one bit. Zebra. Kangaroos. Penguin. What will we need to give up next?"

Tapley Horn didn't stand a chance and he knew it. When Edna scruffed him and threatened to turn him into her football, the professor deposited the bird in the crate Cori held open. Then he shouted, "Her name isn't Pippa, it's Beatrix. Check the zoo records."

"Take that, Ivy," Cori said, when I reached her. Then she handed me the carrier. "And take *that* back to Happy Haven."

"Now? We need to find her Polo. Seeing and hearing Pippa will help find him."

"His name isn't Polo." Professor Horn made a disgusted sound. "Do you think she'd come in voluntarily if her mate was in the vicinity? Penguins are monogamous."

Clutching the carrier, I glared at him. "I know that. But it doesn't mean anything bad has happened to him. He just got distracted by freedom. Or carried away by a current."

"That's not how this works," he said. "If a penguin's mate dies, they mourn. She was mourning." He wrestled free from Edna. "Search is over."

I stared around until I found Keats, sitting well back from the water. His paw came up and he glanced downstream with his blue eye. It gave me hope and courage. "Her mate isn't dead. For some reason, he went on alone and we need to go after him."

"How do you know that?" he asked.

Cori watched me watching Keats and nodded. "You don't need to know how she knows. Just accept that she does. Are you going to stick around and sing your song when it's needed or be a jerk?"

Jilly gestured for Cori to simmer down. "Choose the hero route, Professor. I know the way the zoo treated you stings but today you're turning the story around. Imagine the headline, 'Outspoken professor lures stolen penguin home with spot-on vocals.'"

The tension in his shoulders didn't ease. "I'll ride with Ivy to deliver the penguin and come back when you spot the male. Which you won't."

I slipped out of the hip waders without setting the carrier down. Then I let Keats herd me to the truck. The professor tried to follow, boots sloshing, and the dog kept cutting him off. "Come in your own vehicle if you like, Professor," I said. "There's a heavy police presence at the zoo, but it's your call."

The sloshing stopped. "Maybe I should stay to prove Bertie's really gone. For Beatrix's sake. Eventually, she'll move on. Women always do. It's the men who suffer most."

Edna guffawed. "Get down there and get to work, Tappers. Be the hero, like Jillian says. You're a young man and someday you'll find a new lady who's impressed by bird calls. I assume you have the female's song cued up when we find her partner?"

"Of course. And I'm not looking for a new lady. I'm done with all that."

Jilly was still in the water. "I'll wait for you here," she called.

I grinned at her. "Is it something I smelled?" Being confined in the truck with the penguin and me wouldn't be pleasant.

"That's part of it, I can't lie."

The other part was that she couldn't bear to return to the scene of the crime just yet. This one had hit too close to home. Percy was reluctant to leave her but eventually joined me. Keats, on the other hand, was happy to sacrifice the potential of another rescue win to his canine family.

I set the carrier in the back seat and climbed in after the pets. "I'm onto you, Jilly," I called out the window. "You're trying to avoid the relationship guru."

My best friend laughed. "You got me."

Tapley Horn chimed in, too. "Lacey Byle is a—"

The roar of the engine cut off his last word but whatever it was, I suspected the professor and I agreed.

CHAPTER TEN

Kellan met me in front of Happy Haven and held out his hands to take the carrier.

"I'm not surrendering Pippa to anyone but a zookeeper I can brief," I said. "No offense, Chief."

"None taken." He lifted his chin. "*Whoa*. What reeks?"

"The penguin." I'd zipped a windbreaker to my neck but it felt like the stink had seeped into my pores. Even with the windows open it had been a tough ride. "It's the fish diet. I'll need to get the truck detailed. And possibly myself."

My fiancé's smile looked grudging. I was still in the doghouse for starting the search without his go-ahead. Chief Harper sometimes deluded himself about my capacity to follow orders. Fiancé Harper was getting an olfactory reminder of whose finger he'd slid the diamond ring onto, along with the band of red stones that came from Garnet Point. With those rings, he locked down a rescuer and a wealth of opportunities to practice compromise. "The crime scene isn't clear but you're welcome to come inside as long as you stick with me."

"That would be my pleasure." I was happy to be with Kellan even when he was angry over some infraction. I preferred being lectured by him than anyone else, with the possible exception of my dog.

Keats was usually happy to be with Kellan, too, especially at a crime scene. Today, the dog was subdued. His tail was down and he didn't spare a nip for chiefly cuffs as we walked inside. Percy also left Kellan alone, choosing instead to ride on my shoulder. The boys' behavior made me curious and a little worried. Did they sense a change in Kellan I couldn't see? Had I pushed him one bird too far?

We were almost through the front lobby when a familiar voice called out, "Aha, I thought I sensed a couple in trouble. I can smell romantic crisis even in a cloud of—" Lacey Byle knocked her colorful glasses askew in her haste to cover her nose. "My goodness, what is that smell?"

"We found one of the missing penguins and she poops a lot." I directed the carrier her way. "I'd keep your distance. Not sure if penguins can aim but they pack quite a shot."

Lacey wasn't so easily thrown off her own scent. "Chief, you put up with so much, you poor dear. Have you shared how Ivy's antics make you feel? Remember, radical honesty is the cornerstone of a successful relationship."

"Ms. Byle, I don't have time to chat about your theories today. If you've collected what you came for, I'd ask you to leave. Weddings can be planned remotely."

"You seized our computers, so that's not true. Luckily I can polish my book at home. Let me tell you more about it." She got a little too close and Keats backed her off with a flash of teeth. Obviously, she was the reason his mood had soured. Mine, too. "For the sake of your possible marriage."

"Possible?" I said.

Kellan shook his head. "Ivy, please don't engage with Ms. Byle. She's a possible suspect in a murder investigation."

"That's ridiculous," Lacey said. "I was in the party room with plenty of witnesses when Lenard Pembroke died. How could I have killed him? Even if I had motivation, which I don't. Our conversations were limited. I offered my services as a pre-wedding counsellor and he declined. He and Brina seemed in complete alignment."

"Really?" I asked. "Had they embraced radical honesty? Because Brina wasn't exactly honest in all areas of her life."

"*Ivy.*" Kellan's voice was stern and Lacey's sly smile returned. In her mind, our wedding had become even less possible. "Ms. Byle gave her statement to your brother. There's nothing more to discuss right now."

"Poor Officer Galloway," Lacey said. "Never have I seen a man with such intense cravings for a child. Yet he's foiled at every turn. It sounds like he's being radically honest about the matter... but is his wife?"

Rage swirled into a storm in my midriff. This quack could cast doubt on *my* relationship but she could not diss my best friend's.

Kellan clamped down on my arm to stop the flow of angry words, while Keats took matters into his own teeth. He nailed her bare ankle and her shriek reverberated through the lobby. She tried to kick him away but he evaded her easily and went back for another taste of the love guru.

"So sorry, Lacey," I said. "Keats is Jilly's biggest fan and he doesn't like it when someone questions her character."

"As if he could understand me. Besides, I'm only saying it's tragic to see a couple so very close to happiness kept apart by misunderstanding. Your brother's grief—" She hopped again. "Ow!"

"Ms. Byle, stop what you're doing right now, or the dog won't be the only one issuing sanctions," Kellan said. "Take your unsolicited advice and go home. Either willingly or under police escort."

She fluffed her spiky highlighted hair and smiled. "I'll take option B, thanks."

"Chief, don't," I said. "You can't let another officer fall into a Venus flytrap."

"There are Venus flytraps in the arboretum." Lacey plucked a site map from a stand and handed it to me. "Maybe you and the chief could take a walk there to reconnect." She fanned her face with another map. "Although the stench won't help the mood. Ivy, when you smell that bad, you need to be nearly flawless in every other way to compensate. Are you flawless?"

Kellan snapped his fingers at his most senior officer and asked him to take Lacey out. "Don't speak to her," he said. "Not if you value your... Never mind."

My normally composed fiancé was rattled. Lacey was a skilled manipulator indeed.

"Goodbye for now, you two," she called as the older officer towed her away. "I hope you win."

"Don't ask." Kellan towed me in the other direction. "Do not ask."

I couldn't help turning back to Lacey. "Win what?"

"The six-pack of counseling sessions offered in our zoo fundraiser. I entered your names. Plus poor Asher's. I can't wait to sort through the Galloway baggage."

"Pardon me, Ivy," Kellan said. "I'm going to do something very unprofessional."

"Please do," I encouraged him.

Kellan flicked his fingers and Keats flew after the love coach. She jerked her arm out of the officer's grasp and ran out the door.

We grinned at each other on the way downstairs and it felt good to let some of the tension go. If I hadn't been holding the carrier, I might have given in to a belly laugh. That wasn't appropriate, though, when a man had died here only yesterday. Presumably that man had meant something to Jilly's mother. The time for laughter would come. It always did if you were patient.

Kellan put his chiefly expression back on when we reached the bottom of the stairs. "What's the plan for this bird?"

"She can't rejoin her colony until she's cleared for disease and parasites. It's a shame she'll be isolated when she's grieving her mate. They're monogamous, you know."

"I didn't know. What I don't know about penguins would fill a book." Glancing up the stairs, he added, "Seems like anybody can publish one these days."

"And find a tribe of believers. That woman is as irritating as Justine Schalow."

"More. I don't know why but Lacey is harder to dismiss."

I feared the love coach had struck too close to home for him, as well. Justine rarely got anywhere near a target and if she did it was by accident. As much as I wanted to talk through the fears and doubts Lacey had stirred up, now wasn't the time. Both of us had bigger fish to fry.

In my case, I wanted to get some raw fish into Pippa. African penguins typically ate about a pound of food a day and she couldn't have scrounged a fraction of that in minnows during her time at large. "Are the keepers on duty?"

"Skeleton staff. Only those deemed necessary to maintain the residents."

My feet slowed as we passed the otter exhibit. The pair did elegant somersaults, kicked off against the glass, and then came to stare at us. I smiled at them. "Hey, cuties, how are you doing?"

Their intense stare out of whiskery faces was a little unnerving, and Kellan stepped back. "What's wrong with them?"

"Just bored." The voice came from behind us and I jumped. Turning, I found a man wearing tan coveralls with the zoo's zebra logo. He was my age and height, give or take, and had brown eyes and a head of wild dark curls. I probably outweighed him and his pallor suggested he should get outside more. Maybe eat some red meat. "They're used to having spectators all day. Otters are playful showoffs."

"You're Ben Langtry, I believe," Kellan said. "One of the aquatics staff."

"Reptiles," Ben said. "Covering both while someone's off with a back injury. Those tiles are slippery."

As Kellan introduced me, Ben eyed the carrier in my arms. I wasn't ready to surrender Pippa just yet. "Does it bother you to see the animals stuck in the zoo, Ben?"

"Sometimes, sure. You can't work here without being an animal lover, and you can't be an animal lover without wishing to see them free and flourishing in their natural environment." He nodded at the otters. "Especially those clowns. But flourishing is the key word and these two rehab failures wouldn't. They were rescued as infants and couldn't get the hang of fending for themselves, so the zoo agreed to take them. At least it's an opportunity to educate kids. They're the ones who'll inherit the world we leave behind." His smile faded. "There's not much of it left for the penguins, but I'm glad you found them."

"Only the female, unfortunately. My friends are still searching. If her mate is out there, they'll find him."

He blinked a few times and I wondered if he was fighting tears. "I hope so. There are so many predators who'd love to grab a penguin. Particularly human predators. Rare birds are valuable and we live in a collectors' economy."

I'd never heard that term before but it did suit our hill country ethos. Many families were descended from treasure hunters and thieves, so it was probably inevitable. In a way, I was a collector myself, although I didn't profit from my livestock and rescues. Quite the contrary. Runaway Farm sometimes ran at a deficit. Generous benefactors like Hannah Pemberton and my father covered the gap. I never asked. Somehow, they could just pick up on it. The same way I picked up a stray.

Kellan was only half-listening as he checked his phone, so I continued my interrogation. "Ben, do you know Pippa well?"

"Pippa? Oh, you mean the penguin." Ben shook his unruly mop. "I'm the last into the Happy Haven family and they always start you on reptiles. For obvious reasons. If someone's going to get crushed by a python it better be a newbie. No insurance payout."

"That's awful," I said.

He cracked a smile to show even white teeth. "Just kidding about the insurance. Serious about my role, though. The regular guy will be back in a couple of weeks."

I clutched the carrier tighter. "Do you know how to handle a stressed penguin?"

He nodded. "Regular guy sent the emergency protocol. Said she needs to be in isolation for ten days." His thin lips drooped into a frown. "Poor thing will grieve doubly. They're not meant to be solitary."

"That's what I was afraid of. I wondered if you could connect her by live cam to her colony. I've seen how she responds to penguin calls. Professor Horn helped catch her."

"Tapley? Cool." Ben was more animated. "Always liked that guy. Got a bum rap in my opinion. He wouldn't have blown up the zoo." Catching Kellan's eye, he stopped. "Never mind. I like your suggestion of getting a monitor in there. Might lift her spirits."

"Awesome. If you need help with the tech, let me know. My rescue friends are pretty handy."

"Got it covered." He reached out and tugged the carrier gently. "I'll take good care of her, Ivy. I know you by reputation. You're good people. And your friends will—"

"Squeeze you tighter than a python if you mess this up," I interrupted, releasing the carrier.

"Exactly." His teeth gleamed in the display lights. "Bring everyone in when we reopen. We'll have a black-tie penguin party."

He looked down at Keats, who'd parked on my boots. "You're already in costume."

I expected Keats to give Ben a polite swish for the acknowledgement, but he didn't. Instead, he pressed against my shins to move me away. Someone was still grumpy about our run-in with Lacey. Phonies like her always got his tail in a twist.

Kellan put his phone away and spoke up. "Mr. Langtry, once you have the penguin settled, head up to chat to Officer Galloway. He's taking statements about yesterday's events."

"Will do," Ben said, backing carefully through a "staff only" door. "Wish I'd seen something to help. Take care, Ivy."

The long empty corridor had a vaguely creepy vibe that even the playful otters couldn't dispel. Must be the reptiles, I decided, letting Keats herd me to a wall of glass enclosures. The first few held lush plants, moss, logs and bark. They were home to tiny frogs, some no bigger than a quarter. The frogs came in a rainbow of colors and a few had intricate patterns. I spotted red, orange, yellow, green and shades of blue. A sprinkler system misted them and left water droplets to gleam on their smooth skin. "Come see." I beckoned to Kellan. "Frogs like tiny jewels."

My fiancé stayed where he was and I feared he was avoiding the stench. He probably thought it would disperse when the penguin left, but no such luck. "Pass. There's a gator down the way if you want to say hi. I'll wait for you at the side door."

I already knew more about gators than I wanted, so I followed Kellan. It would have been nice to study the frogs a little more and read the information the zoo provided. Keats must have been fascinated by the vibrant hoppers, too, because he lingered there till we reached the door.

Outside, Kellan led me down to the creek. His expression was serious. This was business, not pleasure.

"Can you walk me through everything again?" he asked. "Normally I don't need to hear the story twice but some things aren't adding up for me."

"Me, either. I can't figure out why whoever stole the penguins would just dump them outside. Like Ben said, they're a valuable commodity. Releasing them near a river was throwing money away."

"Maybe it was something else," Kellan said. "Like a misguided eco-warrior."

"I wondered about that, too. Did you get any leads from the baseball cap we found?"

He shook his head. "It's not top of my list at the moment."

"But the pets indicated the cap is a clue. Eco-warriors were my first theory after meeting Professor Horn."

"Ambushing him, you mean." Kellan crossed his uniformed arms. "At least, that's how he described your visit when Asher spoke to him."

Now I'd been ambushed myself. "Mandy mentioned he was a bird expert, so I wanted to recruit him for the search."

"A bird expert who threatened to blow this place up. He needed to be questioned by police before he joined a search I didn't clear."

So, I really was in the doghouse. At least Lacey would be happy.

"I didn't know about his explosive history at the time, Kellan. Just wanted to talk penguins. Good thing I did, too, because he's the one who lured Pippa back."

"That doesn't clear him. He wanted to damage the zoo's reputation and a murder would certainly do that."

The thought hadn't occurred to me but I dismissed it now. "Tapley Horn isn't your guy. He's an animal lover."

"We've already established that animal lovers can do bad things. It's a lesson that keeps on giving."

"He made a half-hearted attempt to run off with Pippa, but that's the extent of his guilt." I raised my hand. "How do I know?

Because Keats says so and Percy agrees. If Tapley had been in the building, they'd have flagged it when we met."

Kellan wanted to protest but sealed his lips. He couldn't choose to trust the dog's judgement only when it suited him. Not without my pointing out the hypocrisy. Instead, he gestured to the leg of my overalls. "I see the penguin left a little something to remember her by."

I looked down and sighed. "As if I could forget that smell. I've heard it really lingers. We might need separate hotels on our honeymoon."

A smile tried to achieve liftoff on his handsome face but he grounded it. "You think the male penguin is still out there?"

"Keats does and every second counts. There's too little food and too many predators, plus the risk of disease. We'll move down the river mile by mile till we reach Lake Capshaw. The team is out in full force."

"That'll keep you busy." He sounded relieved I wouldn't be underfoot. "I'm sure Keats is thrilled about a water search."

He turned to study the dog, who was moving in circles with his nose to the ground like a hound. Percy jumped down from my shoulder to join Keats.

"About as thrilled as Jilly," I said. "But she's out there."

"How's she holding up?" Walking to the puddle I found yesterday, he crouched to look at the muddy prints. "What happened must have been a terrible shock, even if she didn't know Mr. Pembroke."

"Kellan, it's awful. I've never seen Jilly so distressed. She's a model of restraint, as you know, but she lost it for a second out here yesterday. Needed a break to walk it off." I watched Percy head into the shrubbery and Keats followed. "Edna and I worried she'd gone back inside to tear a strip off her mother, but she waited out front for us."

Kellan straightened and his brow furrowed. "Jilly left you here alone?"

"She needed a few minutes to chill out. Can you blame her?"

"Nobody mentioned that when we debriefed. Not you, not Edna, not Jilly."

I shrugged. "Never thought about it. It wasn't relevant."

His dark blue eyes narrowed and his jaw set. Before, he was disgruntled. Now, he was full-on angry. "It's my job to determine relevance. How long was she gone?"

"Just a few minutes, I think. Why?"

"So, she could conceivably have been gone longer. And conceivably have run into Mr. Pembroke when he stepped outside for some air."

"But she didn't. She would have said so." I crossed my arms. "What exactly are you suggesting? Surely you don't think my best friend in the world whipped out a vial of poison? Or slipped Len a kill pill?" I didn't give him a chance to answer. "Because if you seriously think so, I'm going to—"

I stopped abruptly. If he truly believed that I didn't know what I'd do. Jilly was my ride or die, and I would never want to choose between them. My fingers dropped to my side and thankfully, the soft ears were there. Keats' ruff was prickling, no doubt sharing my umbrage. He mumbled something that sounded both insolent and insistent. Percy scaled my back to provide a united front against our beloved.

"I'll speak to her," he said. "I'm sure you're right, but I need to take it seriously. Witnesses say Jilly threatened Mr. Pembroke while leaving the party room."

"A half threat, at worst, because Lenard threw Percy and could have hurt him."

"A few minutes later he followed, possibly to find her. The point I'm trying to make is that Jilly had motive and opportunity."

"And the poison? She didn't bring her purse, Kellan. I'd love to know where you think she stashed it. A hollow tooth, like in the movies?" I didn't give him a chance to answer. "She had no idea about the wedding and you can be quite sure Jilly Blackwood wouldn't voluntarily meet her mother's fiancé for the first time wearing a stained shirt and yoga pants. The sun's more likely to rise in the west."

"Speaking of west, which way did she go?" he asked.

"I'm not sure. I was using my phone and Edna called Cori. Jilly went to grab Percy and left."

"Could she have walked around to the other side of the building? Was she gone that long?"

His eyes were so fierce and cold my legs turned gelatinous. Too bad I'd left Asher's hip waders behind. If I had a little accident, they'd hide the evidence. "I didn't have a stopwatch on her, Kellan. Like I said, I was busy."

"Try to remember."

Percy left my shoulder to jump to Kellan, where he did a swish past his face to stand on the other shoulder.

With Kellan distracted, I tried to remember the details but when it came to rescue my brain hyper-focused. "I don't know. Maybe she went to check out the butterfly garden. Mandy says it's peaceful, and that's what Jilly was after. Peace."

"No doubt, but did she feel the same way when she ran into Mr. Pembroke?"

"If she ran into Lenard she would have mentioned it. Period. Jilly doesn't keep secrets like that."

He pounced on the slight shift in my tone. "But she does keep secrets."

"We all keep a few, don't we? None of us embrace Lacey Byle's notion of radical honesty. Jilly and I wouldn't have lasted in corporate if we spilled our guts freely."

Keats gave a mumble that suggested I was digging myself ever deeper into a hole. Bragging about our capacity to withhold the truth wasn't doing either Jilly or me any favors.

"I keep secrets related to policing," Kellan said. "It's in my job description."

"That's not all. I don't know everything about you. Nor do I need to." I stared at him, slowly regaining the strength in my limbs. "But that's not the issue here, is it? You want to know if Jilly left us here to find Len with the handy-dandy cartridge of poison she carries in case she runs into paramours she didn't know her mom had. To protect the inheritance she doesn't need."

"Or to help her mom escape a difficult relationship," Kellan countered.

I stared at him, not knowing how to feel. He was doing his job and we'd neglected to share something important. I was doing mine as best friend. "You've known Jilly long enough to question whether that fits her general code of conduct, Kellan. Besides, she's married to your second in command. Is my brilliant best friend stupid enough to leave herself open to a murder charge?"

"It's called a crime of passion for a reason." He staggered slightly as Percy made the return jump to me. Kellan was off balance, which meant he was losing steam.

My legs were back in working order. No need for hip waders or incontinence supplies. I snapped my fingers for Keats and started walking away. "If you think Jilly committed this crime of passion then you'd better bring her in for questioning. Don't try to trick me into implicating my best friend."

"I'm not tricking anyone. You're the one who stayed mum on a critical piece of information."

"I forgot, plain and simple."

"And Jilly and Edna?"

"Forgot and forgot," I said. "It was irrelevant to us. You'll do your due diligence and discover that for yourself."

"I will indeed," he said.

"Then we can sit down with Lacey Byle and figure out how radical honesty works. Things could get lively around here."

I wanted very much to stomp up the path with my head high and my cat higher, but Keats was standing very still with his paw raised in a point. My canine boss had something to say. Walking over, I bent to see what he'd found. Percy jumped down and began scraping loose soil over a discarded cigarette butt.

"What is it?" Kellan asked.

"Evidence, I expect. Maybe Jilly's true secret is smoking and hiding it. I'll leave it to you to sniff out the truth."

"I'll do that," he said. "Although you've pretty much killed my nose with—"

An unchiefly squeal told me Keats was back on cuff duty.

CHAPTER ELEVEN

I drove halfway home before pulling over to do what I knew I needed to do even before I left Happy Haven.

"I can't," I muttered. "I can't. I can't."

Keats put his paw on my leg and mumbled something encouraging. I could and I must. Percy swished along my arm and then scraped some invisible dirt over my phone. There was no escaping the ordeal.

Plucking the phone from under the fluffy orange paw, I sent a single message to the entirety of my family that said "Butter Tart 911. Daisy's house."

Then I set the phone down, pulled back onto the highway and got a move on it. I couldn't recall initiating a family meeting, although I'd attended plenty. I loved that my family could rally in a crisis but I was usually the one getting roasted. Today would be no exception. The only difference was that I'd skewered and basted myself.

"It's the right thing to do," I told the boys. "But that doesn't make it any easier. Thank goodness Asher is stuck at the zoo. There's no way I can face him right now. In fact, I think I'll stay in one of Edna's bunkers till this whole thing blows over. Between him and Mom, it'll be hysteria at the farm."

Keats demanded the window be rolled down and I obliged. The stench was probably offending him, too.

"Poor Jilly," I said. "This was already hard enough without being considered a suspect."

The dog turned back and warmed me briefly with his brown eye, telling me we'd survive this. Percy must have felt the same because he curled up on the phone and caught a cat nap.

That was my excuse to ignore the steady stream of return texts and calls that came in before I reached Daisy's house. The only call I intended to rescue from orange fluff was Jilly's and her ringtone didn't sound. I wondered if she'd bother leaving the search site and part of me hoped she'd pass.

"Jilly always says she loves these meetings, or at least the idea of them," I reminded the boys. "Says they make her feel like she's part of something bigger. Guess I see what she means, now. We Galloways share too much but her family obviously shares too little. No way would you slip a wedding under our radar. Can you imagine anyone trying?"

I chuckled at the thought. Maybe that's what Kellan and I should do. Despite how Jilly felt about elopement, we could try to slip away and tie the knot without anyone knowing. Nowadays, any family event had an element of drama, and often a murder attached. No need to bring crime into the happiest day of our lives.

Providing we reached that milestone. The way Kellan and I had left things it was hard to imagine we'd get to the altar. He was so angry at me for withholding information I didn't remember I had. There was plenty of information I deliberately withheld but this time, I got dinged for a genuine accident.

Daisy's house was across town but the traffic was light and I arrived all too soon. My stomach did a nosedive and I groaned.

Asher's police SUV was not only there but blocking Daisy's driveway.

How had he beaten me from the zoo?

After parking up the street, I pulled the phone out from under Percy and glanced at the screen. Ah. That explained the influx of texts. Asher had simultaneously initiated the 911. Kellan got to him first and my brother was coming in hot.

"Boys, I'm going to need full support, okay? No running off to mingle with the ferrets. Usually I'm taken by surprise but today I know what to expect and I may need to deploy both of you. Use your teeth and claws freely, unless the assailant is Jilly. If so, turn the attack on me. If she's mad, I don't think I'll get over it. In all these years, she's never been really angry at me, even after some boneheaded moves. Nothing I've done has ever put her in the crosshairs like this. During her mother's visit, no less."

I was still behind the wheel five minutes later, when the older twins arrived at the driver's door.

"You'd better come willingly, Aunt Ivy," Sutton said. "Mom said to carry you if your legs didn't work."

"We'll need Beaton and Reese," Weston said. "She's heavier than she looks."

"I can attest to that, having carried her before." The boys parted to reveal Edna, still in her scuba suit. The boys kept casting covert looks at her and smirking. "I've always wondered what these shindigs are about and today I get to find out. Do you need a lift, Ivy? We've got the manpower."

"I'm not touching her." Weston backed away. "No one told us she reeks."

Keats gave a small sharp pinch to my upper arm to get me moving. "Hey. I said you could bite *inside* as needed. Don't abuse the privilege."

The boys marched me to the house and flanked me on the stairs to make sure I didn't bolt. "I know you're in trouble, Aunt Ivy," Sutton said, "but don't worry, we've got your back."

Weston shook his head. "I'm siding with Ash on this one. Throwing Aunt Jilly under the bus was a shady move."

"Stifle it, boys," Edna said, bringing up the rear. "Keep your smirks to yourselves, too. Don't think I won't anchor you to a shipwreck in Capshaw Lake." She cleared her throat. "Why, Daisy, you look wonderful. Positively glowing."

My eldest sister stood in the doorway wearing her rubber gloves, with a chamois in one hand and a bottle of vinegar spray in the other. Nearly five months pregnant, she looked closer to full term and decidedly uncomfortable. Her hair was wild and her complexion blotchy. In short, Edna was being uncharacteristically kind.

"I'm not, Edna, but welcome," Daisy said. "Why people glamorize pregnancy is beyond me. It's a—"

"An honor and a privilege," Edna finished. "But a cakewalk it is not. Do let me know if you need a hand with anything. I've attended scores of births. Once I delivered premature triplets in a swampy ditch after a car accident. And then there was the time... Wait, where are you going, boys?"

She cackled as they kicked off their sneakers and skidded across the kitchen tiles in their haste to get downstairs. They left the door ajar and we all knew they'd eavesdrop from the basement. It would keep our conversation more civil.

Asher was leaning against the fridge in his uniform with his arms crossed when I followed Edna into the kitchen. "What is *she* doing here?" he asked.

"Ivy has a free pass to any and all family meetings, darling," Mom said, from her perch on a stool at the counter. "Did I ever tell you how much you wanted a little sister when you were young?"

I figured Ash would resist the bait but he took it. "I wanted a *brother*, Mom. Someone fun."

My plan to resist also failed. "I'm fun. Just a few months ago we staked out cops together and got shot at. Isn't that the very definition of fun?"

"Sounds fun to me," Weston yelled from the basement. "Count me in next time."

"What about the time Ivy stole your squad car, Uncle Ash?" Sutton called. "That must have been fun, too."

Asher signaled for me to close the basement door. "Not fun. More like lunacy."

I didn't normally follow his orders but Daisy added a flick of her glove, so I clicked the door shut and leaned against it. With enough distance from the others, maybe they wouldn't notice the smell.

"Darlings, don't fight," Mom said. "Especially not in front of Edna."

Edna snorted. "You think I haven't seen them fight before, Dahlia? I broke up a few of them at school. Poppy packed quite a punch."

"Still do." Poppy spoke up from the kitchen table. "Happy to share some pointers."

"I can still take you," Edna said. "I fight dirty."

Asher straightened against the fridge till his fair hair brushed the cupboards. "I was asking why *Edna* is here. She's not family."

"I'm on point to be godmother of your children. That's practically family."

"There's a long lineup of godmothers ahead of you. My kids won't wear camo."

"Shame," Edna said. "I've already got the onesies, and pint-sized replicas of ammo."

"Edna, darling," Mom said. "Asher isn't himself today. Perhaps it's better not to goad him."

That hadn't stopped Mom. Unlike Daisy, my mother truly was glowing. She'd added a dash of rouge to bring up her color to match a scarlet suit that had probably been four different outfits before colliding with my mother's sewing machine.

Jilly finally spoke from her seat beside Poppy. "Asher, please don't be rude to Edna. She was kind enough to leave the river search and drive me here in Gertie's van."

That made Ash bristle more. "Edna doesn't have a license, honey. She's a madwoman behind the wheel."

"You should see Dahlia drive," someone said, from behind the basement door. Probably Weston, since Sutton aided his grandmother to live dangerously on the back country trails.

Mom wasn't fazed. "Some twin is obviously jealous."

Edna crossed her arms to mirror Asher's pose. "Young man, instead of dissing me you should thank me. Your wife was flustered and I left an exciting rescue mission to escort her. That's what a good bridesmaid does. Or have you forgotten my role in your nuptials?"

That was impossible as Ash had framed and mounted several very large wedding photos at the inn. He saw Edna in that lineup every day. After my wedding, the same faces would be shuffled in more photos. The nurse that had terrified him in his youth would be around every corner.

"Of course you were flustered, hon," Asher continued. "How could you be otherwise, after Ivy accused you of murder?"

Jilly caught my eye and gave a faint smile that showed her faith in me. "I doubt that's how it went down. Let Ivy explain."

A nip from behind sent me over to the table. "I'm sorry, Jilly. When I took the penguin to the zoo, Kellan wanted me to go over what happened yesterday. I mentioned you'd taken a short walk to clear your head and that landed you on the suspect list. Lenard Pembroke must have been poisoned at around the same time."

"Speculation," Asher snapped.

"Whatever, brother." I rolled my eyes. "Kellan lost his temper and said I was withholding the truth, but I was just fixated on penguins. I forgot about Jilly's half-hearted threat when we left the party room, too."

Jilly rubbed stray curls off her forehead wearily. "He thought we colluded because none of us mentioned my walk in our statements."

"It wasn't relevant," Edna said. "Unless you lost your mind and killed Len, Jillian. Did you?"

"Not that I recall." Jilly's smile returned with a little more oomph. "I walked around the building and stopped for a minute to watch the butterflies through the glass. It was so peaceful."

"Exactly what I predicted," I said. "Either that or the aviary."

"Too noisy, even outside. The macaws were screaming as if..."

"Someone had just been poisoned," Edna supplied, cheerily. "Which was exactly what happened. Did you see Lenard outside during your perambulation?"

Asher uncrossed his arms and waved. "I'll ask the questions, Miss Evans." His expression softened as he looked at the wife he adored. "Did you see anyone during your walk, honey?"

"A few people, none of them Lenard. But I wasn't paying attention, either. I'd just found out my mother was getting married without cutting me in on the secret."

"The people you saw... were any of them smoking?" I asked. "Keats found a butt of interest near the creek."

That didn't come out as I intended but only the snickering twins noticed.

Jilly's nod was tentative. "I think so. And I feel like there were a couple of people wearing hoodies, although it was warm."

"Makes sense if smoking on the property is against zoo staff policy, which it probably is. Did you—"

Asher shoved himself off the fridge and interrupted. "I'll ask the questions, Ivy."

"I don't know anything else," Jilly said. "Kellan already spoke to me and I told him I couldn't describe anyone. I barely remembered taking a walk, let alone the details. Maybe I will by the time I get to the police station."

"He wants you to come to the station?" There was a squeak in Asher's voice.

"Kellan hopes seeing some photos might jog my memory." She shrugged. "I hope they do, because I don't like being a suspect."

"You're not a suspect." Her husband's squeak turned to indignation. "Not really. It's just—"

"Due process. I know." She stooped and picked up Percy. His fluffy paws were against her knee but he spared her the climb. "It doesn't look great, though. Some could say I had motive."

"Jilly, darling, what possible motive could you have to kill that man?" Mom asked.

"He treated my mother poorly and seemed to be rushing her to the altar. People could say—probably *are* saying—that I was worried about being cut out of Mom's will."

"No one would say that!" Asher was outraged.

Poppy raised her hand. "Sorry, bro. I overheard someone at the hardware store say just that."

"And at the salon," Iris said. "My client was more tactful, since I was holding scissors."

"I heard the same thing at Mandy's store," Violet added, with an apologetic glance at Jilly. "In the absence of a real suspect, they latch onto anything."

"People always want to bring the Galloways down a peg," Edna said. "Don't take it personally, Jillian."

My resilient best friend found a smile. "If folks are suggesting I killed a man, it's hard not to take it personally. Do they have theories about how I pulled it off?"

Violet nodded. "They said it's not the first time you poisoned someone, because of the lumberjack incident."

Edna chuckled. "I called that, Jillian. Too bad I couldn't save you by saving the victim this time."

Asher ran his hands through his hair. "That's terrible. It's not even the same poison."

"What poison is it?" I asked.

My brother shaped his fingers into the same hand pistol that got his wife into trouble. "Never you mind, Ivy. Your job is to find the penguins. Mine is to exonerate my wife. Do not get involved."

I started to remind him that Jilly was my best friend for a decade before he met her and then stopped. He was wringing his hands now. My brother felt helpless in one of the hardest moments of his life. I didn't need to make it worse.

That didn't slow Mom down. "Asher, darling, wouldn't it be wise to get Ivy's help to clear Jilly's name? Your sister's so—"

"Twisty," Asher interrupted. "And lucky. Sticks her nose in at the right time and facts fall into her lap."

"Who wouldn't want a lapful of luck right now?" Mom persisted. "Don't let pride get in the way of resolving this matter quickly."

Jilly rocked Percy harder than the cat enjoyed but he took it like a champ. "Dahlia, I appreciate your concern but I'm confident the police will clear me soon enough."

"Why so confident?" Edna asked. "Haven't we beaten them to the punch before? As much as I hate to agree with Dahlia, this feels like a job for Ivy and team."

I shook my head. "Kellan came down on me hard earlier and I don't care for a second helping."

"Since when has that ever stopped you?" Edna asked.

"Since Lacey Byle started pointing out flaws in our relationship," I said.

Edna's mouth puckered. "Lacey? She's full of hokum. There's nothing wrong with you and Kellan. Healthy as any relationship can be today."

Iris spoke up again. "I follow Lacey's socials and she has a few words of wisdom."

"She isn't even married," Poppy said. "What can she possibly know? Relationships aren't easy."

"That's for sure." The words arrived on a spritz of vinegar spray as Daisy finally weighed in. "Anyone setting herself up as an expert in love is bound to fall."

"I don't know about that," Mom said. "My class was very successful and it only ran a few months. Three women credit me for supporting them into their perfect match. I wonder if this Lacey can say the same."

"She has lots of testimonials," Iris said. "I've considered taking her weekend seminar."

"Don't." The word shot out from Jilly and me at the same time.

Asher went back to hair churning. "We're in the middle of a crisis. How can you even talk about romance?"

"I can always talk about romance," Jilly said, getting up. "Because I found the best match ever."

He was only slightly mollified. "This is serious, hon."

"I know." She handed me Percy as she circled the counter. "But the pets have declared me innocent, haven't they, Ivy?"

"You bet, bestie. Your mom's in the clear, too, according to my pet judges. Brother, I'd focus on the attendants if I were you."

His blue eyes narrowed. "And if I were *you*, I'd focus on the escaped birds. We don't need to be fixing your mistakes."

My so-called mistakes had saved his butt on at least one occasion. Keats mumbled a suggestion that sounded appeasing, however. It must be in our best interest to let it go. The dog didn't often spare Asher's pant cuffs when he used that tone.

Daisy fired more vinegar spray into the air. "Can I have my house back, please?"

"Ease up on the spray," Asher said. "I can't go back to work smelling like pickles."

My sister patted her growing belly. "I hate to be the one to bring up the elephant in the room but something smells horrendous. The baby deserves better."

"She does," I agreed. "I'm the guilty party. A gift from a penguin. Let me give you some breathing room."

Jilly looped her arm through my brother's. "Will you drive me to visit the chief? Ivy and Edna are going back to the creek, I expect."

"All hands on deck," I said, directing my words toward the basement. "Junior Galloways, grab your water wings."

There were groans and muttered backtalk beyond the door.

"Old enough to eavesdrop, old enough to join the rescue party," Daisy said, opening the door. "Especially when two of you are certified lifeguards. Go with your aunt."

More grumbling ensued and a few human yelps drifted up the stairs as a sheepdog rounded up the belligerent herd.

"Nothing more rewarding than helping an animal in need," I told the quartet of sullen boys as they trailed out of the house.

My nephews stopped beside Gertie's van and Edna shook her head. "There's room for all of you in Ivy's pickup."

Weston scowled. "Not a chance. She stinks."

"Besides, like Asher said, you don't have a license," Sutton said. "I'll drive."

"You will not." The keys were in Edna's hand, and fit as she was, this warrior was no match for four tall teenaged boys trained in martial arts.

"You can ride shotgun, Miss Evans," Sutton said as he hopped behind the wheel. "Let's deploy."

"I'm the best driver," Beaton argued. "Even Dad says so."

Weston snorted. "Let him say so when you're legal. Everyone's a star driving around empty barrels in a farm field."

"Ivy Rose Galloway," Edna called after me. "Control these hooligans."

Keats gave a pant-laugh as I got the truck rolling.
I'd finally found an upside to reeking.

CHAPTER TWELVE

My search for the male penguin met a roadblock after three hours and as many spills in the creek.

I didn't give up, but a silent vote among my friends sidelined me as I floundered on slippery rocks. It was a warm evening but I was shivering anyway. My entire body was pruning up from the chilly stream that came down from the hills. This creek ran right past my grandparents' home nearly two hours' drive away. Bocelli and Clippers liked to drink out of it and the thought gave me strength to push myself up one more time.

"Dagnabbit, Ivy, you're of no use to anyone if you bash your head in again," Edna said. "I have better things to do with my time than feed and water your livestock if you're bedridden."

"Back off, Miss Evans," Sutton said. "Aunt Ivy can't help it if she's old and clumsy."

There was a long pause as everyone looked from Edna to Sutton to me and back. His earnest expression showed he wasn't making fun of me. In this moment, he actually saw me as old—perhaps even part of Edna's cohort. Meanwhile, I had yet to reproduce.

"Clumsy, yes, but not old." It was Cori who took on the challenge of educating my nephew. "I'm Ivy's age and still doing aerial stunts that would make your head spin."

Weston stepped forward as spokes-twin. "Can you teach us, Ms. Hogan? We're good with heights."

She fluttered black and neon orange gloves in their direction. "Do I seem like a teacher to you? I'm a dog trainer, and only to give the dogs a fighting chance against stupid people."

Remi Malone laughed. "She's my trainer. Make of that what you will."

"Even experts fail now and then." Cori shook her head at Leo. The beagle was lying on his back on a fleece blanket while the other dogs—and one inspirational cat—worked hard. "But Leo is right. Time to call it a day."

I let Sutton and Weston pull me to my feet and then put my hands on my hips over the waders. "We can't give up now. Polo is still out here on his own. He could fall into the jaws—or greedy hands—of predators."

Keats mumbled agreement with me from high up on the bank. His muzzle pointed downstream and his paw came up in a point.

"I see you want to roll on, Keats," Cori said. "And I admire your fortitude given your hydrophobia. But finding a half-black bird in the darkness would be nearly impossible. We'd lose soldiers and I can't risk that. Better to get a good night's sleep and come back fresh in the morning."

"Maybe I could go a little further with Edna and the boys," I said.

"We're in," the younger pair chorused. Beaton and Reese weren't as outgoing as the older twins and I felt like I didn't really know them yet. I made a mental note to rectify that. Someday I'd want this foursome—quintet, when my forthcoming niece joined the team—to visit me in a retirement home. Not as soon as *they* imagined, but sooner than I'd probably like.

"I meant the pets," I said, smiling at them. "Your mom would have my head if I took you downstream in the dark. We need to manage her stress for the baby's sake. I'll drive you home now before she—" Five phones pinged. "Oops. She's onto us."

The crowd dispersed and by the time I turned into the farm's lane, the moon was rising. A police SUV brushed passed me with barely an inch to spare. It felt deliberate. Not my fiancé, then, but a brother willing to exchange the chip on his shoulder for a chip on my truck. I couldn't see the driver's face but Keats' happy pant made me wonder if Asher had borrowed Cori's trademark gesture.

Outside the barn, I parked and texted Jilly. "Everything okay?"

The thumbs-down emoji came first, followed by, "Mom's here."

Her mom, not mine. Asher must have dropped off his mother-in-law and fled back to the crime scene.

I'd planned to change my damp clothes in the barn and spend some quality time with manure but Jilly's next text arrived quickly. "Help."

Keats raced up the path to the house where Percy was already waiting at the front door. This cat didn't require a text to know he was needed. The screen door cracked open just enough to let him in and I had no doubt the orange fluff of consolation spilled from Jilly's arms before I reached the stairs.

The dog turned back suddenly. His paw came up and he froze. We waited a few minutes on the steps and soon a bronze car roared out of the lane and right up onto the grass. Elsa, the late model sedan, belonged to Janelle Brighton, Jilly's cousin. The woman who emerged and picked her way over the grass in stilettos looked very much like Jilly, only with chestnut curls. She wore a stylish gray dress and a featherweight pashmina in fuchsia. I loved cashmere but it was off limits, except for date nights. I wondered how Janelle protected her fine fabrics from the claws of the pint-sized scrapper under her arm.

Mr. Bixby, a black-and-tan dachshund, yapped a warning at Keats. The two dogs tolerated each other but neither had a fondness for fellow canines. They were working dogs. Mr. Bixby didn't hunt badgers, as he'd been bred to do, but he'd helped sniff out several criminals in Wyldwood Springs. His vocalization as Janelle joined me on the stairs seemed to suggest his role was bigger than I could imagine.

"Settle down," Janelle said, setting the dachshund on the landing. "Ivy's our friend. Save your attitude for Aunt Brina." She hugged me and then pulled back to stare with piercing green eyes. "Tell me you didn't leave them alone in there."

"Just got home," I said. "I have the feeling Asher did a dump and run."

Her laugh sounded just like Jilly's. "You'd almost think he knew Aunt Brina."

"She didn't seem that bad when we met." I was in no hurry to go inside and Janelle didn't rush, either. "Except for the fact that she was sneaking to the altar without inviting her own daughter."

Janelle's smile faded. "That part isn't like Brina at all. She hasn't had a date since her ex left, at least according to my mother. Mom hasn't either. They both got burned hard in the marriage department and then turned their bitterness on each other."

"Yet somehow managed to raise two awesome daughters," I reminded her. "How did you know Brina was here?"

"Felt a shift in the force." Her white teeth showed in a grin as she threw her shoulders back. Jilly didn't believe her cousin had any psychic powers but Janelle's predictions often panned out. Most recently, she'd foretold a baby in the family and then Daisy announced her unexpected pregnancy. "Let's go in. United front."

When I opened the door, Mr. Bixby walked right under Keats, through my dog's front paws and entered the house first. He was making the strange sounds vaguely akin to Keats' mumbles and Janelle nodded as she passed in front of me, as if she understood him.

Keats hopped as if he'd been scorched by the dachshund's

touch. It wasn't hard to understand the yip he let out while rushing after the smaller dog into the family room. This was Keats' turf and he didn't intend to let a wiener dog get one over on him. Shiny black ears flopped as the smaller canine glared back at me with chocolatey eyes. It was almost as if he stated his objection to the word "wiener."

"Mr. Bixby!" There was no mistaking the surprise in Jilly's voice and her eyes rose from the strutting dog to his owner. "Janelle. You're here."

To anyone else, my best friend's tone would have sounded positively chilly. I knew it was apprehension. Despite their vastly different world views, the two cousins were fond of each other.

Brina Brighton stopped pacing across the hardwood and turned suddenly. "What are you doing here, Janelle?"

"Lovely to see you after all these years, Aunt Brina." Janelle's smirk pretty much said the opposite. "My family's in trouble. I came as fast as I could. When a Brighton's been accused of murder, we put aside old grudges."

"Since when?" Brina attempted a smirk and failed miserably. "And how did you hear about this?"

Janelle walked over to stand beside Jilly. "Mom's worried about you, Auntie."

"That would be a first," Brina said. "Shelley hasn't given me a second thought since we argued when you girls were kids."

"Untrue. Very much untrue." Janelle looped her arm through Jilly's free one. "But let's talk about the murder. I half-expected you to be in the clink, Auntie."

Brina turned to Jilly. "How did Shelley find out? Did you tell your grandmother?"

"What if I did?" Jilly dropped Janelle's arm. "It's a family emergency."

Janelle stooped to pick up Mr. Bixby. The small dog directed a warning growl at my fluffy cat, who was now too close for comfort. Percy turned green eyes away, as if the dachshund were beneath his notice. "It doesn't matter who knows what and how, Aunt Brina. When I found out you were in trouble I came running with Mr. Bixby. Here we are, ready to help."

"I'm fine. Can't a woman get left at the altar without the army rolling in?"

The rest of us stared at each other and I spoke up. "No, Ms. Brighton. That's not how our army rolls. We always have each other's back, families included. Besides, you didn't get left in the typical sense of the word. Someone poisoned Lenard, and—"

"Did me a favor," Brina interrupted.

Mine wasn't the only mouth that dropped open in shock. The only sound was a conspicuous pant-laugh, followed by a sharp yap from Mr. Bixby. It sounded like a rebuke of Keats but what did I know about dachshunds?

Janelle gave the smaller dog a little shake. "Never mind, Bixby. This is serious. Aunt Brina, what do you mean about Lenard?"

Brina's eyes had widened, as if she was shocked she'd said anything. She scanned the room. "Is this place bugged? Nanny cam?"

"No," Jilly said. "When there are babies to nanny, maybe."

"Do not have children, Jillian. It's the hardest job in the world."

"Ms. Brighton, how can you say that? Jilly is incredible. Brave, talented and loyal. The best friend anyone could want."

Brina glared at Janelle. "And I had to break up with my own family to make sure she turned out that way. You can't imagine how much it hurt—"

Janelle cut her off with a wave. "I can imagine, because I was on the other end of that breakup, Aunt Brina. But let's stick to the more recent breakup, namely yours. You were going to marry this Lenard today. How can you be happy he's gone?"

"Not happy. Relieved." Brina started pacing again. She was wearing the same blue suit as yesterday and it had become limp and rumpled. "I was starting to have doubts about Len but he said he was certain enough for both of us. He swept me off my feet, you see. Gifts, trips, flowers, you name it. Said it was destiny."

"More like love bombing," Janelle said. "You're supposed to ride the brakes when dating, Aunt Brina. Pace the guy until he proves himself. Otherwise, you can get in over your head."

Jilly didn't disagree. She had paced my brother hard. He would have married her on the day they met. "Did you try to slow things down, Mom?"

"Belatedly, yes. It all happened so fast. We were only together about a month and I'm, well... rusty when it comes to dating. After all this time alone, it was nice to have someone romance me."

"But then you got worried," Jilly prompted.

"I told him we needed to slow down a little." Her strides lengthened. "That's when he surprised me with this trip. Planned it all with Theo and Vanessa, and hired a private plane from Boston. I didn't even know where we were going. When we landed in hill country I figured he was planning to surprise you with a visit. That you might be in on it." She turned back at the patio doors and stared at Jilly with haunted eyes. "Next thing we were at the zoo and I was trying to figure my way out of the trap."

"Why didn't you call, Mom? We would have come for you."

"I wanted to, but I hadn't found the words."

Janelle started pacing, too. "I would have had powerful words for Len. He wouldn't have known what hit him."

Mr. Bixby added his two cents in a garbled grumble that startled Brina. "We don't use words like that, Janelle. Don't believe in them." Her voice was brittle but at the end she added more softly, "Even when a hex might be warranted. And convenient."

"Mom, did Len ever..." Jilly couldn't finish the sentence.

"Abuse you?" Janelle held Bixby closer and he complained about that, too. "Emotionally or physically?"

Brina's heels clicked harder over the hardwood in heels and despite the circumstances, Jilly winced. Every ding in those floors was a ding to her heart. "Technically, no. It was like he put a spell on me, girls." She caught herself. "Not a magic spell, of course. But with all his—"

"Love bombing," Janelle supplied.

"I couldn't think straight. Before Len came along, I was perfectly happy being single. Independent. Then he showed up with flowers and fine words and made me feel—"

"Special," Janelle said.

Brina nodded. "I suppose I never felt special in our family. Shelley was the special one. And then you, Janelle. I was barely average." She cast a quick look at her daughter. "Even Jilly thinks I'm a dud."

"Mother, I never said that." Under cover of Keats' ha-ha-ha she added, "To you."

Janelle caught Brina's arm as she passed. "Mom and I aren't special. Certainly, not where romance is concerned. Jilly's the only special one in the family. Look at her. Happily married. A skilled chef. And now a cat mother."

It was a decoy and it worked. Brina stared at Percy in Jilly's arms. "What is it with the animals? Jillian, we were never pet people."

"I am now, Mom. Runaway Farm is an ark. It's sink or swim."

"Well, it's ridiculous. You gave up a wonderful career in the city to—"

"Run an inn with me," I interrupted. "And build a wonderful community. We tell each other every day how lucky we were to escape the rat race. Have you ever been happier, Jilly?"

"Never." Jilly clutched Percy to her chin. "At least, until yesterday."

Brina started to speak and I signaled Keats to bring her in for questioning. It was time to get some answers and I was probably the best one to do it. "Ms. Brighton, it sounds like you were starting to feel desperate to escape Len's spell. I mean, influence."

"Not desperate enough to poison him, if that's what you're suggesting, Ivy. I didn't kill Len or even want him dead. But a wedding at Happy Haven? That was not the destiny he talked about. Not mine, anyway. I just couldn't think of a graceful way out. I felt as trapped as the animals in the zoo." Keats maneuvered her in front of Jilly and Brina finally touched her daughter's arm. "I didn't want you to know because I was ashamed."

"It's okay, Mom. We've all done stupid things for love." Jilly looked from me to Janelle. "Right?"

"Sure," her cousin said. "But we need to know *how* stupid, Auntie. Did you set up a prenup? Is it possible Len was after your money? I know you have a share of the Brighton fortune. Cousin Liberty told me."

Brina flinched at the name. "There's no prenup because I hadn't planned to get married. Regardless, I made legal arrangements to safeguard that money when Jilly was a child. With the strange mishaps in our family, it seemed wise. Liberty disappeared for decades and I was afraid something like that would happen to me, so I set up a trust. Len couldn't have known about the Brighton money."

"If he's born and bred in hill country, he might have heard rumblings," Janelle said. "I'm sure you haven't forgotten our top-notch grapevine."

"Was Len hard up for cash?" Jilly asked. "Even your house in San Francisco would be worth a bomb."

Brina's hand pressed against her eyes and when it dropped, tears glistened. "You think I've been played like a gullible old fool."

After a moment's hesitation, Jilly offered what she could. Namely, Percy. The cat's fluffy paws came out, claws sheathed, and Brina reluctantly accepted him into her arms.

"No one thinks you're a fool," I said, over Percy's sonorous purring. He was trying to cast a different sort of spell over her. A calming one. Feline magic usually worked and Brina was no exception. The furrows in her brow eased slightly. "We've seen people duped so often we've become cynical, that's all. Did Lenard need money?"

Brina started moving again and Keats let her pace. She had Percy to slow her down now. "Len ran a successful business and always seemed to have plenty. But after this discussion of love bombing, I can't help but wonder."

"There must have been a reason for the rush," I said. "Do you think his business may have been in trouble?"

She paused at the patio doors and stared into the darkened backyard. "Not that I'm aware of, but I'm only beginning to realize how little I knew about Len. He told me he was from a small town but I didn't realize it was here in hill country till yesterday. Maybe he held back because I spoke about my miserable youth in Wyldwood Springs." Her eyes filled again. "I did more of the talking. It was so nice to have a companion again. Loneliness made me an easy mark."

Janelle walked over to touch her shoulder, thought better of it and dropped her hand. "Aunt Brina, I was on the run for nearly fifteen years so I know exactly how you felt. What happened in Wyldwood made us lone wolves. But I'm learning to connect again and you can, too. Start with us. Expand to friends. Then you can open your heart, with all due caution."

"There aren't many single men for women of my vintage. Len was the first to take initiative in years. We met during a lecture series at the museum. He seemed like a gentleman." She turned back. "I'll never trust my instincts again."

"You don't need to when you have us," Janelle said. "And there are plenty of eligible men around. Ask Ivy about Dahlia."

Jilly held up her hand. "Don't. Please. Good thing she stayed in town tonight."

I laughed. "My mom's been the belle of hill country mid-lifers,

Brina, and she'd be thrilled to share her dating tips. For now, let's see if we can put all this behind us."

"You'll find his killer, Ivy?" Brina came over and pinned me with the Brighton green eyes. "I know you're a genius at solving crimes."

Keats gave a loud mumble and I pointed. "He's the genius, along with the cat in your arms. Your daughter's no slouch, either."

"Janelle has her own beat in Wyldwood," Jilly said, to deflect the praise.

"You're all so brave," Brina said. "I admire that, because I always played it safe. But I worry about you, too."

I gave her my most reassuring smile. "Don't worry, we've got the best pets in the world. Have you considered getting a dog, Brina?"

She walked over to Jilly and handed the cat back. "I have allergies."

"Since when?" Jilly asked.

Brina faked a sneeze. "Always, Jillian. That's why we couldn't have a pet when you were growing up. No matter how many times you asked. And you were dreadfully persistent."

Jilly's face flushed and Janelle signaled me to walk her to the front door. "Let them fight. That's the only way forward with Brightons. Ask me how I know."

"You've healed the rift with your mom?" I asked, letting Keats herd us down the stairs to Janelle's car. Bixby leaned over her arm and yapped at my dog. I sensed he didn't like their being treated like common sheep.

"A work-in-progress." She opened the door and set the dachshund on the driver's seat. "Helps that she's staying with Gran down south. She's saved my bacon a couple of times long distance, though. I'll give her that." After Bixby moved to the copilot's position, she slid behind the wheel. "Sorry to leave so soon, Ivy. There's a situation in Wyldwood right now and I don't feel comfortable being gone long. I'll be back as soon as I can."

"I'll come down and give you a hand after we solve our situation here."

She shook her dark curls. "Don't worry about it. I've got Sinda and Ren."

"And Drew Gillock?" I gave her a sly smile. "How's that going?"

"Slowly." Her teeth flashed in a grin. "He's pacing me. Zero risk of love bombing."

"That's the trouble with lawmen. They're slow and steady." I sighed. "So slow you get a little worried."

Closing the door, she reached out the open window and touched my left hand. My rings, to be precise. "Don't worry about Kellan. The wedding and babies are locked and loaded."

"Boy and a girl?" I asked, grinning back.

Now she laughed. "I love blurting predictions, but this one is better left to unfold naturally."

"Ugh. Twins. I knew it."

"I didn't say that." The car rolled forward a little.

"You didn't *not* say that."

"Worry about the triplets later." She pressed the brake and stuck her head out the window. "Find the penguin first. It may have gone further down river than you expect."

"Did you hear something?"

Bixby gave a few yips from the passenger seat.

"I always hear things," she said. "I also got a strange feeling when I was driving here. Passed a cute little town with a bronze seagull on the sign. There's probably a good sized pond, at least. I could come back to help."

"Nope, you've done enough. I wasn't sure how to navigate the tension between Jilly and Brina and you've got them talking. Where there's communication, there's hope."

"The Brighton women are a handful. Maybe that's why the men don't stick around." Sighing, she added, "I hope Jilly and I can break the pattern."

"You will. But if you're worried, I've got a couples therapist you could talk to. Now, that woman's a handful."

Keats gave a ha-ha-ha and Janelle laughed, too. "Beware of false prophets, Ivy. Like I said, you and Kellan are fine." Mr. Bixby made a strange noise and she added, "For the moment, we've got bigger things to worry about than romance."

"Maybe that's what the older generations of Brighton women thought, and we *should* worry more about romance."

Mr. Bixby squished between the steering wheel and Janelle's cashmere shawl and bared his teeth at me through the window. Keats rose on his hind legs like a circus dog and flashed some fang back.

"On that note, I should be going." She lifted her dog into the passenger seat. "If you ruin another pashmina, it's coming out of *your* trust, Bixby."

We both laughed as she hit the gas. Elsa tore a patch out of the lawn before they vanished into the dusky lane.

CHAPTER THIRTEEN

Mandy's store was still dark when I drove by early the next morning. I expected that but it was still disappointing. After being up half the night worrying about the penguin, I craved caffeine. Excitement would need to suffice today. Janelle's tips had a solid track record in my experience, so I was eager to do reconnaissance and be able to make a case for changing the search plan by the time the crew gathered. Cori didn't shift gears without a good reason, and a psychic's prediction wouldn't qualify.

Gull's Glen was our destination. It was barely a blip on the map, and further than I expected the penguin to venture so soon, especially alone. Babble Creek widened into a large pond there, which would likely provide a better food source. After being hand fed three squares a day, Polo would be struggling to feed himself. I couldn't sit around with a triple order of pie while he went hungry.

Keats was uncharacteristically quiet as we turned onto the highway. He asked for the window to be opened and then didn't use it. I glanced at him periodically and after a few minutes, found him wracked with convulsive shudders.

Water.

That's what he was worried about. Not a scouting mission by

road to Gull's Glen. Judging by the time of onset, I guessed that he wanted to stop where we left off the search yesterday and collect a boat.

"Good thing our life jackets are still in the back," I said. "What's your fancy, buddy? Canoe, rowboat or kayak?"

He was sunk so deep in misery over the prospect that he didn't even fire off a blue glare. His legs slid out from under him and he hunkered in what anyone else might mistake for physical pain.

"Keats, we could just stick with the plan and walk around the town. It would be stupid for us to boat down there without backup anyway. Especially before full light."

Percy gave a lazy meow that sounded ironic. When had "stupid" ever stopped us before?

A low and slow mumble from the dog suggested we needed to do the right thing for the penguin even if it was the wrong thing for him.

"You're a hero, my friend." I reached out to pat him but he leaned away. "I know how hard this is for you. We'll call Edna and Gertie to join us. I don't want to take Jilly away from home today. She needs kitchen therapy and I'm hoping Brina will mellow when she sees the chef she raised."

I found my way to the place where we'd ended the search easily enough without help from Keats. His navigational system was temporarily offline. Indeed, his eyes closed and I sensed that if dogs could pray, that's what he was doing. I couldn't offer the comfort he needed when we both knew my water skills were negligible at best. If Cori or Edna were at the helm, he'd likely feel calmer.

His blue eye opened briefly, as if to confirm it.

"We could wait for them. This is your idea."

The blue eye closed again. Evidently, we were casting off alone. It had to be done and done now.

All the vessels were piled up on a trailer. Cori and crew had looped everything they could together with a long metal cord and locked it. The only thing accessible was an inflatable dinghy that sat like a cherry on top.

Not Cori's military grade dinghy, but the one probably liberated from a backyard pool.

"I was hoping for the rowboat but it's at the bottom," I said. "I'd have to use bolt cutters, take the whole pile apart and drag the boat to the water. Plus, there are plenty of thugs who'd love to get their hands on the good stuff if I leave them unlocked. We'll cross fingers and paws that the cheap inflatable is seaworthy for what looks to be an easy ride. And hey, it beats a kayak. I think."

Keats remained standing while I put on his life jacket, which spoke volumes about his commitment to the mission. Then he slunk down to the shore, where Percy stood waiting, orange tail high. The seafaring cat was chuffed and stepped happily into his life jacket.

I found the paddles, shouldered my backpack and dragged everything we needed to the water. The eastern sky was catching fire, so it wouldn't be long till there was enough light to spot a penguin. My dog's nose would narrow the playing field.

Before climbing in, I checked my phone for coordinates. "It's less than ten miles by water and all downstream. Should be easy-peasy. But this is your last chance, buddy. Speak now or forever hold your peace."

Keats lifted his nose and sniffed deeply. Thoughtfully. Only then did he step into the dinghy and crouch. Polo had obviously left a scent trail. Who knew penguin scat could come in so handy? It certainly was pervasive. Even after a couple of showers it clung to me.

I texted Edna, wrapped my phone in a couple of dog poop bags and slid it into the front pocket of my overalls. Then I put on Asher's hip waders, still wet from yesterday. If we found the penguin, I needed to be ready to climb out and use a collapsible net to secure the bird until help arrived. Finally, I topped off my ensemble with a life jacket of my own. While I was optimistic about our voyage, I was also realistic. There was a reasonably good chance I'd end up in the drink.

It felt good to be prepared. Even cautious. With my pets on board, I couldn't afford to be totally reckless. So, I checked and double checked everything before stepping onto a rock and then easing into the dinghy.

"See? Not a hair out of place on either of you, boys, and the water level is just right to avoid hitting rocks. This is going to be a smooth ride."

At first, it was.

The dinghy floated sedately downstream for a mile or two without much intervention from me. I pulled in deep breaths of pleasantly mossy air, scanning the shallows and banks on either side. Plenty of houses backed onto the creek, most with high fences. It seemed a shame to block a view like this. With so few tributaries in hill country, people should prize their access. If I owned a house there, I'd build a dock and sit in an Adirondack chair, letting the melodic stream rush past to carry my worries away.

Rushing.

Yes. That was the word. The creek had stopped ambling and begun to hurry.

While I was caught up in my hypnotic creekside fantasy I'd missed the acceleration. A mumble had warned me, I realized, and it was louder now. The dog gave my sleeve a shake with his teeth in case I missed the urgent memo.

"Right, right, things have picked up speed, haven't they? But we're riding straight down the middle. Don't worry at all, boys."

Percy wasn't worried. He stood with orange paws on the edge of the dinghy watching the world whip by. The cold spray that slapped my face didn't bother him at all.

Keats was bothered. Very much so. He half-stood to shake off the water and then slumped to the bottom again.

Hearing Cori's voice in my head, I feathered the small plastic paddles. They were like kids' toys and no match at all for the swift current. There wasn't much I could do except keep the boat as steady as possible.

"It's good, all good," I said with forced optimism. "What an adventure! Too bad we'll never get to talk about it, because Jilly and Kellan would kill me. Even Edna would have my head, because we're not wearing helmets."

Was there such a thing as a dog helmet? A cat helmet? I hoped I'd get a chance to find out.

"Not sure this was a great idea, Keats. I mean, I'm not blaming you, because I'm CEO and take responsibility. But still, you've steered me better before."

It came out as a shout, either from nerves or because the noise of the water was louder. Or both. Either way, I had to chill out enough to think logically. I could throw myself overboard but I'd risk tipping the pets. I could scream for help, but the houses were gone and by the time anyone heard us, we'd be gone too.

The only option, it seemed, was to ride this out.

Maybe Babble Creek knew its travelers would be in a panic by this time because it threw us a buoy of hope. Up ahead was a deep bend that would slow us down naturally.

And it did, for a few blissful moments of relief.

Then we reached the next hairpin turn and slowed even more.

It was going to be fine. One more turn and I might even be able to step out without capsizing. The stream had narrowed till it felt almost possible to touch both shores.

"I should try to end this," I told the boys.

Babble Creek, unfortunately, had decided to end us, first.

The narrowing was merely a chute to eject us into a roaring waterway.

The acceleration began as soon as the banks opened up.

Rapids.

We were caught in rapids that looked just like the photos in tourist brochures. The ones where passengers in a massive dinghy raise their arms and cheer while skilled guides navigate.

No one was cheering here. No one was navigating either. Mother Nature was at the helm.

The water gushed over the sides and the dinghy rose and fell, rose and fell, each time with a bigger smack. At one point, we caught air and my stomach did a spectacular somersault. Good thing I'd missed breakfast because Mandy's pie would doubtlessly be lost to the River Babble. I could only hope Polo the penguin enjoyed the ride more than we did. Unlike us, he was built for marine adventures.

"Hold tight, boys," I called out, frantically wielding the oars. "Not so tight that your claws puncture the boat."

The oars weren't helping much, but it was still heartbreaking when the creek snatched one right out of my hand. Now it was Ivy against river with a single cheap plastic oar.

Both pets splayed on the bottom of the dinghy. Keats looked boneless, as flat as the dog toys meant to defy hard chewers. Even his ears and tail were pressed down. His brown eye rolled my way and pleaded with me to do something. *Do anything.*

I was little more than a toy myself as the creek spun the boat around and sent us on our way again, this time backward. If anything, we picked up speed, bouncing off a few rocks to add spice to the trip.

One more bump and I'd lose a pet. The thought was enough to make me grab the remaining oar with both hands and feather like my life depended on it. It very well might. If the pets went in, I was going, too. It wasn't melodramatic, it was fact. I'd rather drown myself than lose Percy and Keats.

Muttering a few fervent pleas, I plied that oar like I knew how. If I'd earned any points for putting bad guys away, I wanted to cash them in now.

Finally, the dinghy turned the right way around.

And that's when I saw the bridge.

It wasn't much. Just a footbridge for locals to cross on their woodland strolls. It had surprisingly little clearance for those barreling down Babble Creek. If I stretched both arms, I might just be able to stop the dinghy long enough to inch over to the bank. My upper body strength might be sufficient. All that physical labor would pay off in spades.

The dinghy spun around once more and snatched that option away. The only thing I could do was duck and hope for the best. A second later a shadow crossed over us and we plunged onward to Gull's Glen where I could only pray there really was a placid pond to welcome terrorized boaters.

We spun around and around till I was dizzy and even more seasick. Surely, we were nearing the town by now. It felt like forever since we'd shoved off.

A few seconds later, the creek sent the dinghy careering sharply to the right. I saw the crash coming but there was nothing I could do but rest a hand on each pet. Percy evaded my grasp, however, and when the boat ran aground he catapulted ashore. Landing with his usual aplomb, he promptly scaled the bank without a backward glance.

I pushed myself up to follow but my legs didn't receive the order.

Instead, I collapsed into the shallows.

CHAPTER FOURTEEN

The water rushed around me and I stared at the sky, wondering about the point of it all. Not just the wild water ride, but my very existence. Why get up when I was only going to get knocked down again? It seemed like a lot of work to keep going. Every time we rescued an animal or caught a killer, the next crisis arrived. If I couldn't win the game I might as well enjoy the water. It wasn't that cold once you got used to it.

Keats didn't intend to get used to it. With his paws on land, he reanimated. This wasn't the time to loll around asking big questions of the sky. His teeth pierced the hip waders to tell me so.

"Fine, fine, I'll get up." I didn't move. "Sometimes it all just feels a bit much, you know? I could just be a farm wife raising the triplets Janelle predicted. No hair-raising escapades. No secrets from my loved ones. A radically honest life well lived. What do you say, buddy?"

He said his piece with his teeth, this time in my submerged wrist. If the dog was getting his feet and muzzle wet, he meant business.

And he was right. One member of our trio had gone rogue and I heard the roar of a truck's engine above. Percy could be in danger.

It took a fair bit of floundering to get myself moving. The hip waders were full and it felt like I'd suddenly gained 20 awkward pounds. No wonder Daisy looked weary these days.

"Wait for us, Percy," I called out, staring up the steep bank. "Keats, go after him while I tie up the boat."

The dog listed to one side and then the other as he tried to find his "land legs." My own were still wobbly so I started on all fours, cutting my finger on a sharp stone.

There was no time to nurse my injury with the cat out of sight and the dog scaling the bank slowly. My first aid kit hadn't survived the journey anyway. Somewhere along the way I'd lost the backpack Edna filled with everything we might need in a crisis—probably even anti-nausea drugs. Not that I would need them for the ride back. The chances of paddling upstream were nil, even with two oars and a better boat. Gertie would need to ferry us home on the highway.

I took a long look around before going after the boys. It was almost a relief not to spot the penguin because anything that might help in Polo's rescue had gone down with the backpack.

Cresting the bank, I got my first glimpse of Gull's Glen. The town was as quaint as their marketing material suggested. Stores with large windows lined the far side of what was likely Main Street. They'd left the river side free, perhaps to enjoy what there was of a view. I doubted you could see Babble Creek from the shops unless the water ran very high, which it probably did in spring.

An orange tail beckoned to me from across the street at the Gull Café. My hip waders sloshed slightly as I walked and I wished I'd left them in the boat with the life jacket. My overalls were soaked, however, and this felt slightly more presentable. Many—my mother chief among them—would argue otherwise. Hopefully it wouldn't be long before my friends arrived and they probably had a change of clothes in the van. Camo would fit the bill nicely.

Behind the iron fence of a sidewalk patio, Percy performed a flashy figure eight between the legs of a woman seated at a café table. She looked to be around my mother's age, but that's where the resemblance ended. This woman wore a flowing paisley print dress over her slim frame and was letting her gray hair grow out. As a hair stylist, Mom abhorred what she called "the graying." She would fight hers till the zombies took her down.

I held a more charitable view, especially since the woman was cooing to Percy and showering him with attention. "I see you've met my cat," I said, sloshing up to them.

She straightened in her seat and stared at me with big blue eyes in a thin face. "Oh my goodness! Were you fishing?"

"Not exactly." I ran a hand over my wet hair and decided "presentable" was beyond reach. "I rode down from the Clover Grove area in a dinghy. Got a little rougher than I expected."

"Only the kids do that now," she said. "With helmets and safety gear."

Percy and Keats were still wearing their life jackets, and the dog was using the railing to try to scrape his off. I hoped she didn't see me as a terrible pet mom for taking the risk. "I wasn't aware of the rapids when I set off. Never was much good with maps."

"The rapids aren't on most local maps." She found a smile, mostly for Percy, who had landed lightly on the table beside her mug. "To avoid turning it into an attraction. There have been accidents."

"I'll bet. We're okay, but I feel a bit queasy."

She patted the chair next to her. "Rest for a few minutes, dear. I'll get you some ginger tea."

"That's so kind, but I'm embarrassed to sit out here in my wet clothes. And I'd be more embarrassed to sit inside."

"Well, you can't go back the way you came. Do you have friends to help?"

I reached into my pocket and peeled back the poop bags to reveal my phone. Scanning my messages, I nodded. "They're on their way but it'll be at least half an hour. Told me to wait right here, in fact."

Percy flexed his claws through the woman's sleeve and she looked down. "He's wet. Cats don't like to be wet."

This cat didn't particularly mind but the damp dog at my knees sure did. "It's going to be a nice day, so we'll take a walk and they'll dry off. I thought there was a pond here."

"It's down the road a ways. Probably best to wait for your friends so you don't miss each other."

It made sense, and Keats wouldn't be so focused on wrecking his life jacket if the penguin were waiting for us. I was beginning to wonder if Janelle was wrong about the destination and Keats about the route.

The dog stopped scraping to rumble objections. It wasn't my place to doubt. My role was to ask the questions he couldn't.

"Maybe I will sit down," I said. "I'm a bit lightheaded."

Shaking her head, she pushed her chair back and rose. "I can't have you sitting here soaked, even on a nice day. That's no way to treat a hill country hero. You're coming to my house to warm up and drink tea."

I stuck out my hand and smiled. "Ivy Galloway. You've met Percy and this is Keats."

"Dixie Squibb," she said, gesturing to the sidewalk and moving ahead of me. "If you weren't looking for white water, what brings you to Gull's Glen?"

"Penguins. Two escaped from Happy Haven. We recovered one upstream yesterday but the other is still at large."

"What a shame. I always loved visiting the penguins when my kids were small. They're all grown up now. One day I might get to do the same with grandchildren."

Turning right at the first street, she picked up the pace. I did my best to keep up but the waders weren't built for speed, nor concrete. Keats was well ahead though, white tuft aloft. This adventure suited him far better than rafting. Percy stuck close to Dixie and it was obvious he'd taken a shine to her.

"That's a pretty little café," I said. "Do you go there to watch the sunrise?"

"As often as I can. That creek may not look like much but it attracts a lot of birds and other wildlife, especially at dawn. I like to be the first one there and enjoy my coffee in peace. People are so irritating." She looked surprised by her own admission. "Not everyone, of course, but if it weren't for Percy, I would have left when I saw you. I keep to myself, mostly." Keats turned up a path and she slowed. "How did he know that's my house?"

"Good nose. You travel the route often."

He fanned his tail before climbing the stairs and an orange bullet shot past him to reach the front door first.

"What delightful pets you have, Ivy. That doesn't always come across in news coverage. Justine Schalow's reports sometimes feel a little mean-spirited."

I struggled up the stairs after her. "Especially when she disses my pets. They've helped rescue so many animals in need."

"And bring wrongdoers to justice." She twisted the doorknob and it opened easily. Gull's Glen was apparently a community where doors could be left unlocked. In Clover Grove, most of us had alarms and security cameras. "I always read the stories about you. You're a legend."

I laughed as I followed her inside. "Tell that to my fiancé, please. To him, I'm often a wrongdoer and always a rogue."

"He's lucky to have you and I hope he realizes it. Some never do, I'm afraid." She directed me to the main floor bathroom. "You take a hot shower and wash off the creek slime. My son left some old clothes behind when he moved out and I'll leave them by the door."

As much as I wanted a shower, I didn't take her up on the offer. Leaving the pets alone with a stranger felt wrong, but bringing them into her bathroom felt wrong, too. Instead, I scrubbed myself with a facecloth and braided my hair. Cracking the door open, I found Keats standing sentry beside a pile of fleece. Dixie's son and I were about the same size, right down to his castoff rubber water shoes. That was convenient, if not flattering.

I followed the sound of clinking china into the living room, where Dixie had arranged a tea party fit for royalty. She perched in a battered armchair and I took a spot on the couch. My nausea had abated, so I happily helped myself to an oatmeal cookie when she passed them.

"You have a lovely home, Mrs. Squibb," I said, taking the steaming mug she offered.

"Call me Dixie, please. Squibb is my maiden name and I haven't been a missus for a very long time."

"Understood." I watched Keats watching me and continued. "So, you raised your children here?"

She smoothed a chip in the coffee table. "Can you tell? My son was wild, and my daughter was a pet lover, like you. There's hardly a thing in the house without damage, but every dent or scratch holds a memory."

"That's what I tell my best friend, who runs an inn with me." I smiled at Percy, who sat by my feet, purring loudly. "This guy has an entire forest at his disposal and uses the dining room table leg to sharpen his claws. No one leaves without orange fur on their behind."

She laughed. "Perfection is overrated, and not even achievable for a single mom. I did the best I could, cobbling jobs together in a town with few options." Adjusting a misshapen lampshade, she sighed. "My son says he raised himself, but I did my best for him and so did his sister. She's a nurse in Dorset Hills."

I nudged Percy in her direction to offer comfort and he invited himself into her lap and began purring. Her fingers trailed over him and the feline hypnosis set in almost immediately.

"Sounds similar to my family. My mom really struggled to raise six of us and I couldn't see that till I came home after a decade. Now, we're becoming quite close."

"Your father was out of the picture?"

"For many years, yes. He's back, but it was an adjustment."

Her hand lifted off the fluff and hung there. "I certainly hope my ex doesn't come back. That would be a terrible shock."

Percy rubbed against Dixie's hand but couldn't get her to reengage. After a few passes, he left her lap to explore.

I plucked Percy off the end table but he hopped right back up. "So sorry. He can be quite rude." The cat swatted an ornament, which landed on the carpet at my feet. Bending to pick it up, I found a little frog sitting in my palm. It looked hand-carved. "How adorable! Did your son do this?"

She shook her head. "Bought it at a flea market when he was a child. It became the first of many frogs." Her hand swept around the room. "I have quite a collection now."

"Why frogs?" I asked.

She folded her hands in her lap and sighed. "That boy practically lived in Babble Creek. I couldn't keep him away and there were always tadpoles in a jar on his windowsill. As I said, it wasn't the easiest childhood and watching those tadpoles turn into frogs brought him joy. I let him do what he liked within reason. Some said I spoiled him but I was trying to make up for what he lost." I set the frog on the table and she stared at it. "Took him a long time to grow his own legs but he's finally swimming, and I feel like I can relax."

Percy scaled the wall-mounted shelves and found another treasure. It came down fast and I snatched it out of the air just in time. This figurine looked hand-painted and I turned it over. "Aha! A Mabel Halliday creation. I have an ever-growing ceramic town she made for me. It's supposed to be a Christmas display but we love it so much we leave it out year round."

Dixie's smile came back. "Another collector? I don't feel so embarrassed about all the frogs now."

"Miniatures are a good choice," I said, standing to retrieve the cat before he could do real damage. "My pasture is full of livestock collectibles." Tugging on the cat, I grunted, "Would you give it up, Percy?"

He would not give it up. On the contrary, he selected a red-and-blue glass frog to flick in my general direction.

"Oh, dear, don't break that one, Percy," Dixie said, as I caught the missile. "It was special for my sixtieth birthday last year. Hand-blown by a local artist at my son's request."

"It's so beautiful. Like ruby and sapphire."

"My son has his moments. Now that he's launched, I actually miss him."

Percy landed on the couch and I grabbed him. "I'd better get this menace out of your house. My friends will be here in a few minutes and we'll go check out the pond. I take it there have been no penguin sightings?"

"Not that I've heard and as much as I sidestep gossip, things like that get around."

"What a shame. I'm so worried about him. The female, too. Penguins mate for life."

A shadow crossed Dixie's face and I wondered if a penguin love story raised more regrets about her failed marriage.

"I remember that," she said. "Happy Haven may be a bit..."

"Cheesy?" I suggested, bringing her smile back.

"Lame was the word my son used. Yet some of our happiest family memories are there."

Keats gave my knee a nudge so I took a last sip of tea before saying, "I hear the aviary and butterfly garden are nice."

Another cloud crossed her face. "I was married in the aviary. It *is* lovely, if loud. The macaws are raucous."

"They are. My friend Buckley has a stunning bonded pair."

This time she winced and I mirrored it. I couldn't seem to stop lobbing happy couples in Dixie's direction. Percy was rubbing off on me.

My host rose and led me to the front hall, where I collected my things. "I'll walk you back to the café, Ivy. I'm sure you could use a hand with those hip waders."

"I've got it, Dixie. You've already done so much for me. I'll launder and deliver your son's clothes the next time I'm down this way."

"He won't even notice they're gone, but I'd welcome another visit." She winked at me mischievously. "Next time, you might come by land."

I laughed. "No more rapids for me. My back aches."

"You're lucky that's all that aches. You could have gotten a concussion."

She was right. I could have easily added insult to head injury and destroyed my chances of a normal life.

Keats herded us out of the house and we walked down the road together. I insisted on wrangling the hip waders, while Dixie carried my soggy clothes in a tote bag.

Staring around, I said, "Gull's Glen seems like a hidden gem of hill country. No one ever talks about it."

"I'd love to keep it that way. The bigger the population, the bigger the problems and the higher the crime rate."

"My fiancé would probably agree. Clover Grove is growing too fast for its infrastructure."

As we approached the Gull Café, a shout made me turn. Edna Evans strode up the creek's bank wearing a life jacket over her camouflage jumpsuit. A pink floral shower cap peeked out from under her helmet.

"Those rapids were a hoot," she called, clomping across the street in army boots. "I don't know what you were whining about, Ivy. The spray was bracing."

Dixie laughed and held out her hand. "Bracing. That's one word for it. I'm Dixie Squibb."

Taking my host's hand in a waterproof glove, Edna cackled. "I have others. Like invigorating. Or rejuvenating. I feel years younger than I did an hour ago. Why haven't we met, Dixie? I'm Edna Evans and I know almost everyone."

"I live a quiet life here. But you're making me think a little bigger, Edna."

My prepper friend stood back and took Dixie's measure. "You don't look a day over seventy, Dixie. We can turn back time with a basic revivification program." She unzipped one of many pockets and plucked out a business card. "My website will give you a simple list to get started."

Dixie flushed over the decade Edna tacked onto her age, but she studied the card. "How interesting. I should try something new."

A white van pulled up and Gertie jumped out. Her poncho and long braid made Dixie recoil, which earned a smirk from both my friends. "We'd better ship out, crew," Gertie said. "Captain Hogan has a lead on the penguin."

I clutched the hip waders tighter. "We're taking the van, though, right?"

Edna cackled again. "You'd never make it back by water, since you punctured the dinghy." She jerked a thumb over her shoulder. "Found your go-kit, though. Packed with care by yours truly and tossed like fish to a penguin."

"Do go and save the escapee," Dixie said, handing me the tote bag. Then she held up the business card. "Edna's given me homework."

"I'll get you scaled back to sixty pronto, Dix," Edna said, hopping ahead of Keats. "By the end times, you'll be kicking—"

I interrupted Edna with a kick to the derriere. It knocked me off balance and I sank quickly under a pile of clothing and hip waders.

By the time my friends stopped laughing and helped me up, Dixie was long gone.

CHAPTER FIFTEEN

"You weren't my first choice or even my third," Cori told me, as we left the others and walked toward my truck at the meetup point. "Especially after stealing and destroying a perfectly good dinghy. It's because of renegades like you we can't have nice things."

"I already said I was sorry about that ride." I felt no remorse over the dead dinghy but I did regret taking the pets downriver, especially when it was a bust. The missing penguin wasn't in Gull's Glen and may never have been. Hopefully that meant Janelle Brighton was also wrong about the triplet prediction. "But if someone has a void in their backyard pool, I'll buy them some water wings. Why choose me at all if you have better options?"

"Can you stop shivering, please? You look like a delicate flower and I need someone tough."

"I'm as tough as any of your friends. Caught a chill, that's all."

She shrugged off her jacket and handed it to me. "Wear this. I don't need black leather to exude toughness."

I put it on over the sweats I'd borrowed from Dixie Squibb. Of course, it was several sizes too small. I could barely get the domes clasped and breathing became a luxury. "There. Better?"

"Marginally. Don't stretch my jacket. Unfortunately, no one had spare gear that conveys the right message."

We stopped behind my truck and Keats kibbitzed around the trainer, excited to be part of the elite mission. "Exactly what message are we trying to convey? And to whom?"

"A thug message. To a thug." She waggled her gloved fingers. "I've got thug covered but you still pass as a lady farmer."

"A lady farmer?" I tried to throw my shoulders back but her jacket constrained me. "That's insulting. I've taken down a ton of killers and it wasn't with a genteel foxtrot."

She tipped her head. "I always wonder if you win by accident. You're notoriously clumsy."

I let my umbrage go. There was no room for it in the tight jacket. "It does feel accidental sometimes. Okay, most times. Like the deadbeats walk right into the weapon of choice. Afterward, I can never explain how it happened."

Cori stared up at me with her crow-like eyes. "Divine intervention, I guess. I don't say that lightly, but I think it works in my favor sometimes, too. I should be in jail by now."

I laughed. "Me, too. Good thing we have our pets to keep us out of the clink and helping animal-kind."

"And that's why you're actually here." She gestured to the truck. "I needed a double order of furry thugs and you come with the package. Clem is an amazing dog but he's not bloodthirsty."

My umbrage tank refilled. "My pets aren't bloodthirsty. There's more finesse in our work than you imagine."

"That's what Jilly said while you were gallivanting in my dinghy. I'm giving you the benefit of the doubt. This mission requires a careful balance of finesse and thuggery. Can you handle that?"

Keats mumbled confirmation that we could and would. His excitement could barely be contained by his furry tuxedo. Even

Percy felt the vibe and scaled Cori's petite frame to perch on her shoulder. It felt good to see her wince under his claws.

"I'd like to be briefed before accepting the gig as your muscle. Or is it triggerwoman?"

She held out her glove, palm up. "Keys."

"It's my truck. You're not driving."

Her fingers waggled. "Keys. I'm not going to sit back while you treat this sweet beast with stick shift brutality. It belonged to Hannah Pemberton and is part of the Mafia. Unlike you."

I tried to cross my arms in the tight leather and failed. "My truck is part of the Mafia and I'm not? After all my efforts to support you guys?"

"The Mafia is a team. A pack, if you will. You're a lone wolf, Ivy. None of us would head down the rapids alone at dawn in a dinghy. You don't always play well with others. Despite all the support you have, you go rogue."

Her words hit home and I handed her the keys. "I'm just impatient. When I get an idea I can't always wait for everyone else to have breakfast and fall into formation. Besides, I'm never alone. I have Keats and Percy."

She shook her sleek short hair and hopped into the truck, as agile as a monkey. "There's a word for people like you."

"Oh yeah?" I got into the passenger seat and patted my lap for the pets. "Reckless? Impulsive? Rash?"

Cori managed to flick an orange finger while turning the key. "*Crazy*. You make me look tame, and that's saying something. But the real reason you're here is that our target is crazy, too. I think you'll be able to meet her on her level."

"I don't even know what to do with all this flattery."

"Does your ego need a boost? Fine. As much as I hate admitting you do anything better than me, you have a certain talent for pulling facts out of people. It's that sneakery your brother complains about."

"There's no sneakery involved. I just ask questions and listen very closely to the answers."

"I ask questions and nobody answers," Cori said. "Not honestly, anyway."

"If you're flipping them the bird, what do you expect? Even criminals want to be heard. They have their reasons, even if we don't agree with their actions. I just try to understand them."

"I guess. My patience for fools is in short supply."

I smiled. "Your patience for humans in general is in short supply."

"True that. Most *are* fools and animals suffer the consequences."

"There are more good than bad by far, but it takes some sifting to separate the gold from the garbage. Remember, I worked in HR for a decade. As a baseline, I presume people are lying. The lies are often harmless. When they're not, I have a good nose for the truth, and Keats' is even better."

The dog gave a ha-ha-ha of agreement.

"You'll need it today. Our target is a liar by trade." She flicked more fingers. "Before you ask, watch the video I sent."

I hadn't checked my phone since leaving Gull's Glen. Cueing up the video now, I watched it closely. Then again. And again. The screen was too small to make out much detail but it looked like someone wearing a zoo uniform and cap was in the penguin enclosure with the colony. "I'm not really sure what I'm supposed to be seeing here. Is this from today?"

"Two days ago. What you're seeing is someone kidnapping two penguins."

I gasped. "What? I thought there was no suspicious footage on the security feed."

"There wasn't by the time Fergus Shay got to it. But someone got to it first and digitally edited it. Luckily, I hacked in the second he called me and downloaded what I could. Took my guy some time to clean it up. There are several fragments, including one that shows this gal putting a penguin in a gym bag."

"That gym bag is gonna stink something fierce," I said. "Too bad we only have a view from behind. It must be a man. Kellan said there aren't any women on the zookeeper staff right now."

"It's a woman. Look at her wrists." She held up her own. "Not much bigger than mine."

I held the phone closer to my nose. "Is that dirt or a tattoo on her forearm?"

"Her second big mistake, after being caught on camera at all," Cori said. "I know that tattoo. It's overlapping initials for an extremist environmental group. They've been involved in some of the biggest rescue efforts in the world, including oil spills in South Africa. But they don't play nice and most have a police record. Wynn Hartwell is the only member I know who hails from hill country. I heard through my traplines that she's back and on parole."

I turned to her quickly. "Did you tell Kellan?"

"Do *you* tell Kellan everything? I hear you're all about radical honesty now."

Keats laughed for me. "Not so much. But I would definitely tell him about criminals stealing penguins near the site of a murder."

"Saved you the trouble. The chief and I grease the wheels of rescue by sharing intel, so I couldn't hold back. When I got the clips this morning, I sent them to you both at the same time. Of course, I didn't expect you to be riding whitewater and now he might be ahead of us."

Keats slumped and grumbled. "Kellan's probably got the jump," I said. "While the penguins aren't his first priority, someone like Wynn is a hot lead. Maybe she ran into Len while leaving and offed him. He might have gone outside more than once."

"Doubtful. Radicals like Wynn don't back away from

confrontation but they don't go out of their way to hurt random citizens, either. Bad press harms the cause."

"Hopefully the police have left and we can question her privately. We're after different information." Keats stood and his tail swished in my face. "Someone's optimistic."

"Maybe the dog senses a little something I held back from Chief Uppity. I gave him the last known address for Wynn but she moves around a lot. My moles tell me she's been seen in Stoat Crossing a few times lately."

Keats mumbled an order to hurry and Cori pressed the pedal down. There was no question my truck performed happily for her, just as my pets did.

"Why do you think this Wynn stole the penguins? Anti-zoo sentiment? Free the caged and all that?"

She shrugged. "Her group is definitely anti-zoo but there's no way they'd release one into the wrong environment for it to thrive. Sacrificing an animal to the cause is anathema. Something must have gone wrong."

"Maybe Wynn has it stashed in her bathtub. All we have to do is find her and get inside."

"Piece of cake." Cori laughed. "Wynn is going to love you."

I watched the clips over and over until Cori skillfully backed into a spot on Main Street in Stoat Crossing. There was a pretty bit of green space in the town square with a canopy of century-old trees. Keats and Percy catapulted out of the truck and ran up to a woman sitting on a park bench facing away from us. Her arm draped casually over the back of the bench and a cigarette dangled from her hand. A tattoo peeked out from the sleeve of her denim shirt.

That was easy. Too easy. When suspects fell in our lap it usually meant the next steps were hard. Whoever pulled my puppet strings liked to keep me on my toes. A complacent sleuth was a lazy sleuth.

"Oh, hey," she said, as Percy landed beside her. "Where'd you come from?"

We walked around to face her and it was obvious Wynn Hartwell didn't love me at first sight and didn't care much for Cori, either. Her black hair was in twin braids and there were half a dozen studs in one ear, another in her lip and one in a nostril. Wynn's features were attractive but her expression seemed hardened. I guessed she was in her late thirties but looked older.

"Thought you'd be tough to find, Wynn," Cori said. "You're getting sloppy."

Wynn dropped her cigarette on the grass and ground it out with a work boot. "I have nothing to hide, so there's no reason I can't enjoy a sunny day in the park."

The tiny trainer kicked the eco warrior's boot. "Get up. We want to speak privately. Your place or... your place. Those are the only options."

"Whatever you want to ask, do it in public." She eyed Keats warily and then glanced at me. "I know who you are."

"Then you know he means business," I said, signaling for Keats to get her moving.

Wynn's toughness faded quickly with the sheepdog nips. Her little yelps probably attracted more attention than she liked because she got up and started hopping. Quite literally. Percy, meanwhile, led us directly to an old house just a short walk away. He stood on the porch till we got there and brushed against Wynn's ankles to end Keats' assault.

"How did you—?" She ended with, "Never mind."

"Happy to answer," I said. "They smell penguin guano. I do, too. Unless it's stuck in my head permanently after getting spritzed myself."

Cori shrugged. "You both stink, but good rescuers willingly suffer for the cause. Right, Wynn?"

The pig-tailed warrior took her sweet time unlocking the door until Keats delivered motivation to her butt cheek. He didn't pull that move often but he must have sensed I'd let him get away with it today. The assignment was to thug and we were thugging.

Inside, she stayed ahead of him by a hair and was puffing when we got to the upstairs landing. "Call him off, Galloway."

I signaled for the boys to fan out. "Find the penguin, please."

"There's no penguin. I don't know what you're talking about."

Keats stopped first at a gym bag and went into a point. "Evidence," I said. "We saw your bag in the footage from the kidnapping."

Unlike me, Wynn had no trouble crossing her arms over her chest. "Still don't know what you're talking about."

Cori cued up the video and held it out. "Your tattoo is available for viewing. And the police have the clips, too. Is animal abduction a violation of your parole order?"

Wynn glanced at the video and turned away, her expression stony. "Not me. Lots of people have tattoos."

"I do," Cori said. "But not for an eco militia group. That's pretty rare. I hear you have to do some pretty fine stunts to earn admission. I'd love to hear the war stories. Not today, but after we recover the missing penguin."

"Good luck with your search." She subtly covered the tattoo wrist with her other sleeve. "Afraid I can't help you."

"Keats?" The dog came back from his reconnaissance with tail down. It was another bust, but Wynn had more information. I could sense it. "Have another go at her, buddy. Leave her hands alone. There's already a wound. Probably a gash from a penguin beak."

"Let him bite if you want," Wynn said. "I won't hurt a dog. But I don't know anything, can't say anything."

"You won't hurt a dog but you hurt two penguins?" I said. "That's against the rescuer code of conduct."

"Is there a rule book for you guys?" she asked. Her face was nearly immobile, a skill I didn't see often. "No one told me."

Cori sighed. "It's no use, Ivy. High-end eco nuts are trained to withstand interrogation, and we're not trained to withstand seeing it. As far as I'm concerned, Wynn's a wounded animal, too."

"I resent that, Cori Hogan." Her stance, with shoulders bent and hands hidden like a child's in an oversized shirt, backed Cori's statement. Whatever Wynn had been through, she felt broken now.

"Tell us where the penguin is and we'll leave you in peace," I said, scanning the books and magazines on her end table. "We just want to see him safe. Pippa's all alone now. She's grieving her mate in isolation and it's so hard to watch. She's not eating."

I didn't expect a tug on her heartstrings to do any good, but Wynn's face gave the slightest twitch. "I don't know where he is and that's all I can say."

"Do you know if Polo's safe?" I pressed. "Is there hope for a reunion? Penguins mate for life, you know."

Again, a twitch. It reminded me of Dixie this morning when I mentioned couples. "That's sad, but I still can't help you."

"Can't or won't? If she dies of heartbreak, do you want that on your conscience?"

"Can't. Won't. Same diff." This time she took a small step back and Keats lifted his paw. There was something here to press on.

"Do you know what heartbreak is like, Wynn? I do, and I wouldn't wish that on my worst enemy, let alone an innocent bird. Finding her another mate would be tough with the small genetic pool."

She half-turned, staring blankly at the window. "Irrelevant."

"Poor Pippa was so trusting she let you stuff her in a gym bag, only to toss her in a creek like trash."

"I didn't do that." The words shot out of her mouth. "I would never."

Time to press harder. "Then tell us what really happened?"

"No idea. Just feel bad hearing about it, is all."

"We know you did," I continued. "The footprint near the creek was your size and boot model. Now Pippa's in mourning and her mate might be dead, for all we know. One less rare penguin on the planet because of you."

"Stop it. Just stop it." Her voice cracked. "It's not like that."

Cori raised her glove in my direction to ease off but my other master's paw was still up. I forged on.

"Well, what is it like?" I asked. "Cori and I know things can get hairy in animal rescue and we've both done extreme things. Maybe you thought this was best for them." Her expression was still utterly blank. I was good with a bland HR mask but her skill was off the charts. "Here's what the police are saying: they think you did it to please a guy and now he's broken your heart."

The mild twitch came again. "You don't know anything. The cops don't, either. If they did, they'd be here."

"I know you'll forget this dude and meet someone new at the next eco disaster. And by then, Pippa and Polo will likely be dead."

Finally, she turned back and her eyes met mine. "Bring in the cops. I'd rather get grilled by them. You're relentless."

I shrugged. "Guilty. And when it comes to animals, ruthless, too. Confirm Polo's alive and in hill country and we'll leave."

She hugged herself tighter. "I don't know that he isn't."

Still, Keats' paw hung in the air. He was the relentless one in search of truth.

"Is Polo still at large in Babble Creek?" I asked. "There's a search party thirty people strong and I suspect you want him found, too. Reunited with Pippa."

Wynn's twitch turned into a small spasm as she snapped, "Those are not their names."

Cori arched a dark swallow-like eyebrow at me and mouthed, "See?"

"It's Pippa. She told me so. Polo I'm not sure about as we haven't met. But at least he's out of the creek. My dog says you say so."

Keats confirmed that with a mumble.

"You're nuts. No one said anything to you."

"Nuts, yes, but not wrong. Thanks to your disclosure, we can redeploy and find Polo."

"You won't," she said. "It's hopeless."

Keats didn't think it was hopeless. Far from it. His bum came up and his tail rose. "My dog says otherwise. So, don't you worry. We'll find that bird and bring the happy couple together again."

Cori aimed an index finger in Percy's direction. "What is your cat saying?"

My fluffy feline was scraping busily at the carpet in front of a painting propped against the wall near the door. There was a box beside it that bulged with books, men's toiletries and a pair of large Oxford shoes. The breakup box, I guessed. She was returning someone's property, including the painting.

"Percy's right, that's a beautiful piece," I said. "It looks like lily pads with yellow flowers."

"Nice try," Cori said. "Anything goes with that modern crap. You can plant your butt on canvas and call it art."

I walked over and bent to take a photo. "I'd love something just like this at the inn. Must be part of a series. It says number two."

Wynn came over and used her work boot to lift my cat away from the art. "Leave that alone, you brat."

Percy continued to scrape busily over her boot, pronouncing her dead to us, or at least pumped dry. I didn't get the sense either pet thought she was guilty of more than penguin theft.

"I'll send the police back for a chat, since you asked," I said. "Let's go, Cori."

Cori swaggered to the door and kicked the breakup box. "Sorry about your broken heart, Wynn, but people like us stay single for a reason. Easy come, easy go. If you do take him back, get him to buy you some real art. This dandelion painting is lame."

"Lighten up," I said. "That's art and it means something to Wynn. She's stressed enough about the penguins."

"I'm not stressed." Wynn eased her boot out of Percy's imaginary litterbox. "Never felt better."

"Great, then you won't mind if we visit again," I said.

"Go ahead. Don't be surprised if I've moved."

Cori laughed and walked out the door. "See you at the next rally, Wynn."

"Not if I see you first, Cori. And I'd take that jacket back from your hulk friend unless you want it to be permanently stretched."

"Noted." Cori waited till we were at the truck before crooking her finger. "Surrender the jacket. Wynn's not wrong."

"That I'm a hulk?" I said, indignantly.

"You know that's why I brought you. For the very thuggery you and your pets displayed. It was like a torture scene in a thriller movie. I had to close my eyes."

"Please. It was just a chat. I probably would have gotten more out of her if you hadn't been riding the brakes."

"You're all bloodthirsty." She shook her head and went to the driver's door. "Guess that makes us a dream team. I got the moves, you got the screws."

I followed her to the driver's door and used my muscle. "Give me the keys. I'm driving my own truck."

"Fine. Touchy much?" She climbed in ahead of me and crossed nimbly to the passenger seat. Cori wasn't wrong about her grace. Whenever I crawled through the cab, it went far wrong. "Open your mind and you'll see it's a compliment. I never learned how to do what you do. The fine art of sneakery offends my sense of honor but I see its value and admire anyone good at her game. My genius —and I am one—is knowing where I need backup, so welcome to the Mafia shortlist. And it's a very short list."

The pets jumped in after her and I slid behind the wheel.

"Shortlist? I've been helping the Mafia for two years, both directly and indirectly."

"Yeah, but it's a closed membership and has been for a while. Plus, with you being first lady of law enforcement, you're a risky choice." She reached up to pat Keats' head. Seated, he was actually taller than her. "That said, we need you."

"On the dream team of animal rescue?"

Keats pant-laughed and leaned into Cori's hand. "It's a privilege to be part of something this awesome," she said. "There's a temporary opening with Hannah still overseas. But fair warning, there's an admissions test."

I thought about it. Then I thought about Kellan's views on my making it Mafia official. I did consider it an honor to be considered, but for now I was happy on the periphery.

"Hannah's coming back soon, Cori. My dad offered to parcel off a few acres so she can build next to the farm and I hope she'll go for it."

"With two kids, she can't work for us at full capacity, but we are loyal above all else. So that makes you official backup."

"In other words, everything will continue as it was."

"Exactly. Why fix what ain't broke?"

I smiled as I turned onto the highway. Cori would always have my back if I needed help. And if my ego ever got too big for her jacket, she'd be right there to deflate it.

CHAPTER SIXTEEN

I dropped Cori off to break down the search and headed back to the farm to see how Jilly was faring with her mom. It was a welcome break that would give me time to ponder our next move in finding the penguin. The world was a big place to hide a bird, no matter how stinky.

When we rolled out of the lane, there was a police SUV parked outside the inn on the very patch Janelle had left in the grass. Did no one respect lawns anymore?

"Moving to plan B," I told the boys, spinning the truck and shifting to reverse. My default plan B was to hide in the barn. I'd needed that option so often it had only made sense to clear out the brush to create a parking spot beside the barn. The truck was virtually undetectable from the house. If someone really wanted to know my whereabouts they could walk down to find me. It deterred Mom one hundred percent of the time. Out of sight, out of mind. "Sneakery at its finest, right?"

I expected a pant-laugh and didn't get it. Keats was on alert, though his flags were down.

"Something wrong with the livestock?" I asked, checking my

watch before letting him out. "Charlie's away, but Poppy's supposed to spell Dad off soon."

The dog didn't take off as we slid around the truck in its tight hollow. Instead, he nipped at my cuffs repeatedly to manage my speed. This farmer sheep had no choice but to surrender control.

Percy was under no such law and took off like an orange bullet to investigate. He had many highways and byways in the barn to permit recon and surveillance. With his beacon fur, he had to go one step further—and usually higher—than most cats.

The journey through the barn was slow and choppy. Stop, go. Stop, go. Keats had a destination in mind that required utmost stealth and my footfalls would normally be a giveaway. The rubber-soled water shoes supported the cause.

Finally, we got close to the very last stall. It was normally vacant, and the one I used as a bedroom when there was an issue with the livestock. Today, two people were whispering inside. A man and a woman. Were Poppy and Travis having a private moment in my makeshift bedroom? On work time? My sister would get an earful.

Keats wasn't trying to prank them, though. His hackles came up and his blue eye told me to listen harder.

Not Poppy.

Not Travis.

There was an imperious tone in the woman's voice that took me in another direction. It was Vanessa Greer, the maid of honor at Brina's bridal hostage-taking. The man was probably Theo Radcliffe. Why they were lurking in my stall was anyone's guess. Maybe they were the ones overtaken by romance. Vanessa hadn't tried that hard to hide her interest in Theo.

Keats eased me into the next stall. At night it housed goats but they were outside now. I crouched and pressed my ear to the wood, telling myself it wasn't really eavesdropping if they were hanging in my stall bedroom. If my dog wanted me here, it must be about something important. Keats could barely tolerate my romance with Kellan, let alone anyone else's.

Glancing up, I saw Percy in the rafters. He had hunkered down above us for a good listen.

"We've got to make this quick," Theo said. "Colonel Harper will come down looking for us and we have to get our stories lined up."

Vanessa giggled over Kellan's new title. "Guy's full of himself, no question. Didn't try very hard to get Brina to let us in the house. What a drama queen and after all we did for her. That dowdy spinster was about to land a fine man, thanks to us."

Theo paused. "Brina's not dowdy or a spinster. Gullible, for sure. Lenard wasn't subtle enough in grooming her. I told him a dozen times to slow his roll."

"He was desperate. You two couldn't hide this problem forever without losing the business. Len got you into it and it was his job to get you out. Brina wrecked everything. She's so loaded she'd never miss it."

My knees gave out and I sank into the straw. What was wrong with these people? They were enough to challenge my always-tenuous faith in humanity. I wanted them out of my barn before they polluted the air my livestock breathed.

But I wanted to know if they killed Lenard Pembroke more, so I sealed my lips and hit record on my phone. They were quiet, but I might capture some of the conversation.

Theo came to Brina's defense again. "It wasn't her fault. She would have followed through if her daughter's posse hadn't arrived. One more day and the deal would have been sealed. Brina's the kind of woman who stands behind her man and I'm sure she would have helped him out."

Vanessa clucked in disgust. "Those nosey ruffians and their pets. Can't help wondering if Brina cued them up."

"Doubt it. She was so upset about her daughter finding out this way. I just wanted to hug her."

"Hug her? Maybe *you* should marry her then, Theo."

He laughed quietly. "Thought about offering her a shoulder to cry on, but I can't work my charms from out here."

"You'd really do that?" There was pain in Vanessa's voice. She'd fallen for Theo and he was oblivious.

"You bet I would. Brina's way too good for Artie and it would still solve our problems."

I glanced at Keats and mouthed, "Artie?" Was that their nickname for Len? Len*ard*. Artie. It was a stretch, but I could see it.

"Fine. Try. The wedding's still paid for." Her tone was clipped but I suspected Theo would be oblivious to that, too.

"Maybe I could twist the colonel's arm. Brina likes me but she never warmed to you. How about sitting this one out, Vanessa? For the good of the team."

She was quiet so long I worried they were onto me. Then she cleared her throat. "Theo, I'm beginning to wonder if you took Art out of the equation so you could do the job yourself."

Now Theo paused. "Are you accusing me of murder? Seriously?"

"Seems like you have motive. You had the hots for the bride and you doubted Len could pull this off. You even followed him out of the room when he left. Both times. That's probably when you—"

"Pulled out my poison capsule?" He snorted. "I went to the restroom! Vanny, we've known each other ten years. Is that what you think of me?"

"Well, someone killed him and you make the most sense."

"You two fought all the time, especially after you found out what he'd done. This could be—what do they call it?" I mouthed the words and he finished, "A crime of passion."

"Except I didn't leave the room, Theo. No opportunity. No

means. And no motive, since this marriage would have kept me from bankruptcy."

I didn't need to press my ear to the wood anymore because their voices were raised. I barely heard the mumble beside me and missed the footsteps behind me.

"Oh, hi Ivy. Fancy seeing you here." I sat back and stared up at Lacey Byle. She crossed her arms over my stall and smiled. "Hope you're going to be honest with your boyfriend about eavesdropping."

She'd downgraded Kellan from fiancé. It was another mind game and a good one. But if Kellan ever downgraded me we wouldn't be going back to casual status. That would be us over. I could not bear to be around him if he changed his mind about marriage.

Keats reminded me of our present crisis with a none-too-gentle poke. "Hey, Lacey. It's my farm and my job to pick through straw for anything that might harm my livestock. You can't imagine the mischief goats get into."

"I can barely imagine what *you* get into, Ivy. You're a mystery waiting to be solved. In couples therapy."

Vanessa and Theo came out of the next stall. Both looked pale, as well they should. Let them wonder about what I'd overheard. I wouldn't give Lacey the satisfaction of knowing.

Luckily, Kellan arrived before things got ugly. *Uglier.* "What's going on?" he asked.

The question was directed at me but Lacey elected herself spokeswoman. "Your girlfriend was sitting in the hay with her phone. I'm sorry to tell you that she may have been recording Theo and Vanessa. Isn't that illegal?"

"I was taking pictures of manure, Lacey," I said. "Once you establish a baseline with goats, you need to monitor it daily. Would you like to see some pics?"

By the time I got to my feet, Lacey had backed away but she wasn't easily foiled. "Show and tell? Sure, what fun."

Kellan's expression turned as flinty as Wynn Hartford's earlier, making me fear I might wind up on the receiving end of verbal manure, but Keats shot out of the stall and went after the therapist. Having felt his wrath before, she left the barn at a run. The dog came right back for the others and started herding.

"Separate them," I said. "Quickly."

We followed them and found Asher getting out of his SUV. "What's up, Chief? Jilly says her mom's upset so I came over."

"That'll have to wait," Kellan said. "I need you to drive the others back to town and don't leave them unattended for a second."

Asher looked from Kellan to me and then back. "I wouldn't leave Ivy unattended for a second either, Chief. She's my twistiest sister. Capable of untold sneakery."

Kellan sighed. "Ain't that the truth."

CHAPTER SEVENTEEN

The visitors left in a cloud of dust before the scolding began. Kellan gestured to follow him into the barn. My father came in from the pasture, took one look at us, and walked right back out again.

"Was Lacey right?" Kellan asked. "Were you recording a conversation without someone's consent?"

"You bet I was. And was Lacey right about my being downgraded to girlfriend? You didn't correct her."

His eyes widened. "I didn't even notice, Ivy. Lacey caught you in a compromising position. She's right about it being illegal."

I shrugged impatiently. "I record killers all the time and you don't complain."

"In those conversations you're a party and grant consent. If you were just sitting here in the hay having a listen, that's different."

"Fine. Does that mean you don't want to hear about Theo and Vanessa accusing each other of murder?"

He pursed his lips. "I'm open to hearing your account. Eavesdropping isn't illegal. Only recording said conversation."

I thought about sulking longer but Keats told me with a nip to hurry it up. We still had a penguin to find. Percy was more supportive, coming down from the rafters to accost Kellan's uniform with fluff. It was always easier to face the chief when the cat was on his shoulder to take some starch out of him.

"I got home from the penguin search, saw the police SUV and decided to stay in the barn," I said. "Keats let me know someone was in the stall, the one I sleep in. I realized it was Theo and Vanessa having a private conversation and yes, I hunkered right down to eavesdrop on them."

"Without texting me?"

"Then the conversation wouldn't have continued. I wouldn't have known that their business was in trouble, or been sure that Len was only marrying Brina for her money. 'Grooming' was the word Theo used. Vanessa wouldn't have suggested Theo take over and marry Brina, and Theo wouldn't have misunderstood that she wants him for herself. Then Vanessa wouldn't have accused Theo of killing Len—they were calling Lenard 'Art' by this point—and Theo wouldn't have countered with his own accusation. I didn't need to listen hard by this time. Even Lacey could have heard that, depending on when she arrived. She's got sneakery nailed."

Kellan rubbed one hand through his hair and then followed with the other. It was a two-hander, no question. "Can you go through all of that again? Slowly?"

I shrugged. "Sure. Or you could just listen to the recording. That way you won't miss a single scintillating detail."

"With your phenomenal memory, I'm sure there won't be a stone left unturned."

"I certainly remember Lacey downgrading me to girlfriend. You're right about that."

Percy slowly crossed Kellan's face to the other shoulder, perhaps trying to ensure the maximum injection of dander into his nostrils. "Can we stick to the criminal issue?"

"Of course." All he had to do was laugh off Lacey's comment and toss me a scrap of reassurance, but the chief was all business. I could do that, too. In retelling the story, I slowed it right down, dwelling on every pause, every tonal change, all the subtext Theo didn't pick up but Keats, Percy and I did. "You're missing a good convo," I said, at the end. "I can't do it full justice."

"A seasoned actor couldn't do better." He cracked a smile. "What great timing that you happened to be here."

"Wasn't it? But this is my safe place and I didn't expect to find it sullied with sleazeballs. Did you know their business was on the brink of disaster?"

He nodded. "Theo had a primary stake and he had every reason to be angry over Len's mismanagement. My working theory was that he planned to take drastic action if the marriage scam didn't work out. No one was coughing up details."

"Being in a stall tends to lower inhibitions," I said. "When I came in, I feared Poppy and Travis had lowered theirs too far. Never occurred to me it was Theo and Vanessa, and at first I thought they were canoodling, too."

His jaw relaxed a trifle, although it was hard to see with Percy leaning in so hard. I could hear the purring from five feet away. "They haven't had a moment to speak privately and I guess they wanted to get their stories straight. Sounds like that didn't work out too well."

"The manure was flying by the end, Colonel. That's Theo's nickname for you. Is 'Art' a nickname for Lenard?"

"Actually, no. Lenard wasn't his real name, nor was Art. He had a number of aliases and as many failed businesses. Theo and Vanessa probably didn't know the extent of it, or they wouldn't have backed the business or this scheme."

I crossed my arms on top of the stall and rested my head on them. "Poor Brina. She was a mark."

"I'm afraid so, and it happens too often. She's far from alone."

"I doubt that will make her feel better. Not right now." I raised my head. "At least you have more to go on with Theo, and possibly Vanessa. Brina and Jilly are off the hook."

"Not quite." Keats didn't like Kellan's curt tone and told his cuffs so. "We need an actual confession. Proof."

"Let me help. Tell me more about Len's aliases. Was he even from hill country, like he said?"

He smiled at last. "Nice try. I'm not letting you run off to dig up dirt on this guy. He was practically a phantom before he was even a phantom."

I smiled, too. "Good one. If there's dirt to dig he must be hill country born and bred."

"I did not say that."

"You didn't *not* say that." His smile held position so I tried a new tack. "Asher said you'd identified the poison."

"Asher says too much sometimes." His smile flickered and turned off. "Particularly since the findings are preliminary."

"Cyanide?" I guessed. "The old reliable for kill pills?"

"Something less common. Perhaps from a backyard garden."

"Like holly or yew? We've been there before."

He shook his head. "More like rhododendron. Ever heard of 'mad honey'?"

I came around the stall and walked over. "No, and I can't wait."

"I knew that would tickle your bee-loving fancy. Pollinators take the toxic nectar back to the hive and when a human consumes it, they can become quite addled and even hallucinate." He looked around, as if the livestock might eavesdrop and get big ideas. "We get the odd case, but it's uncommon. No fatalities on record here, but Len may be the first. Especially if he had a preexisting health condition."

"Huh. So it wasn't a bad oyster at lunch but a sweet trip."

"Not so sweet, from all accounts. I doubt he was a frequent user or Brina would have noticed. His game was too consistent and calculated."

I reached for Keats and found his ears waiting. He was willing to offer support but the grumble beneath my fingertips told me he was impatient to be doing. "You know I'm going to google the heck out of mad honey, right?"

"Don't you have your hands full with the missing penguin? I'm sure I'd have heard if you'd captured it. Make that smelled. I mean, I can smell it but it's stale now."

Percy decided another pass was warranted and earned a chiefly sneeze for his efforts.

"Eau de stale penguin," I said. "No wonder I got downgraded."

He pulled out his handkerchief and mopped fluff off his face. The fact that he still carried one, and with a monogram yet, was part of his old-school allure. Even this "ruffian" hobby farmer loved knowing her gallant man might whisk it out at a poignant moment. "What are you smiling at?" he asked

"Nothing. Just you."

The full-on Kellan smile arrived in all its glory. "I honestly didn't notice what Lacey Byle said, Ivy, and you shouldn't listen to her either. I've met some poor therapists in the line of duty but she's gotta be the worst. I can't imagine a single couple has benefited from her advice."

"She was right about Mandy," I said. "Lacey's not always wrong."

"Lacey Byle?" A voice behind us made me jump. Keats hadn't seen fit to alert me about Poppy's arrival. "She's a hack. A scorpion. Can you believe she predicted Travis and I would never go the distance?"

I gave Kellan a significant look. He wouldn't admit to sharing my concerns about that particular relationship but I knew he did. "I do believe it, because she's entered us in a draw for a six-pack of couples therapy sessions."

Poppy laughed. "Guess she has to give them away. No one's

going to pay to hear they need to be radically honest with their partner. Or radically anything else."

I figured Kellan would leave but he hung on, while gently dislodging Percy.

"Pops, I'm pretty sure you complained Travis wasn't honest enough with you not so long ago."

"That was then. After a few weeks of way too much information, I backpedaled. Now we're on a need-to-know basis." She grabbed a pitchfork to start her shift. "I mean, it might work for some, but not people like us."

She pointed from herself to me.

"What's that supposed to mean?" I asked. "Galloways in general?"

"Not every Galloway. Asher's an open book, pretty much. But some of us need to keep a lid on it or blow things up, like Lacey says. And not in a good way."

"Is there a good way to blow things up?" Kellan asked.

Poppy shook her head. "Better to pick your way around the landmines. That's my view, anyway. I know everything I need to know about Travis to go all in."

Kellan and I exchanged another glance and Poppy caught this one.

"Never you mind, Chief Judgypants and Farmer Do-Right. Some couples get stuck with one foot on the gas and the other on the brakes. That's not us. Full throttle, baby."

Kellan's phone rang and he looked relieved to have an out. He walked through the back door to take the call near my manure pile.

"Are you engaged, Pops?" I asked. "Like, formally?"

"Not something I'd share with doubters like you guys. Date with the door open but commit with the door shut." She went over to the stall where Theo and Vanessa had duked it out. After peering inside, she hooked the door with her foot until it slammed. "Door shut. Get it? Losers like Lacey can quack outside but never hand them a key."

I watched as she tossed hay into Florence's stall. It was such a nice day the old blind mare had willingly gone outside. "Who are you? And what have you done with Poppy?"

The next forkful came in my direction. "She grew up. You should try it, little sister."

Keats was past done with relationship talk and ended it with nips as sharp and fast as a rattlesnake.

"Too much, buddy," I said, waving to Poppy. "Got the message already."

The message was bigger than his boredom. With Kellan distracted, it was time to slip the truck out of its shady hiding spot and get back to shady business.

CHAPTER EIGHTEEN

On the highway, I turned my mind to our visit with Wynn a few hours ago. It wasn't easy to push what had happened in the barn out of my head but Theo, Vanessa and Lacey weren't going to carry me closer to my goal of finding the remaining penguin. Wynn Hartwell just might. True to her eco warrior status, she'd held her ground and divulged very little. Even warriors had hearts, however, and hers seemed to be broken. Was it possible the relationship rupture had come from the penguin incident? Maybe she had plotted the theft with her partner but something went wrong and they lost the birds. And maybe, to earn back her trust, he'd recovered the male penguin and was keeping him safe somewhere. I sensed that she was conflicted about her ex, so he may have redeemed himself somehow.

"I think I know Wynn's guy, boys," I said. "The Oxford shoes in the breakup box were a clue. Let's drop by and see if he's got the penguin. If it's there, you'll be able to sniff it out. If not, we'll need to twist his arm to find out where he stashed it."

Keats mumbled encouragement. We were definitely on the right track. For the first time since we shipped out on the inflatable dinghy, I felt in control of our destiny. More or less.

"I guess Cori isn't wrong about us being lone wolves, with all due respect to you, Percy. While I trust my friends, operating alone is usually faster and easier. I can't think clearly when there's too much clamor. Or when someone's stuffing me into a leather jacket that doesn't fit. I thought I was going to suffocate."

Now I felt comfortable. I hadn't had a chance to change out of the castoff sweats Dixie had loaned me. Despite all the excitement in the barn, I still had a slight chill.

"Figured I'd miss my overalls, but these soft pants aren't bad at all. If I can get used to a drawstring, I may ultimately be able to tolerate a waistband and move into hard pants again. Becoming a married woman might inspire me to up my style game." Keats pant-laughed, so I added, "People do strange things for love, buddy. Like steal penguins. Or give up their sloppy overalls."

Just before we arrived, I pulled over and texted Jilly. This wolf might be a loner, but she was learning to check in with her pack before descending on someone she suspected of committing a crime against penguins.

We parked down the road to preserve the element of surprise and walked up the front stairs. By the time the door opened, I had my biggest, fakest HR smile strapped securely in place. This would take some fancy footwork. Good thing I'd swapped out my work boots for water shoes in Gull's Glen. This lady farmer was going to foxtrot.

"What are you doing here?" The door cracked open enough for Percy to slip past unnoticed.

"Is that any way to greet a friend?" I said. "We did good work together, Professor Horn."

He started to close the door and I stuck my foot in the gap. That move worked better when I had steel-toed work boots, so I pulled back the water shoe quickly. I'd need to get Percy out another way.

"We're not friends, Ms. Galloway. I was there to help the

penguin, not you. Then you betrayed me by taking her back to freshwater prison."

"I had no choice, Professor. She belongs to Happy Haven, and the police would have come after her. And you. There were a lot of witnesses."

"And now you're back here to ask for help to find the male, aren't you? Well, you're wasting your time. I won't be duped a second time."

"Duped? No one said you could keep her. Did you dupe yourself?" I held up my hand to stop him. "No offense, sir. I dupe myself all the time about animals. I actually thought I could keep a trio of kangaroos at Runaway Farm. And if I thought I could install a marine system, I'd probably try to keep penguins, too. Like most collectors, I get a dopamine hit with each treasure."

"I'm not interested in your hormones, Ms. Galloway. You're making me anxious and I need to go and ground myself."

With that, he slammed the door in my face, trapping my cat inside. I knocked a few times and then tried the doorbell. Percy would eventually interrupt Tapley's meditation to demand release but I didn't care to wait.

So, I kept pressing the doorbell. Over and over and over. It was a loud one, annoying even outside.

Keats slipped through the railings and went around the house. We invited ourselves into the backyard just before Tapley locked the gate. Percy wasn't there, so he must have found something interesting inside.

"Professor—"

"You drove me out of my own home," he interrupted, walking back to his garden. "Like an entitled, lazy student. If you can't find the other penguin, that's your problem."

"What if I didn't come about the penguin at all?" I followed closely and then backtracked when he picked up a hoe. There was a dent in his downspout from tossing smaller garden tools at me earlier. "What if I came to collect dirt on the zoo? You might call it lazy, but discussion with experts is a key part of a student's work. It can be the most expeditious when there's a tight deadline."

"Only when said expert is a willing participant. Pounding his doorbell won't garner cooperation."

"Apologies for my impatience," I said, pulling out my phone. "There's something I want you to see."

He came over reluctantly, still clutching the hoe. "Is that... Is that Beatrix?" His greedy gardening glove tried to snatch the phone but I stepped away.

"Pippa, yeah. Chief Harper gave me access to the penguins' closed-circuit TV system. I know you're disappointed about what happened but she's safe. I mean, she looks miserable there grieving alone, but she's safe."

Turning away, he started whacking the dirt with his hoe. "So, this is about the missing penguin, after all."

"Actually, I'm here about Lacey Byle."

The hoe stopped. "Ms. Byle? What about her?"

"I'd like to get her fired, that's what. She's planting seeds of dissent in otherwise happy couples."

He went back to whacking. "I don't disagree with you about her therapeutic skills. She gave me harmful advice about my last relationship and it didn't end well."

"Let me guess," I said. "Radical honesty?"

A derisive snort confirmed it. "Even radicals can't handle that much honesty."

"Exactly! Thanks to her, I'm doubting my own relationship."

Bending, he yanked out a few weeds and tossed them aside. "That said, some relationships aren't meant to grow."

"Are you talking about the chief?" I asked.

He kicked at the discarded weeds. "Always so self-absorbed, Ms. Galloway. It was a general observation."

"You're right, it was rude to focus on myself. Especially given *your* situation."

He turned, startled. "What situation?"

"Your recent breakup, sir. Was it radical honesty that wrecked your relationship with Wynn Hartwell?"

There was no sun hat now to shield his expression but he had enough skill to keep it neutral. "Wynn Hartwell? Wherever would you get that idea?"

"I met her today and she dropped a few hints. A magazine on her end table had a photo of you on the cover. It seemed like a treasure."

A flush rose from his collar. "That's an old journal of ornithology, not some teen zine."

"I could totally see you and Wynn together. You're quite distinguished, sir. I'm sorry you had to let her go. Was she too... well, radical for you?"

Shaking his head, he went back to weed-whacking. "You're grasping at straws, Ms. Galloway. I know Wynn Hartwell, yes. We met first at rallies and later at an overseas rescue. I'll even admit I admired her, at first. But Wynn's a true activist, willing to put her principles on the line despite the law. I'm an accidental activist. A blundering fool who gets emotional and says too much. Teaching was my calling and I lost it because of a few stupid words. I'd never blow things up for real, whereas Wynn and her colleagues already have."

"That doesn't mean you can't love each other. You share much in common."

He turned again and met my gaze. "Needs to be the *right* things for it to work, at least in my limited experience. Principles, values, shared purpose. If you must know, my ex is a high school teacher who shares my love of learning. And yes, the radical honesty that landed me in the press and left me jobless also lost me the girl. Impulse control is still an uphill battle, as you saw, but I try to choose education over activism."

Keats turned his warm brown eye on the professor and I knew the man was telling the truth.

"That's so sad, sir. Maybe you can win your teacher back. After we get Lacey fired."

He tipped his head skeptically. "This isn't really about Lacey, is it? You're as twisty as your brother said when he came by earlier. Just ask me what you want to know so I can reclaim my peace."

I gave up the game and sighed. "Honestly, I hoped you and Wynn were a thing, and that you did something heroic to capture the penguin. Do you think she stole them?"

"I think she's capable, but I have no reason to suspect she did. It would certainly be out of character for her to release them into Babble Creek. She cares about animals a little too much. Like me."

"And me. But what if she did? What if losing them was an accident she's trying to fix? Where might she stash the missing bird?"

He dropped the hoe and came toward me. "Do you have proof she stole them? I agree she's capable, but do you know it to be true?"

I reached down to touch Keats' ear to cement the truth in my vault. "Just suspicions, sir. She has the most motive."

"Lots of people have motive. I'm on the suspect list and there are plenty of previous thieves to investigate. I wish it were Wynn, because she would find a soft landing for that male."

"I wondered if that soft landing would be here," I admitted.

He actually laughed. "You think there's a penguin in my bathtub? I'm not lacking a certain courage, Ms. Galloway, but I couldn't live with that stench. Perhaps when I was a younger man, but now I value my creature comforts too much."

Keats didn't flag a lie, so I'd have to believe Tapley, unless Percy said otherwise. "Presuming the penguin has been recovered from the creek—"

"Why presume that? We have no evidence. I think you called off the search prematurely and intend to continue on my own."

I gestured to Keats. "There are half a dozen dogs on the case who never give up. And they gave up. The penguin is gone."

"Gone out of their range, quite possibly. But as you saw for yourself, it takes someone with my skill to capture one." He held up a gardening glove. "I haven't succeeded with the male but I'll keep trying."

"And if you did succeed and wanted to hide that penguin, where would you keep it?"

He rubbed his graying hair with the glove hard enough to create static. "There's nowhere safe for a penguin. Not for long. Backyard ponds, perhaps, securely fenced. Swimming pools, if the thief is misguided enough to risk the chemicals. But you know they're raucous birds. It wouldn't stay a secret from the neighbors."

"I'm sure he's destined for another home, if not already there. I was hoping the person would lie low for a few days and give us an opportunity to catch up."

"If someone managed to capture him, they know what they're doing and have a plan." He sighed. "Neither of us is going to like that plan."

"Black market?" I asked.

"Probably, and that never ends well. Very few creatures stolen from Happy Haven are recovered."

"Fergus said they'd only lost a few reptiles and some parrots."

"Do you think he'd tell the whole truth?" Tapley bristled with indignation. "Fergus is a decent guy but he's paid to toe the party line. When I worked there, I heard about dozens of thefts. Admitting it publicly would tarnish the zoo's reputation and in the case of reptiles, alarm the public. That's one reason they wanted me gone. Too vocal."

"That's so sad. I guess it's about the money."

"The missing macaws are worth tens of thousands, and pythons fetch a good price, too. Another hot ticket is the dart frogs. Easily concealed and impossible to find."

"Those cute colorful little guys are valuable?"

"Cute and deadly, Ms. Galloway. The golden poison frog is one of the most toxic creatures on the planet. The batrachotoxin a single frog secretes is said to be enough to kill ten men. That's a collector's dream."

Not this collector. "How could anyone handle them?"

"Very carefully." My expression made him smile. "At one time, the indigenous peoples of South America used a frog's poison on the tips of their blow darts. Hence the name. The poison derives from their natural diet of ants, termites and other toxic insects. That's how wild frogs evade predation. Their bright colors scream, 'eat at your own risk.'"

"Fascinating," I said. "I can see why they'd be a prize."

"Fortunately, frogs in captivity aren't normally toxic because of their safe diet. But they still have cachet." He shrugged. "Or so I hear. I'm a bird man, as you know." I thought he might continue to educate me and I was happy to learn. Instead, he turned back to the garden. "Can you show yourself out, Ms. Galloway?"

"Of course, sir. There's just one more thing."

He threw down a glove in exasperation. "Seems like there's always one more thing with you. If I do as you ask, will you promise not to assault my doorbell again?"

"That I can promise. And I'll leave you in total peace if you just let my cat out of your house."

"Out of my house. That's a..." He sputtered in outrage. "An utter violation of my privacy."

"It's only a cat, sir. When you opened the front door, he slipped in under the lecture."

I wondered what Tapley was so anxious to hide from an inquisitive cat, but I doubted it was a penguin.

He stomped over to the back door and when Percy didn't emerge, went inside with a slam of punctuation.

"I wonder if he'll eject Percy from the front door instead," I said. "Not sure what to do here."

Keats knew exactly what to do. He stepped into the garden, walked to the flowering shrubs Percy had investigated on our first visit and raised his paw.

The bushy plants had colorful blooms in pink and mauve.

Rhododendrons.

CHAPTER NINETEEN

Percy trotted around the side of the house to let me know we'd been summarily dismissed. Professor Horn didn't come back and I couldn't blame him. The longer I stayed, the greater my chances of asking him about his magnificent rhododendrons and the production of mad honey. He was probably an expert on that, too, although there were no hives in the yard. You could rent plots of land for bees in our area and lots of people did. I'd learned quite a bit about honey when I helped rescue a major bee operation, but somehow, the topic of mad honey never came up. It was something I'd love to know more about. For the moment, I settled for taking pictures and texting them to Kellan.

"Do you think Tapley killed Lenard Pembroke?" I whispered to the pets as we walked back to the truck. "Yesterday, I got the sense he knew more about Len. Or Art, or whatever name he went by when he lived in hill country. Len was a scammer and may have bilked the professor at some point, too."

Keats' mumble sounded unconvinced. Obviously, the flowers were of interest but the boys would have flagged an alert if I'd been chatting away with a killer.

Unless killing Len had been a one-time revenge hit for Professor Horn. A crime of passion that didn't leave me at risk.

I had half a mind to go back and hammer his doorbell again to continue my "homework," but the strategy was unlikely to work a second time. Tapley Horn would probably prefer to go deaf than deal with any more of my questions.

"He could have supplied the toxin to someone else to do the job, I suppose. Hired and armed a hitman. Or maybe he just provided mad honey to someone more motivated to take out Lenard. Seems like Len left a trail of grudges behind. Thank goodness Brina escaped his trap."

We drove back to Clover Grove, since I had no leads on the penguin. The professor was probably right it was gone from the region already. It would be difficult to hide a loud smelly bird, even though it wasn't that big. I could only hope that its value would prevent someone from housing it in squalid conditions. What's more, that Polo would get a happy ending in a home that saw him as a treasure. Maybe they'd even find him a new mate, if only to produce more eggs for sale.

"Wildlife mercenaries," I said. "Maybe someone should serve them mad honey. Someone more radical than me."

Keats mumbled what sounded like a pep talk, something he didn't indulge me with often. I was supposed to keep my own spirits high so that he could dash cold water on them.

He turned a blue eye on me. It was too soon for jokes about water, even silent ones.

"You're the one who wanted to go downriver," I reminded him. "I can't see the point of shooting the rapids if Polo was never there."

The blue eye didn't leave my face.

"Well, was he there? Because you didn't point him out for us. You seemed happy to pursue a new mission with Cori."

He turned back to the window and applied his nose to the

crack. Like the professor, the dog wasn't going to do my homework for me.

I continued to muse aloud. "I suppose it's possible someone got to Gull's Glen before us this morning and captured Polo. Or even last night."

The blue eye flashed in my direction once more.

"Tapley Horn would have the skills and so would Wynn. Together they'd make a dynamic duo. I don't trust either of them. Those Oxford shoes in Wynn's breakup box looked just like what a professor would wear to go courting. Not that Wynn seemed the type to be impressed by scholarly footwear."

Keats let me ramble myself quiet before raising a paw to suggest a troll through town before going home.

"Sure," I said. "I'm in no hurry to get back to Brina. She's not one for dramatics, so it must have taken a lot out of her to ban Theo and Vanessa. I wonder if Lacey got past the threshold. I'd hate to think Lovebirdy was contaminating the inn."

That earned a pant-laugh from Keats. Lacey was beneath his notice, unless she got in the way of our business.

I thought about calling Jilly for an update but Keats was pawing at the glass now and Percy got up to take a look, too.

At first, I thought they wanted to stop at Bloomers, the salon Mom and Iris ran together, but when I parked and let them out, they hurried straight to Hill Country Designs.

"You wanna visit Teri?" I asked, although the answer was obvious. "The store's about to close, boys."

Indeed, Teri Mason was turning the sign on the door when she saw us and smiled. The day had passed in such a blur I didn't realize it was dinnertime already. I hadn't eaten all day.

"Come in," Teri said, locking the door after me. "The sign doesn't apply to friends."

She was wearing her usual floral caftan and her short spiky hair was freshly colored with pink and blue streaks. I wondered if Lacey had copied her hair, because no one else in town got it done like that. With Teri, it was a natural reflection of her inner artist and joie de vivre, whereas Lacey probably did it to stand out on social media.

"Can I ask you something only a friend would?" I said, following her to the counter.

"Always." She grabbed tubs of dog and cat treats from under the counter and came around to offer my pets some. They didn't often accept food gifts but they did from Teri.

"Do you have any human treats?" I asked. "I'm starving and don't want to go home."

She laughed. "Let me see what I can find."

While she was gone, I strolled around the store checking out her new designs. I'd never had much interest in art before coming home but Teri had changed that. No matter what medium she used, she produced vibrant pieces that conveyed her exuberance. As a result, there were several of her paintings at the inn, and other bits and pieces. Jilly and I didn't always agree on décor but we were all in on Teri's work, as well as Mabel's miniatures. If we hadn't called a moratorium on new acquisitions, I'd be seriously tempted by the framed watercolors that caught the late day sun from the window.

"Love those," I said, pointing to the paintings before accepting the protein bars she offered.

"Sorry, Ivy. That's all the food I could find. I'm trying not to overstuff my caftan, you see."

I ripped one open. "Gotcha. That's why I fight against the waistband. A drawstring is as close as I get."

"Wouldn't have recognized you without your overalls if it hadn't been for these handsome fellas." Percy was on the counter to receive some pats but Keats had gone to stand under the paintings.

I chewed and swallowed before questioning Teri. "Those don't look like your usual stuff."

"They're not, but about eight months ago I had what I call my 'impressionist phase.' It didn't last long before I moved on.

Customers ate them up but you know I don't really work for the money. At least, beyond the money I need to keep the lights on. I need to love it and I didn't."

I took another bite before pulling out my phone. "Reminds me of something I saw earlier today. I got a pic."

Flipping past the rhododendron series, I found the painting that sat beside Wynn Hartwell's breakup box.

Teri took the phone from my hand and nodded. "Yep, that's my work. You have a great eye, Ivy."

"The yellow water lily spoke to me. I'm eager to get my pond launched at the farm and see the real thing close by."

She laughed. "That's not a water lily, my friend, but I'll let you keep the compliment about your good eye, because it's impressionism. It's fair to see anything that resonates."

I joined in with sheepish laughter. "What is it, then?"

"A frog. It was a private commission. I did a pair of them."

The next bite of protein bar went down like sawdust and I had to wait for it to pass before speaking. "Did the customer know it was a frog?"

"Requested it specifically. A small yellow frog against a green background. I did my best, but maybe it's a good thing my impressionist phase passed."

"It's beautiful," I said. Beautiful and deadly, perhaps, like the golden dart frog it probably represented. "Can you give me a name? I'd really like to talk to this guy."

"Don't know that it's a guy or even have a name. The request came by email with full payment in advance. All I did was paint and ship it." She studied my face. "I'll share the address with you if you promise to pass it along to Kellan, as needed. I suspect this means more than you're willing to say."

"Depends what I find when I get there," I told her. "But yes, you have my word I'll share it with the police if it has any relevance at all."

She searched for the address on her computer while I did a search of my own online.

I tried to take another bite of the protein bar but my throat had closed for business. After Teri's email arrived, I mouthed thanks and let Keats herd me out.

———

I WAITED till I was in the truck before checking Teri's email for the address. My first guess was that it would lead me right back to Professor Horn, but it didn't. Nor was it the place in Stoat Crossing where we'd found Wynn Hartwell today. But that didn't mean anything. Cori said Wynn moved around a lot, and Teri had shipped the art six months ago. The customer could be anywhere by now.

Keats rested a paw on my leg and mumbled. The time for musing was when the truck was in motion, not when we were still parked on Main Street.

"Got it, but let me check the map. This address isn't familiar to me." After getting the truck rolling, I said, "Outskirts of Dorset Hills, not far from Professor Horn. People in Dog Town do love their art. Whether they also love toxic frogs remains to be seen."

The dog mumbled an order to hurry things along. Turns out the time for musing and conversation wasn't when the truck was in motion, either. Not this evening. He had a bee in his bonnet and it didn't seem to be about mad honey.

I continued chatting anyway. "Do you think it's a coincidence that the poison in rhododendrons is similar to what a toxic frog produces? Possibly similar enough to be mistaken by forensics? That may be why police haven't finalized the results. Rainforest amphibia probably didn't top their list. Especially when they aren't toxic here."

Now, Keats mumbled. The message sounded like, "Don't be so sure."

"I suppose someone could feed frogs the right stuff to make the wrong stuff, but it would take some work. There are easier ways to find natural poison. It can be as close as a backyard garden."

We drove a couple of miles as I mulled.

"You know what I've learned, boys? People will often take the hard way *just because*. It's about the challenge. And I can't help thinking that an academic who prides himself on knowledge mastery would be best positioned to hack a frog. If Tapley Horn has managed to put the killer back into the dart frog, he's going to be a very rich man. And rich men score all the girls. I don't need Lacey Byle to tell me that. The teen zines prove it."

It was as good a theory as any, and since Keats elected not to encourage my speculation, I pressed the pedal down and rushed into the dusk.

The small bungalow on the secluded street was in near-darkness except for an eerie glow emanating from the basement. It probably wasn't that eerie but it felt that way.

After parking up the street, I did the right thing and walked to the front door and knocked. Then I pressed the doorbell a few times. If Professor Horn was here, he'd blow a gasket.

That realization made me pull out the phone and text my coordinates to Jilly. There was nothing worthy of reporting to Kellan just yet. All I had was a head full of swirling pieces that hadn't coalesced into anything concrete. I'd already over-texted him today in the name of radical honesty. There was no reason to hit him again until there was something substantive.

This morning, Lacey had made a social media post about how to keep the allure alive while withholding nothing. It boiled down to "leaning back" or whatever catchphrase she used. Issuing a nonstop stream of texts kept a guy from wondering about you. Create the wonder, she said.

Keats mumbled now and it didn't sound complimentary. Of either Lacey or me.

"Sorry, buddy. I'm ashamed I even looked her up."

I walked down the stairs and thought carefully about our next step.

And that's when I did the wrong thing.

CHAPTER TWENTY

The basement window at the side of the house suggested it was worth going in for a look. I'd assumed the eerie light might indicate a grow op but it looked like the only thing growing lived in an aquarium. Perhaps a vivarium, as the frog literature recommended.

Jilly responded with a series of question marks but there was no way to explain briefly why I was thinking about breaking into a house to check out frogs.

Not just thinking about it. Doing it.

One window happened to be open to let in the evening breeze. Unfortunately, it was also the smallest. The bathroom, I suspected, from the mottled glass. On the bright side, the screen was already frayed and splitting so it felt even less like a break-in and more like a visit. A visit to someone's private zoo, if my suspicions panned out. It was probably a rental and the tenant could be anyone's guess.

Percy went in ahead to scout and I waited until he gave what sounded like a meow of clearance.

"Sorry, Keats, you're going to need to stand guard," I said. "It'll be hard enough to get in there alone and I want to make this fast. If there's something worth seeing, I'll open the side door for you. Promise."

Keats was unhappy to be left behind. So unhappy that he nipped the cuffs of the sweatshirt as I backed into the window.

"Stop that," I hissed. "This is hard enough. Wynn was right about me being a hulk. Either that or this window was meant for elves."

My feet landed where I hoped they would, specifically on the bathroom sink. The rubber soles of the water shoes came in handy for traction. This endeavor would have been harder in work boots.

Once I was steady, I turned and hopped down. Percy waited in the doorway and then led me into the hall and straight to the furnace room, with the lights.

The vivarium I saw from outside was just the opening act, as it turned out.

Here, the walls were lined with them. Far more than I saw at Happy Haven, though not as big. Many pretty yellow frogs had private accommodation, with some doubled up in couples' suites.

I didn't linger to make their acquaintance. Anxiety was tossing the protein bar around in my gut. This was feeling like more than a quirky hobby. Raising golden frogs appeared to be someone's job, or at least a side hustle, and probably a lucrative one. Even without the poison upgrade, this model would have strong value on the black market.

Percy escorted me to shelves on the other wall that were lined with plastic cups. In each sat a tadpole at various stages of metamorphosis. A dozen in tipped cups had sprouted all their legs, with only a tiny bit of tail remaining. In a few days, they'd hop right into new digs.

"Where's the food, Percy?" I asked.

There was a long workbench at the end of the room holding what appeared to be candy jars. Percy jumped up and strolled among them, pausing to scrape invisible litter around a few.

Frog candy turned out to be ants and termites, among other insects I didn't care to identify. The protein bar took another perilous turn inside. Soon I'd be using the bathroom for more than an exit.

I snapped a few photos, but my hand wobbled so much they were blurry. Frog candy was small. I needed to focus. Focus my energy, focus the phone camera lens.

Capturing the tadpoles took focus, too, but the adult frogs were easy-peasy. These bright little blobs begged to be photographed. Or painted with an impressionist's brush.

A yip from outside told me the visit was over. I wondered how long Keats had been trying to get my attention because he always started with mumbles. Percy was still trying to cover the frog candy.

I ran back to scoop the cat up and his paws kept moving as I carried him to the basement stairs. We were going out the easy way.

But then Keats whined. It was high. Piercing. A warning.

Sure enough, there were footsteps upstairs.

It was time to see if the upper body strength I bragged to myself about could deliver me from a tricky bind.

I hopped onto the toilet seat, stepped to the sink and popped Percy outside.

The window that had felt small going in was miniscule going out. Had it shrunk while I was exploring, or had I grown like Alice in frog wonderland?

Halfway through, I got stuck. Without gravity working in my favor, there was nothing to push against and nothing to pull me forward. My hips were jammed and the drawstring loosened.

Keats grabbed the sweatshirt and pulled. The shirt ripped, but it did no good.

His mumbles went from urgent to pleading.

Get out. Get out.

I had to get out before someone pulled me back in, where I'd probably smash my head on the sink as I went down. And lose my pants, too.

Rock.

The word landed in my consciousness, perhaps from my reptilian brain. The keeper of instinct and impulse toward action. Fight or flight.

I rocked. And rocked some more. Finally, that tipped the balance in my favor and I got myself unstuck.

Scrambling to my feet, I yanked up the sweatpants and fled by way of a neighbor's yard.

CHAPTER TWENTY-ONE

"Well. That was exciting."

There was no response but a lazy meow, because Keats wasn't speaking to me and Percy was recouping his energy for the next escapade.

"No more escapades tonight, my fluffy friend," I said. "I've already used up my stress hormones, yet I don't even know whose frog farm we visited."

I'd continue to use the word "visit" till forced to be radically honest about what had happened. It probably wouldn't be long before I had to cough up specifics, because I'd stopped a few miles outside Dorset Hills to send the photos and a brief explanation of what they contained to Kellan.

After a suitable interval, I gave the chief a call, relieved when it went straight to voicemail. I left him a cheery message that went on so long about dart frogs the phone system cut me off. I let it go at that. Kellan could fact check and get back to me.

If all went as I hoped, he'd scope out the frog farm and delay questioning me till morning. By then, I'd be on the road hunting for the penguin. Maybe we'd drive down to Gull's Glen again to try the pond. Polo's ship could have come in after we left.

I felt the blue eye of doom on me. Keats had no intention of exploring the creek again. We'd have to find new options. But not tonight. Tonight, I was heading home.

The mumble suggested I rethink that decision.

"Tonight? Really?" My voice sounded whiny, even to me. "But where?"

He stared straight ahead so I kept going. And as we drove into the deepening darkness a few of those amorphous pieces started stitching themselves together in my mind. Not in the reptilian part of my brain, but the later add-on, the prefrontal cortex. Both were coming in handy tonight.

"Got it," I said, reaching out to touch his side. He leaned away from me, so I added, "I'm sorry I left you outside. And I'm sorry I didn't hear you right away when you sounded the alarm. But we made it out safely and that's what counts. I'll do better, buddy."

A grumble let me know I was still in his bad books. When he put his paws on the dash, I got the impression our new mission was more urgent than it needed to be because I hadn't listened to my handler.

"Is the frog farmer coming after us, Keats? Because I wouldn't want to meet them alone. Not where we're going. I mean, we can probably take the professor down now that I know some martial arts moves. Wynn Hartwell, not so much. Bet she's mastered a spinning sidekick with a stick of dynamite in each hand."

I tried calling Jilly and got her voicemail, too. After leaving a message, I moved on to Edna. Where was everyone tonight? Did I miss an invitation to a party?

After spreading the word about our destination, I hurried to get there. Professor Horn had inadvertently given me an idea about the penguin's whereabouts. Presuming the thief was stashing Polo temporarily and wanted to keep him healthy, backyard pools and ponds were out. But there was at least one big pool I could think of that might just do the trick for someone with a long memory and a little ingenuity. Anyone raising and selling poison frogs had ingenuity in spades.

"How do you think you get the poison from the frog?" I asked. Neither pet entertained me so I speculated alone. "It comes from bodily secretions, so the people who used it probably rolled their dart tips on the frog. Maybe someone could do that now, once they engineered the right toxic snack to get production started. I don't want to think about how they tested it. The research said a golden frog has enough fire power to kill twenty thousand mice. A little goes a very long way. There were enough frogs down there to clear out all of hill country's bad guys and some of the good ones. Feels like the frog farmer started with Lenard Pembroke, but why? Proof of concept? The frog's value would skyrocket, for sure. Especially if the poison is so hard to identify. There's no antidote for batrachotoxin." I chuckled. "No pronouncing it, either."

Keats' next mumble suggested he no longer found me amusing. He was all out of pant-laughs, but he was a professional, and as such would get the job done.

Hopefully the job was just finding and rescuing the penguin. We would take the service entrance I'd seen on the Happy Haven map earlier. A few good sniffs would tell Keats whether we were on the right track.

"Maybe Len's murder was a grand anti-zoo statement, especially when combined with the penguin theft. Great way to grab headlines. Parents are worried about taking their kids there, now, which could ultimately drive the zoo out of business." Covering the last mile at high speed, I sighed. "I don't get it. My reptile brain is still at the wheel, but that's probably for the best right now."

Keats threw me a bone by mumbling in a more reassuring tone as we took the winding road down into the expansive grounds. It felt like he was telling me the story would unfold as it should, providing I followed his advice.

I was happy to do just that after what happened at the frog farm. My midriff hurt from thrashing through the window.

The dog wasted no time in alerting me that we were in the right place. His nose was in the window crack and he pulled back with paw raised.

It was go time.

Even though it took an extra couple of minutes, I hid the truck in the bushes. If the frog farmer was onto us, they knew where to come. But I wasn't going to make it easy for them to vandalize our getaway vehicle.

It was more about outrunning them now. There had better be enough adrenaline left in my tank. I put my reptile brain on notice as I collected the spare go-kit. My first pack was drying out from its dunk in Babble Creek, but Edna never left me unprepared.

I pulled out my phone to check the map but only needed it for light. Keats knew exactly where the old hippopotamus enclosure was on the vast property. They should have filled that pool in before someone got hurt. If it was big enough for a hippo, it was too big for me. I was the Goldilocks of rescuers tonight. No space was just right.

Keats drove me across the grass with a nip and then surged ahead with Percy. I followed the bobbing bits of white and orange till we reached a tall, iron fence.

Of course there was a fence. That was as it should be, if the hippo pool was still open for business, but it made things harder for me. I heaved off the backpack and opened it. What would saw through or pry open iron bars? Nothing I could use quickly, I was sure.

Edna was ahead of me, as always. Folded neatly on top of the pile was a rope ladder with carabiners to secure it. In a side pocket sat a hunting knife. I took that and stuck it in my side pocket. With the potential for potent poison, I had to arm myself with more than clever conversation.

Scaling the bars easily, Percy did his recon and announced success with eager meows that spurred me on.

"Don't fight me on this, Keats," I said, pulling out his backpack. "If you want to come in, this is the only way to do it."

He took it like a champ and adrenaline kept my fingers steady as I strapped him in. Then I swung the ladder onto the fence, secured it, and tossed my go-kit over. There was a collapsible net in the backpack, among other things I might need to nab the penguin.

Finally, I hoisted the dog onto my back and started climbing. Perching awkwardly on top, I pulled the ladder up and over and descended safely.

We were in.

Now to grab and go.

If the hippo pool had been paved over after all this, I think my heart would have broken. But the cement hole was only covered by a tarp and the familiar fishy smell told me Polo had left his mark. I hoped he was still leaving it, and even welcomed another shot.

Keats snipped the ropes securing the tarp and started yanking it back without my help. Directing the light inside, I saw the black-and-white bird on a platform that covered a portion of the water at the bottom. The water didn't look deep, but the pool itself sure was. Probably 10 feet and 12 across. Didn't seem like much room for a hippo, which was probably why they retired him to a sanctuary, but poor little Polo looked like a child's toy from up here. Or a ceramic miniature for my village.

"Oh man, how am I going to get down there? There's nothing to hook the ladder onto." Percy thought about jumping down but I stopped him. Scaling back up the concrete walls would be challenging, even for my athletic cat. Plus, I didn't want to frighten the bird.

I set the pack down and pulled out the net. It was nowhere near long enough to snag the bird. There was another long, sturdy rope, however, and with some ingenuity I might be able to tie it off on the iron railings and hook up the ladder.

"I've got ingenuity," I muttered. "Not poison frog farmer ingenuity, but Edna's rubbed off on me. Let's MacGyver this situation. Or Tarzan. Whatever works."

Thank goodness I'd been an A-student in Edna's knots seminar because I had to use them to get everything secure. My adrenaline continued to serve and my fingers worked nimbly and fast.

"This I do alone, buddy," I said. "It's a one-person job and I need Polo to stay still. If he gets in the water, it's going to be way harder."

The bird got in the water.

Of course, he did. I would too, if I were him. And now I'd probably need to do the same.

I left a flashlight propped on the side of the pool, pulled on a headlamp and then shimmied down the ladder with the net and gloves. It was still very dark down there, and the headlamp showed the water was deeper than expected.

Deep enough for the penguin to dive, and he could hold his breath for more than two minutes. Polo poked his head up, took one look at me, and vanished again.

I had two minutes, but that was about it. Keats' worried mumble above told me so. When the penguin surfaced, I had to nail him fast. There was no time to lure him with mimicked calls.

In the gap, I pulled out my phone and called Edna again. Reception wasn't great in a hippo hole, as it happened. All I heard was a crackly, "Dagnabit, Ivy! I'm on my—" before she cut out. There was no clue about how long it would take her to get here. If she was cursing me she wasn't nearly close enough.

The gloves were on and the light raised when the penguin surfaced. I muttered a fervent prayer and scooped.

One try! I captured Polo with one try!

Pulling the bird in, I brayed a little penguin tune while wrapping him swiftly and carefully. Maybe my soothing vocals helped me avoid getting gouged by the hooked beak. It didn't stop the stream of guano, however. I could hardly blame the little guy. The protein bar Teri Mason gave me wanted out, too. Stress was a GI killer for penguins and rescuers alike.

Then I stared up at the ledge and my stomach dropped.

A pet carrier wasn't something Edna could pack in a go-kit. How was I going to climb back up while holding this rare treasure?

"Keats, your backpack. Nudge it over, buddy."

It came down so fast I knew he was ahead of me. Or at least wanted to get rid of it.

By the time I was done slipping the bird out of the net and into the pack, there was no denying my hands were shaking. Adrenaline only takes someone so far when trapped in a hippo pool.

"Ready to climb," I said, trying not to worry about how I'd get both penguin and dog over the iron fence. That was a problem for five minutes from now. We were working a minute at a time here.

A growl and a yowl above announced the stakes had changed and the clanging of iron confirmed it.

We had company.

CHAPTER TWENTY-TWO

"Tell the dog to back off or I'll make him."

It was a man, so Wynn was off the table. Professor Horn was still on it. The braying bird lover from the creek would have a dark side if he engineered poison frogs as his moneymaker. Re-engineered, I supposed, since they were born to be poison before a modern diet robbed them of their natural defense.

Focus, Ivy.

I wasn't sure which part of my brain the voice came from. For all I knew it was a silent shout-out from Keats. But I heard it and I listened.

Now felt like the right time for clever conversation. I reached into my pocket and pressed record on my phone so Kellan could enjoy my repartee, later. This time I had consent from one party and I hoped the mic would work better than cell reception.

"Hey there," I called, trying to project confidence. "I could use a hand down here."

He stayed out of reach of my headlamp's beam. "Pass. I'll wait while you bring up my penguin."

"He's not yours and I won't deliver him right into your hands."

"You will if you care about your dog. Do it or he dies."

Criminals always said that. What they lacked in originality they made up for with savagery. It worried me, though. The iron had clanged twice, meaning Keats was still shut in a cage with no way out. The only positive was that my adversary hadn't mentioned Percy. That meant there was an orange bullet nearby with the man's name on it.

"Polo belongs with his mate and he's going back to her."

There was a long pause, and then, "His name's not Polo."

"Sure, it is. I told you that yesterday."

"You didn't tell me anything."

Not the professor, then. Tapley would remember our battle of words at Babble Creek. That left only the man I'd suspected since my visit to the frog farm. It would have been sooner if I'd picked up on the boys' signals. Tapley Horn wasn't the type of guy to give Wynn Hartwell an impressionist portrait of a frog. A hummingbird, maybe. He said himself he wasn't a frog man.

But I knew a frog man, or at least *of* him.

I was wearing his sweatshirt. And his drawstring pants. Even his water shoes, which came in handy again on the slippery wood over the water.

"I was sure I mentioned that on our unofficial Meet the Keeper Day. My dog didn't like you, Ben, and I should have listened. You're not as much of an animal lover as you said if you're threatening to hurt him."

Ben Langtry's mop of curly dark hair appeared over the side of the hippo pool and he reared back quickly when the beam of the headlamp hit his eyes. "Fine, you tagged me. I borrowed the penguin and now I'm going to put him back. Make it all good again. I was just waiting for the cops to clear the building."

A smile flashed across my face, despite the circumstances. We shared the same goal and that was half the battle. "Awesome. I can't wait to see him reunited with Pippa."

"Her name is not Pippa. And get up here."

I stepped over to the ladder. "You could be a little nicer, Ben. I've done the heavy lifting for you."

"I got the bird in there safely and I could get him out, if you weren't clogging up the works."

"Yeah, maybe. But you didn't do so well with the birds the first time. They got away on you. Slipped into the creek."

He glanced from me to the dog and back. "That wasn't supposed to happen, but everyone has an off day."

"Wynn Hartwell was so upset," I said. "She stole those birds and then lost them because of you."

The shot hit home and he knelt at the pool's edge. "Wynn didn't steal them. I did."

"How gallant, but the security footage says otherwise. Someone hacked in before you erased it and we saw the tattoo. Same emblem that was on the baseball cap we found downstream, now that I think about it."

More of his face came into view and Keats crept over to him. I could see the white tuft of the dog's tail and knew he was boldly close to the pool's edge. "You're not pinning this on Wynn," Ben said. "No way. I'm the one who broke the rules and got her inside. I'm the one who let her down and got her so flustered she dropped the gym bag. Little monsters slashed the fabric and ran off. We couldn't catch them."

I laughed. "Sounds like a great video. Viral post, guaranteed. Lacey Byle would be jealous."

He spit over the edge and it came down a few feet away with a small plop in the water. "Lacey *is* bile. Steered me so wrong."

"Let me guess... she told you to be radically honest with Wynn and it backfired."

He wiped his forehead with his sleeve, proving he was more rattled than he let on. "Did it ever."

I had a good idea exactly what had backfired but it was too soon to go there. With no timeline on my friends' arrival, I needed to drag this out a bit.

"I bet Lovebirdy's behind a lot of breakups," I said. "Potentially mine, if she keeps messing with my head. But you can still get Wynn back, Ben."

"I don't think so. She dumped me on the spot and took off alone in the dinghy. I went back inside to erase the security feed and followed in my kayak when I could. Chased the girl, just like in the movies. They're supposed to love that."

Another viral hit if it had been filmed, but I kept the observation to myself. "She was just worried about the birds and I'm sure you can't blame her. They're so rare. And so valuable."

"She wasn't going to sell them, if that's what you're implying." His voice rose as he defended his girl. "Wynn is super principled. She cares about animals."

"I know she does, because I met her this morning. But she didn't share her plans for the birds. The police already have the security footage and I'm sure they'll go easier on her if they know she had a good reason to steal them. Can you tell me?"

Ben got up and started pacing on the deck. I couldn't see my dog anymore, but I knew he was crouched and ready. If I weren't standing down here with a penguin in his backpack, Keats would have sent the zookeeper for a dive already.

Finally, Ben answered. "The birds were destined for a sanctuary down south, where they'd have more space and freedom. We have plenty here and more to come, whereas they need genetic diversity for their small colony. It's part of a global effort to save them. A noble cause."

"I agree, and I see why you'd put your job on the line to help. And you're right to defend Wynn. She loves you, I could see that, and I really think there's hope for you guys. You could try a grand gesture, like in the movies."

"I recaptured the missing bird. Wasn't that enough? She won't take my calls."

"Grander," I said. "Reuniting the penguins safely in the zoo will help but I think you should take it a step further."

After looking around for the dog, he stooped to listen. "Like what?"

"How about you steal Pippa again and deliver both penguins to the sanctuary yourself? Even a warrior like Wynn would crumble with a gesture like that."

He didn't answer for a long moment. "That might work, actually. All she cares about is animals. Nothing else will get through to her."

"Then do it. There's no time like the present."

"Now?"

"Tonight, yes. The police have cleared Happy Haven to reopen tomorrow and you need to move Polo anyway. It's not safe for him here. If he gets sick, your grand gesture goes down the toilet."

He stood, staring into the distance, and decided. "Okay. Bring the penguin up and I'll go get the female."

"Alrighty." I climbed the rope ladder slowly, both for Polo's sake and because my legs were wobbly. When I reached the top, Ben helped me step over the edge and stand up straight. A real gentleman, if you didn't scrape below the sticky, poison mucus. "I'll come with you and help."

He took a few steps back and I quickly crossed my arms over my chest.

"You're not coming, Ivy. No way, no how. I know exactly what you're like. We walk in there and you'll hand me right over to your fiancé. I'd be *your* grand gesture."

I smiled. "You don't know me that well, Ben, or even the chief. Radical honesty isn't much of a thing in our relationship. He only knows half of what I do and it's better that way. So, yeah, I'd be happy to help you reunite the penguins and send them to this sanctuary."

His curls swished a negative. "Don't trust you. Give me the bird."

"Look, if any officers are there, who better to decoy them? You must have heard enough about me to know I put animals first."

He started pacing again and pulled out cigarettes. "Let me think about it."

After lighting one up and inhaling deeply, he offered the pack. I shook my head. "Quit years ago, but don't think I wouldn't love a good menthol. When I worked in HR, I picked up the best gossip hanging out with the smokers. Never believed it was that dangerous."

"It can be, but I don't let fear stop me anymore. Wynn and I are alike in that respect." He bent to pull up the ladder and unclipped it from the rope sling I'd made. "I'll take you up on your offer. You come, but the dog stays. Tie him to the fence."

"Dude, I can't leave my dog. It's dangerous."

"He'll be fine locked up here. When we get back from the sanctuary, you can be reunited, too."

"That wasn't part of the bargain, Ben. I only offered to help you get Pippa out. As a bonus, I'll run interference with Wynn for you. I do love a good happily ever after."

He shook his head. "My way or nothing."

"Okay, fine. But I'll take that smoke now." With a side order of stalling, please. As a lifelong nonsmoker, I hoped I wouldn't choke.

Reaching into another pocket, he pulled out a different pack. "It's your lucky day. I've got menthol. Wynn prefers that, too."

"We have a lot in common." I reached out to take one and Keats stepped in front of me, growling. "Oops. The boss says no."

"Tie the boss up now, and you can have your smoke while we walk." He threw me the rope. "And by the way, I'm the new boss."

Things might have gone fine if I hadn't dropped my arms to

catch the rope. But I did, and he saw it. Indeed, he stepped forward for a closer look.

I stepped back, getting a little too close to the pool for comfort. "Personal space, Ben."

"Is that my sweatshirt? There's only one like it."

"Found it in a thrift shop." I dipped my shoulder forward. "Does yours have a tear?"

"It didn't when I left it with my mother for safekeeping. Those are my sweatpants, too."

"What about the water shoes?" I poked out my foot. "Got the bunch for two bucks."

Puffing furiously on the cigarette, he stared at me. There was enough light to reveal the gleam in the brown eyes he'd inherited from his father. The crazy train was chugging out of the station. Now it was about damage control.

"Give them back," he said. "Give them all back. They mean something to me."

"I can't walk into the zoo naked and go unnoticed. At least, I hope not. No gentleman would suggest it."

"Lady, I'm only a gentleman with Wynn. And my mother."

In the distance, I heard a motor. It sounded like Edna's ATV. Gertie must have brought it over in the van. Now, I could start pressing. Edna was my muscle, just as I'd been Cori's today, and Gertie was my triggerwoman. I just hoped they could find me. There were two other shuttered water exhibits. My octogenarian thugs didn't have Keats to flag the right one.

"Your mother's so kind," I said. "And yes, she let me borrow your clothes after my spill in the creek."

"You met my mother?" His voice was incredulous.

"This morning, at her local café. She took me home and served me tea. I noticed the frog collection and she told me all about your childhood fascination. We hit it off so well that she invited me to come back."

His Adam's apple bobbed as he digested this information. "That ain't gonna happen. Tie up your dog and give me my clothes. That's option one. Option two is I kill your dog and take the clothes. You choose."

"Option one it is." I carried the rope to the fence and looped it through Keats' collar.

This wasn't a rope he could snip easily with his teeth, so I tied a knot he could break. "On my cue, buddy," I whispered. Then I looked up at Percy perched in the corner under overhanging boughs and delivered a silent message. He would understand what was needed and when, just like always.

I slipped the backpack off my shoulders and set it beside Keats. "I think I'll take that smoke after all," I said, heading back.

Ben's teeth showed in a dangerous smile. "Be my guest."

I reached out again and then stopped. "Wait. Did your dad bum a menthol? That didn't work out so well for him."

Pulling out his private pack, he lit another from the first. There was a noticeable tremor in his hand. "I don't have a father. Never did. Deadbeat scammed the wrong guys and left my mom with two young kids."

"Mine wasn't so different," I said.

He took another long drag and his eyes narrowed. "Did you kill yours, too?"

"Not yet. But I might take a little frog poison in case he tries any funny business. Looked like you had enough to spare."

Smoke blew in my direction. "So you're the one who broke in. Just missed you. It got me worried about the penguin."

"No one answered the door and I was curious. Tapley Horn told me about golden poison frogs earlier and it was fun to see how it all works. Making any money yet?"

"Enough. Wynn's eco group will never lack funds thanks to this anonymous donor."

"Why stay anonymous? That's even grander. Think about how

Wynn will feel knowing she's behind saving species on the brink. With an unlimited supply of frogs, you could do so much good."

"The poison's unlimited but the clients aren't. Not yet, anyway. People never see the genius of frogs. That's why I had the sweatshirt made. Rana Potentia. Latin for frog power, more or less."

That was a clue I'd missed and I'd been wearing it all day. Granted, the lettering was stylized and cracked from washing.

"People don't know what they don't know," I said. "A poison that has no antidote is priceless."

"Should be. I'm counting on it." He patted his chest pocket. "How about a candy? There's a toxic toffee in my pocket with your name on it. Breath mints, too. Even some lip balm if you're dry from talking so much."

"You had lots of options for Lenard. How'd you know he'd be there?"

"I didn't. Met him by accident while I was waiting for Wynn to come out. He bummed a smoke and introduced himself." One hand sank into his curls and churned. "It was like the world fell out from under me. I knew about his aliases because I hired a private investigator last year. Couldn't believe he had the gall to come back to the site of my earliest memories with another woman."

He started pacing again and Keats watched closely for his moment. The rope had already fallen away. Meanwhile Percy had relocated to stand on the fence over the dog. The cat was impossible to miss, except by someone locked in a fight with his past.

"You know this woman—Brina—was just a mark, right? It doesn't mean he didn't love your mother. Or you and your sister. People like him are still capable of love, hard as it is to believe."

"I gave him a chance. All he had to do was say one nice thing. To show he was human. Instead, he joked about his bride's gullibility. Called her his golden goose." Ben patted his pocket of poison again. "So, I decided to give him a different type of gold. Didn't do it, though. Not then. Because Wynn came out."

Ah. I'd wondered about the timing. "Then you walked her down to the water."

He nodded. "Told her what happened. That I met my dad. That he didn't even recognize me. And what a dirtbag he was, scamming that lady. I blurted it all out, right down to my plan to share a special cigarette."

"You *told* her?" I was genuinely shocked. "Too much honesty, Ben. Way too much."

"Blame it on Lacey. She helped me when Wynn and I were first dating and I wanted to do the right thing. I thought Wynn might understand, because she's had a hard life, too. But that's when she dropped the penguins. She took off after them in the dinghy. I went back in to clear the security feed and decided against the poison. But then I went upstairs and saw that lady. The blonde one. She looked so helpless. Trapped."

"That's exactly how Brina felt," I said. "She wanted out but didn't know how. He'd love bombed her. Was after her money to bail out his latest business."

"That's what he did to my mom. Stole every cent she inherited from her parents. Drained our education funds and put a lien on the house." His chin came up and his expression settled into resignation. "So I decided to wait outside for him. In case he needed another smoke."

"Do you always carry poison around? What if you'd given Wynn the wrong menthol?"

"I'm not stupid, Ivy. I was meeting a client later." After a second, he added, "But I also didn't know exactly how it would work. It's all new and hard to gauge. Thought it might only give him a bellyache—enough time to let his bride escape. Didn't know he died till later, after hours of searching for the penguins. This stuff is insanely powerful."

"Well, you did Brina a favor, Ben."

He ran his free hand through his curly hair and then followed it with the cigarette hand. It was a risky move, but he'd probably done it before. "Just wish Wynn saw it that way. When she heard he'd died, that spelled the end for us."

"That's so sad, but even now, I think you can salvage this. Tell Wynn it was accidental, since you didn't know how potent the poison was yet. When you explain your success with the frogs, she'll be impressed. I sure am."

It looked like he was teetering on the brink of believing me. He *wanted* to believe and in a strange way, it broke my heart to lead him on. Thanks to the man I met as Lenard Pembroke, Ben's brain was broken—despite his capacity to re-engineer poison frogs.

"Okay, I'll try Wynn once more," he said. "You've given me great advice, Ivy, and I appreciate it." He took a final drag and then stubbed out the cigarette. "Shame I need to kill you."

CHAPTER TWENTY-THREE

It was a shame he needed to try, because in an odd way, we'd really connected. But if Ben Langtry thought it would be easy to shove a poisoned toffee in my mouth, he was wrong.

He would lose at least one ear.

And a portion of his scalp.

Wynn wouldn't find this man at all attractive by the time my pets were done with him.

Ben ran at me and I danced back. Now, I missed my boots greatly, because the kick I wanted to land wouldn't have nearly the same impact with water shoes. Still, the spinning sidekick I'd practiced ad nauseum with my nephews should knock the frog man off balance. Then I could keep him at bay with the hunting knife.

If he got anywhere near the penguin, I wouldn't hesitate to jab him in the leg. Both legs. Enough to keep him down till the ATV arrived.

"Don't make me do this, Ben," I said.

He watched as I got into position, shaking his head. "Do what? Kick me with my own water shoes?"

"Actually, yeah. Plus I'm packing a little poison of my own."

"You don't say. Is it as good as mine?"

"Nothing is as good as yours. But mine is plenty effective."

"Take the toffee, Ivy. Otherwise, I'm going to slip your dog a special treat. Do you want to watch that first?"

"I don't like your chances, Ben. You'll have better luck with me."

He took me at my word and came at me. I dashed away and faced him from the other side of the pool.

Only a few more minutes. I could see the lights from the ATV in the distance but I couldn't hear its engine over the din.

The din of braying, to be specific. Polo the penguin had sliced through the backpack and was waddling around yelling. Now I was on the wrong side to protect him.

"Don't hurt the bird," I said.

"I need the penguin for my grand gesture, remember?" He came after me and I ran around the pool again. "Stay still," he bellowed.

I thought about taking that kick, but what I'd recently gained in skill, I'd lost in confidence. The more I learned the more I realized what I didn't know. If the first rule of self-defense was "run," the second was "don't wear water shoes."

Fail and fail.

The third rule I nailed: keep your opponent guessing.

I ran around the pool twice more with Ben on my heels. On the third pass, Keats intercepted.

One lunge was all it took to send Ben reeling backward. Arms pinwheeling, he toppled into the hippo pool, landing with a splash and a volley of curses.

Keats ached to leap after him but I kept him back.

There was no way the deranged zookeeper could get out without the ladder he'd already removed. Even from the platform Ben had built for Polo, it was more than a seven-foot jump. He could never make it.

Only he did.

Or he would have, had a certain sheepdog not shown the

savagery previously directed at him. Every time Ben popped up Keats brought the hammer down. The man's ear was in tatters even before Percy joined the fray.

Like any cat, Percy teased his prey with taps and whacks until he finally got his chance for a whirl in Ben's curls. The cat went down into the pool with the man but unlike Keats, Polo and me, Percy had springs. Before I had a second to scream, orange paws appeared and the cat hoisted himself onto the deck.

He yowled a challenge down at Ben. *Bring it on.*

Shockingly, the man did. His screaming as the pets continued the punishment drowned out the penguin calls. Was Ben fueled by rage, love, or sheer insanity?

I would never know, because the next time he popped up, someone shoved him down into the hippo pool and joined him with another splash.

It happened so fast that I didn't see Edna go. When I turned to find Gertie, it was actually Jilly who stood with open arms.

From the depths of the pool, I heard Asher read Ben his rights. The lack of "dagnabits" suggested my brother had gotten the jump on Edna for once.

"How's Ash going to get Ben out of there?" I asked, hugging Jilly hard.

"Not a problem." She led me out the iron door my brother had unlocked. "Plenty of backup."

Edna clomped past us now in full army gear, helmet included. The pack on her back would bring most people to their knees.

Gertie was right behind her, Minnie primed to take a chunk out of Ben. Flipping her poncho aside, she crouched by the pool and took aim. "Need some leg irons, Officer? I believe we have some in our kit."

"Grab the penguin, Edna," I called.

"Grab the penguin, Edna," she replied in a singsong voice. "Always with the scut work. I'm not the Galloway janitor."

"And Polo is not trash. He's very precious and we need to get him back into the zoo right now."

Edna grumbled as she considered her options. "He tore up a perfectly good pet pack."

"I bet he won't get through yours," I said.

"You're right about that. I refuse to sacrifice a military grade backpack to the cause. You can't commandeer everything, Ivy."

Jilly raised her hand. "Got it covered. Percy's carrier is tied on the ATV."

"Hear that, Edna? Jilly knows the meaning of sacrifice. Now, remember what Cori said. Scruff the penguin, support his butt, and then tuck him like a football under your arm. Watch out for the beak."

"Why don't you do that? You have all the experience."

"Because no one wants an ugly bride, Edna."

Jilly laughed as she towed me to the ATV. "You okay?" she asked.

I nodded. "Fine, all things considered. I'm surprised Asher let you come."

"He didn't get a say. I told you I wanted to see this put to bed, and thanks to the braying penguin, we did. We stopped at the retired polar bear pool first, you see. And then the sea lion pool. That's when we heard the clamor."

"I'm sorry the fight wasn't bigger," I said. "Sometimes, there are gymnastics."

She looped her arm through mine and swung the carrier with the other as we walked back. "I saw all I needed to see. My best friend and my best pets ridding hill country of a deadbeat."

"In all fairness, Ben took out his father partly to save Brina from the fate his mother suffered. Dixie Squibb is the one I feel sorry for. She adores her son and never would have wanted this for him. That abandoned boy's pain turned into a passion for frogs and a little miracle of science. The love of a warrior woman nearly saved him from the worst of himself, but he blew it by making poison frogs and toxic bonbons."

Jilly shook her curls in amazement. "This is quite a tale, but how about we save the full retelling till we get home and Mom can hear it, too. It matters so much to her."

I nodded. "Let's take Polo back to Pippa. At least they can squawk at each other over CCTV until they get clearance to make more chicks."

"I'm guessing you'll want to hurry," Jilly said, handing me the carrier so she could stoop to collect Percy from the grass. "The chief isn't far behind us."

I dropped her arm and ran. "Edna, pop the penguin in here fast."

She mimicked me in the same singsong voice while doing as I asked, and then added, "Ivy, don't get too comfortable. I only have another fifty years on this planet to serve."

I grinned at her over my shoulder as Keats herded me up. "Hope the smell wears off by then."

CHAPTER TWENTY-FOUR

The next morning, I did my chores early and repaired to my manure pile. Despite being stiff and sore from yesterday's adventures, my adrenaline tank was overflowing. It was always like this after a run-in with criminals. Sometimes it took a few good workouts before I crashed and slept for the better part of a day. Most hobby farmers didn't have that luxury but Dad quietly took over when needed. When something criminal was afoot, he didn't go home at all. I appreciated that he protected the farm and the livestock, although I still felt awkward about the notion of him protecting me.

Keats rumbled from below, perhaps as a reminder that protecting me was *his* job. He was restless, too. Soon, he would vanish into the meadow to visit the old dump and try to get me interested in what he'd found there. Someday soon I'd indulge him. Not today.

Only Percy had mastered recovery. Now, as he lay on a haybale in a sunbeam, his switch was in the off position. A fluffy tail covered his face and didn't so much as twitch when I looked at him. Officially off duty, even as comfort cat.

The fact he wasn't needed in the house was heartening. When I went up for coffee, Jilly was whipping up a soufflé while her mother sat on a stool to watch. They only exchanged a few casual words while I was there but I knew they were tentatively advancing toward reconnection. It looked different for everyone. With my mother, there was a constant deluge of words I needed to sift through and with my dad, almost none. The best thing I could do was center myself and presume benign intent. We were all doing the best we could with what we had. Brina Brighton was no exception.

Keats' tail came up and swished. Finally, a little action. Percy moved his tail and cracked a green eye open. Then he closed it again. Still off duty.

The dog disappeared for a few moments and returned with Kellan. We hadn't spoken since the episode at the hippo pool, although I'd sent him the recording promptly and offered a thorough debriefing. My evasion had been more successful than expected but didn't feel as good as I'd hoped. I knew he was busy but nearly 12 hours without contact felt like an eternity under the circumstances. There was so much room in that vacuum to presume intent less benign. I worried I'd pushed things one step too far this time. That Lacey was right about us.

Kellan hopped a few times before backing up to a stall and leaning against it. He must be oozing negativity for Keats to punish his cuffs that hard. Normally the dog liked to work up to it. Save the flash for the finale. It put me on alert. I expected grilling but perhaps there was more. Kellan had proposed right here at the manure pile. Maybe he'd come full circle to collect the rings back for someone less reckless. Someone uncomplicated. Someone who smelled better.

Luckily, I'd left the rings in the house after a good post-penguin scrubbing. He couldn't take them now, and maybe when he cooled off, he wouldn't take them at all.

"Good morning," he said, with unnecessary formality. "Came by to talk about last night."

"Of course, Chief," I said, because he sounded chiefly. Then I dug the spade in deep and kicked it. Felt good to have steel-toed protection again. "Happy to answer your questions."

Happy was overstating it, but there was plenty of adrenaline in the tank to carry me through.

"Can we start with your visit to Ben Langtry's home?"

"Sure, but if I were doing the interrogating, I'd back up to my chat with Professor Horn. That's where I learned about poison dart frogs and got curious. Plus, we discussed where someone might stash a penguin temporarily and it got me thinking. I let you know about the rhododendrons."

He held up a hand. "Slow it down to cop speed, please. My brain doesn't work like yours. It's methodical. Plodding. So walk me through your thought pattern step by step."

I turned another spade full and nodded. Kellan was right. I couldn't even keep up with my own thoughts sometimes. That's why Keats was so necessary. Like any good sheepdog, he was always at least one thought ahead of me. In this case, quite a few.

"I went over to visit Tapley Horn again because I thought he was involved with Wynn Hartwell. That they stole the penguins together. It made sense, because I knew they were both fresh out of a relationship and had a lot in common. Activism, to be specific. He denied it, but when I saw the rhododendrons, I thought he might have used grayanotoxin—mad honey—to kill Len. That maybe Len had interrupted their mission."

"But how did you arrive at Ben's house?"

"There was another stop first. Keats wanted to visit Teri Mason in town. I had seen a pretty painting at Wynn Hartwell's place and thought it might prove a connection to Tapley. Or at least, that the mystery man might have the missing penguin. Turned out Teri had done the painting on a commission from someone anonymous. What I thought was a water lily was a yellow frog. A golden dart frog, one of the most lethal creatures on the planet. All she had was an address."

"So you broke in to see these incredibly lethal frogs?"

"Well, they're only lethal if you feed them right. Plus you have to touch them. Or eat them. I was hungry but not *that* hungry."

I hoped for a smile, but didn't get it. He just rolled his index finger for me to go on with the story.

"Google told me the two poisons were similar so I figured there was a connection to Len's death, but I didn't get a chance to look around. Someone came home and we beat it. Besides, the penguin was my priority, and that's when I remembered the old zoo map Lacey handed me in the Happy Haven foyer the other day. Fifty years ago there were more exotic animals, some of whom required pools. It seemed like the perfect place to stash a penguin, with plenty of space to avoid detection. I feared this was Polo's last stop before getting shipped out to a collector, but as it turned out, Ben was just waiting for the right opportunity to return him."

"You didn't mention you were taking a deep dive into a hippo pool. Did it occur to you I'd want to know?"

I kicked the shovel again. "I called after seeing the dart frogs and you didn't pick up."

"That's when you zero out to Betty."

Finally, I turned to stare at him. "I never zero out to Bunhead Betty. If that means I die alone in a hippo pool, so be it."

"And you say Tapley and Wynn are extreme."

The corner of his lip twitched, a sign that the chief's waxwork expression might melt into Kellan's.

I went back to shoveling. "I have more extreme friends to call on when you're busy, and I did. Keats seemed to think time was of the essence and his nose told him where to go. Honestly, it was textbook rescue, at least at first. The penguin was already in the bag, literally, when Ben arrived. He wasn't on my suspect list, or I would have changed out of his old sweatshirt. That's what sent him around the bend."

"The recording was patchy, but I heard that part."

"Do you know what they call a frog enthusiast? A batrachophile. Just like the poison. Wish I'd looked that one up after meeting his mother."

He shook his head. "I don't understand how you ended up at Dixie's. Was it really a coincidence?"

"Mostly. Janelle mentioned passing Gull's Crossing on her way up to visit Brina and Keats wanted to go downriver to find the penguin. He must have smelled the guano trail, but by the time we got there, Ben had already recovered Polo. It seemed like a dead end at the time but we ran into Dixie. I didn't get the sense she had any idea what Ben had been doing but we talked about his batrachophilia. Not sure that's a word but saying it on repeat will keep my brain sharp."

"And that's how you put it all together from the bottom of the hippo pool?"

"Technically, I was out of the pool when the last bits fell into place. My best thinking rarely happens in a deep, dark hole."

"It happens up there, doesn't it?"

He pointed at the manure pile and I shook my head. "Manure's awesome, but the magic usually happens in the truck. That's where my brain shifts into neutral and makes the connections." I looked at my dog, who was sitting with his tail around his paws and letting the story unfold. "Keats is usually waiting for me to catch up. He tried to tell me he didn't like Ben when we met at the zoo and he was unusually interested in the frog exhibit. I just figured he was annoyed about Lacey."

"As anyone would be."

"That's for sure." I expected him to fire more questions but he was quiet. There was enough tension in the air to rouse Percy, who stretched and gave a lazy meow.

"Ivy, can you come down here?" A nip to his pant cuffs earned the addition of "Please."

"I'm good here. This is a critical part."

"A critical part of manure management?"

"This isn't as easy as it looks, Chief. There's an art to it."

"It doesn't look easy. It looks like too much work, actually."

"You wouldn't say that if you saw Finch Pefferlaw's radishes. They won an award at the spring fair and he credits my fertilizer."

"I didn't mean to undermine your fertilizer, but I do want to talk to you face-to-face. Without manure in between."

I drove my spade in again. "There's always manure in between."

His more immediate concern was the wall of orange fluff in between. Percy had scaled Kellan and begun repeated passes across his face.

"Please come down, Ivy," he said, through fur. "I can see you're upset."

He couldn't see much of anything at this point. "What makes you say that? I'm just putting my all into the work. A job worth doing is worth doing well."

"Keats is attacking me and Percy is trying to smother me. That's usually my first clue you're upset."

I didn't come down and I didn't look at him, but after a minute or so, I blurted, "Brina said you don't want to get married."

"Ah, so *that's* what this is about. I declined the free wedding upgrade the zoo offered her as compensation for her pain and suffering."

"Did you think I wouldn't hear? I figured you'd at least tell me face-to-face that the wedding is off."

He sneezed. "That I would. Even if I suffocated in the process."

"Well, I'd just as soon find out the truth from up here. This is where you proposed and you can bring it full circle."

"Do you want to talk about it now? Or should I just sit down on a haybale and wait for you to cool off? Because I will, even though there's a massive pile of work waiting for me. Work you helped create by going rogue again."

I kept digging and turning, digging and turning. "I guess I understand it. Lacey Byle says our lack of honesty makes us a bad match. Yesterday was just one example. It goes back to our teen years."

"True." His answer surprised and alarmed me enough to stop shoveling. "We've never been fully honest with each other," he continued. "Not even on our first official date, when we left that party separately. I knew you didn't go home when I asked."

I dropped the shovel and it rolled down the pile to his feet. "You did?"

"Yeah. I saw your face when you heard those guys talking smack about a dog. I hoped you'd call in some backup but you didn't."

My feet came down the manure stairs of their own accord. It was like they knew I might tumble if I was intentional about it. "I didn't have backup then. No good friends. Didn't trust my family. So, I went and stole the dog. Found it a good home."

"I figured, when I heard it was gone."

"Where did *you* go?" I asked.

"After the guys, with your brother. The dog wasn't their only target that night and we couldn't stand by."

"So, you stopped it. I never heard what happened because they were expelled."

He nodded. "Asher and I were nearly expelled, too. Let's just say we didn't handle it the way we would now. Far from it."

When he didn't go on, I asked, "Are you going to tell me about it?"

"Nope, and Asher won't either. We made a vow to each other and the principal of the day to keep quiet. I don't need to hear everything that happened to you that night, either. Unlike some so-called experts, I don't believe in radical honesty. Did you really let that quack get in your head?"

"I guess. I'm worried you'll realize Lacey is right and we're incompatible."

Kellan laughed. "We've been compatible since the day we met."

"But I wasn't the real me, then. I was a rule-follower. Quiet. Docile. The hippo pool rescuer is who I really am and I feel like I've duped you."

"Back then, we weren't who we became. But the signs were there. We both took big risks the night of our first date. Do you really think we were incompatible from the start?"

Keats tilted his head this way and that, as if following a tennis game. "I guess I was incompatible with myself back then. I didn't want to be a rule-breaker, like my dad and his family. I wanted to fly under the radar."

"So later, you ran away from me and yourself."

"And became the Grim Reaper of HR." I reached down and touched Keats' ears. "Until another dog reminded me of who I really am."

"And now here we are." He took my hand, without noticing the rings were missing. "Ivy, I knew you were perfect for me *because* you took a risk to rescue that dog. That you were someone with fire. Passion. A drive for justice. When you married corporate life, I didn't fight it because you had to find that out for yourself. And you did. And now we're getting married."

"We're getting married." It was more of a question than a statement and my eyes filled. All along, no matter what Kellan said, I'd felt he wouldn't love me if he really knew me. Yet he knew me all along.

"Of course we're getting married. Just not at Honky Haven. I never liked the idea and even less now, after the murder. I may be a tough-guy cop, Ivy, but I actually care about the—what's the word?"

"Ambience?"

"Sure. I figure we're surrounded by so much crime and death we deserve one day blissfully free of negative associations. I didn't spell all that out to Brina and she misunderstood." His brow furrowed. "Do you really want a free wedding package that much?"

"It's not about the money, although we could have a spectacular honeymoon with what we'd save."

"You don't want a spectacular honeymoon. Last I heard we were touring in a bookmobile."

"I still love that idea," I said, smiling at last.

"I don't." He managed to offboard Percy onto a ledge. "There's some radical honesty for you. If you're not looking to score the freebie, what's this really about?"

I sighed. "I'm worried if we leave it much longer it won't happen at all. We'll turn back into friends."

"That's Lacey talking again. She's a quack." He folded me into his arms and only jumped a little when the nips started below. "We were never just friends. But if you're really that worried, I'll marry you today. Right here in the barn. We'll call an officiant and take our vows on the manure pile to bring you full circle, like you said. How does that sound?"

It sounded heavenly to me. This was my absolute favorite ambience. "While perfect, I have a better idea." Keats applied his teeth to me and I jumped before hugging Kellan again. "We're getting married."

"We were always getting married," he said, through a mouthful of fur as Percy rejoined us.

"But now we're *really* getting married."

CHAPTER TWENTY-FIVE

The indoor butterfly garden at Happy Haven was absolutely enchanting. We stood in the center, surrounded by lush tropical foliage and cascading waterfalls. Hundreds of free-flying butterflies in various shapes, colors and sizes fluttered around until an enormous blue one landed on the officiant's bald head. If he noticed, he didn't let on. A burble of laughter started in my midriff and threatened to roll right over me like a tidal wave.

"Stop it, Ivy," my mother hissed from behind me. "This is a very special day."

Very special days could have laughter and in my view, they *should*. There were enough other days filled with pain and crime and suffering.

A wedding day should get a free pass into hilarity. I didn't understand why more people weren't letting it rip right now. They had more self-control than I did, but that wasn't saying much.

I gripped the bouquet with one hand and reached down to touch Keats' ears with the other. The zoo had fought me hard about his presence here, despite my insistence that he only chewed people. They gave up when I shamelessly reminded them of my contributions, not only to the penguins but the institution's reputation. Thanks in large part to this very dog, the sordid event was behind us. Pippa and Polo had been renamed, reunited and rejoined their colony. It was a time for celebration indeed. And that included a free wedding, where Happy Haven pulled out all the stops.

The blue butterfly strolled around the officiant's head, perhaps trying to find a better grip. It moved to the fringe of hair around the man's ear and began a slow fanning of wings. It looked like he'd sprouted a living bow.

I bit my lip and tried to focus on his words. It was so hot in here I felt lightheaded. The late afternoon sun shone down through all the glass and roasted us in our finest attire. I hadn't worn a dress this tight since... well, never. But with a short run-up I'd had to take what I could get and this gown was elegant, if not comfortable.

"Do not laugh," I whispered to myself, as the butterfly waltzed to the officiant's forehead and made a slow descent to his nose. "Do. Not. Laugh."

This was serious business. These words meant something. "Till death do us part" was no small commitment in hill country. Death was always fluttering around and it never looked like butterflies.

Keats gave a pant-laugh, which only made things worse. He wanted me to crack up and endure my mother's wrath.

And I think the bride did, too.

Poppy looked over at me, her "best woman," and we both convulsed into gales of laughter. That gave everyone permission to do the same. Even Mom giggled.

When the merriment subsided, Travis, the surprisingly dapper groom, draped his arm around Poppy's shoulders and said, "Can we just get on with it, sir? I'm going to explode from the heat and no one wants to see that."

"Just skip to the good part," Poppy said, exchanging grins with her groom.

She looked stunning, but also just like Poppy. I figured she'd eschew white but she went all out with a wedding gown fit for a princess. Mom had stepped in with her sewing machine to make it original. There were satin panels the color of the butterfly throughout the full skirt that flashed when the bride moved. Iris had styled Poppy's hair in a bun, but a vibrant slash of blue took center stage. Only the flowers were traditional, mainly because Jilly took care of that part. We'd all pitched in to pull this together in just two weeks.

The officiant let the butterfly walk all over his face and his restraint suggested it wasn't the first time. "If anyone objects to this marriage, speak now or—"

"I object!"

There was a collective gasp and we turned as one to find Lacey Byle waving her hand.

"These two have no business marrying," she continued. "Their trauma-filled pasts will make them utterly miserable. They need intensive counseling before considering such a move."

Asher, the best man, started to walk toward Lacey but his mother-in-law got there first.

"Keep your opinions to yourself, Lacey Byle," Brina Brighton said. "You told me Lenard Pembroke was perfect for me and he was a deadbeat scammer with a criminal record and at least one secret family."

The groom smoothed his extraordinary head of hair and called, "Go back to shrink school, lady. I know what I need to know and I'm one hundred percent sure my bride and I can work out the rest. Poppy?"

"If I weren't wearing this beautiful dress, I'd kick the—"

"*Poppy!*"

Mom was aghast but Edna's cackle drowned her protests out. "That's my girl. She'll outlive the insects when the apocalypse comes."

"Shall we get on with it, then?" the officiant asked. "Do you—?"

"I do," Poppy said. "I absolutely do."

Travis laughed, the famous Wigg smile gleaming. "I do, too. Without reservation."

Jilly finally spoke up. "Release the butterflies and let's call it done."

The officiant stepped back so that Fergus Shay could open the box holding hundreds of sanctioned butterflies. They flew up and circled the wedding party, making the bride sneeze. That didn't stop Travis from dipping her and sealing the deal with a long kiss.

It was wonderful to see my sister so happy. Once I thought she'd be the last Galloway to marry but she beat three of us to the altar. The free package allowed them to save more for a house nearby. I had it on good authority that our father was going to cough up some of the Galloway treasure to help. Despite choosing to spend much of his time in a barn loft, Dad liked to see his kids in comfort.

Keats herded me outside before the group even broke up, knowing I could only handle crowds for so long without doing something worse than laughing.

While we waited for the rest of the guests to join us, Professor Horn walked across the grass to see me.

"I wanted to thank you, Ms. Galloway," he said.

I grinned at him. "For sending the police to check out your garden and home? Most people wouldn't thank me for that."

"That part was unsettling, I admit. Your brother seemed to be under the impression I was not only selling but using mad honey." He grinned back, and I realized he was attractive under his crusty eccentricity. "Perhaps he'd heard about my convincing penguin impression."

"No doubt. You're famous for it, now, sir. It was good of you to give Justine a clip for Schalow TV."

He shrugged. "My days as a stuffy academic are done. Education goes down easily with a dose of laughter, I'm discovering. No need for mad honey."

"Good to see you back on your old stomping grounds. Happy Haven is lucky to have you."

"Apparently, I'm lucky to have you, since you put in a good word for me. I'm offering twice-weekly lectures for the rest of the year while I work on my book. If Lacey Byle can do it, anyone can."

"Exactly. And that penguin impression is going to make your socials go viral."

I thought he'd roll his eyes but he shrugged. "We all need to do our bit to help animals, even if it means being a laughingstock. One day, I'll be able to fund a saltwater system for the penguins."

"Sooner than you think, I bet. Glad you're a zoobie again."

Tapley drifted away discreetly as the wedding party came out of the butterfly garden. I wanted to mingle with my family and friends, but Lacey got to me first.

"Ivy, I come bearing tidings of great joy. You and the chief won the draw for six couples therapy sessions with yours truly. With my help, you'll be the next Galloway in white. But don't delay, because your boyfriend has more options than any lady in town. Until you put a ring on it, you'll always be wondering."

"I'm already wondering what's in it for you, Lacey. I doubt you're doing this from the goodness of your heart."

Keats took a deep whiff and grumbled. He didn't smell any goodness.

"All I ask is a testimonial for my book and socials. Getting Clover Grove's unlikeliest couple to the altar would be a feather in Lovebirdy's cap." She tittered. "Pardon the quip."

Jilly swept in wearing her best dress and highest heels. Percy was under her arm, while Asher followed with the cat carrier. "Scat, Lovebirdy," she said. "Nobody wants your advice today. And I'll do what my husband was too polite to do and decline your offer of six free therapy sessions."

I turned back to Lacey. "I thought you said Kellan and I won."

Poppy was close enough to overhear. "Only because Travis and I turned her down. We're freestyling our marriage."

"Big mistake, Mrs. Wigg. Big mistake."

"Galloway-Wigg," Poppy corrected. "And I'll stick with Ms."

"There's your first fatal error. A man needs to—"

"Tell us, Ms. Byle." An arm dropped over my shoulder and I reached up to lace my fingers through Kellan's. "What does a man need to do to keep a powerful, passionate woman happy? I think every man here would like to know."

Asher raised his hand. "Me."

Travis followed suit. "Me."

The last hand to go up surprised me the most. "Also, me," my father said.

There was a shout from a short way off. "Me. A hundred times over." Everyone but Lacey laughed as Professor Horn threw back his head and brayed like a penguin.

"It's a shame none of you take relationships seriously," Lacey said. "I—"

Kellan whispered in my ear and I nodded. "By all means, Chief. If you need help clearing pests from the grounds, Deputy Keats—"

The dog was off before I finished the sentence. It was always a wonder to see him work but Lacey's long and perilous departure from the area warmed my heart. The dog was deadly serious but he sure knew how to breathe life into a party.

And a party it was. All the people I loved most were here, because Poppy loved them, too. The music came up long before dinner and Edna was first to take to the temporary dance floor. Her prowess in the field was surpassed only by her ballroom dancing skills and Buckley Brackens worked hard to keep up. Gertie, looking half her usual size without a poncho or rifle, proved just as adept with her dance partner, Wendel Barrick.

Asher pulled Kellan aside for some serious cop talk, and Jilly passed me her phone.

"What am I looking at?" I asked, enlarging the screen.

"A tentative booking at Dundonald Mill in October. I know you were getting fed up with bridesmaidzilla, so I put them through their paces alone and made an executive decision." She winked at me. "As long as you pay, of course."

I hugged her. "Bestie, you rock. October is my favorite month and there's a bit of time to build anticipation."

"We have so much to do," she said. "For starters, you'll want a dress that actually fits comfortably."

I nodded. "Room to laugh, mandatory. Room for spinning side-kicks optional, though highly advisable."

"If only we could get through October without cause for any type of kicking." She laughed and then sighed, as my four nephews moved to the grass and began impromptu sparring. Daisy started to yell at them, then touched her belly and stopped. I suspected she'd just gotten a kick from baby Galloway.

"How long is your mom staying?" I asked.

"Just a few more days. She's renting a car and driving home with a stop at the Briar Estates." My shock must have showed because she added quickly, "Aunt Shelley said she'd head to Wyld-wood Springs for a week or two to give Gran time with Mom. Wouldn't be surprised if she stays, though. Janelle's been working her magic to make this happen." She looked over at her cousin, who'd extricated Sutton and led him to the dance floor. He looked terrified and delighted to have such a stunning partner. Janelle definitely knew how to put the laughter in education as she taught him to waltz.

Jilly handed me Percy. "You look a little pensive, my friend."

I stared around and nodded. "Just wondering how my wedding could ever top this. It's perfect."

"Mine was perfect, and yours will be, too. There's plenty of perfect to go around."

A perfect dog delivered a perfect fiancé to me with a few nips and Kellan hopped as he tried to save his best pants. "All right then," I said. "I'll take an order of perfect, and everything can stay just as it is."

Kellan led me to the dance floor and we joined the others. As the best dancer there, there was no reason for Edna to bump into me, but she did it twice before Kellan twirled me out of reach.

"Never let your guard down, Galloway," she said, coming after me again with a cackle. "There's a quack with an agenda around every corner."

Kellan blocked her next pass. "Once more and I'll cuff you and Buckley together for the evening, Miss Evans."

She subsided instantly and it was pure joy to whirl into the sunset with my beloved. Whatever surprises our wedding day delivered, I had no doubt there'd be plenty of laughter.

When a self-help retreat transforms into murder most fowl, Ivy turns to her pond's new resident for clues. This is one mystery she can't afford to duck. Join the next fun-filled adventure in *Hit the Road, Quack.*

Interested in hearing more about my writing and my dogs? Join the Ellen Riggs newsletter at **ellenriggs.com/opt-in**.

RUNAWAY FARM & INN RECIPES

Sudden Death Pudding

Ingredients

- 1 ½ cups all purpose flour
- 2 ½ tsp. baking powder
- ½ tsp. nutmeg
- ½ cup brown sugar
- 1 cup raisins
- ¾ cup milk
- For sauce:
- 1 cup brown sugar
- 2 tbsp. butter
- 1 ½ cup boiling water

Instructions

1. Mix ingredients to make a soft batter. Pour into a buttered baking dish.
2. For sauce, sprinkle batter with brown sugar, add butter and cover with boiling water.
3. Bake at 375 degrees for 30-35 minutes.

(Author's note: This is a childhood favorite handed down from my English grandmother. No idea why it's titled that way—I have many recipes more inclined to cause instant heart attack—but it's perfect here and no poison required!)

More Books by Ellen Riggs

Bought-the-Farm Cozy Mystery Series

- A Dog with Two Tales (Prequel)
- Dogcatcher in the Rye
- Dark Side of the Moo
- A Streak of Bad Cluck
- Till the Cat Lady Sings
- Alpaca Lies
- Twas the Bite Before Christmas
- Swine and Punishment
- The Cat and the Riddle
- Don't Rock the Goat
- Swan with the Wind
- How to Get a Neigh with Murder
- Tweet Revende
- For Love Or Bunny
- Between a Squawk and a Hard Place
- Double Dog Dare
- Deerly Departed
- Think Outside the Fox
- Mouse of Ill Repute
- Bee All and End All
- Sheep with One Eye Open
- Roo the Day
- Till Death Zoo Us Part
- Hit the Road, Quack
- One Horse Open Slay
- Beg, Burrow or Steal

Bought-the-Farm Mysteries - Boxed Sets

- Bought the Farm Mysteries - Books 1-3
- Bought the Farm Mysteries - Books 4-6
- Bought the Farm Mysteries - Books 7-9
- Bought the Farm Mysteries - Books 1-10

Dog Town Series

- Ready or Not in Dog Town (The Beginning)
- Bitter and Sweet in Dog Town (Labor Day)
- A Match Made in Dog Town (Thanksgiving)
- Lost and Found in Dog Town (Christmas)
- Calm and Bright in Dog Town (Christmas)
- Tried and True in Dog Town (New Year's)
- Yours and Mine in Dog Town (Valentine's Day)
- Nine Lives in Dog Town (Easter)
- Great and Small in Dog Town (Memorial Day)
- Bold and Blue in Dog Town (Independence Day)
- Better or Worse in Dog Town (Labor Day)

Mystic Mutt Mysteries Paranormal Cozy

- I Want You to Haunt Me (Prequel)
- You Can't Always Get What You Haunt
- Any Way You Haunt It
- I Only Haunt to be with You
- All I Haunt Is You
- Do You Haunt to Know a Secret?
- All I Haunt for Christmas
- I Haunt You Back